To Erika,

Blessings,

[signature]

1

The Unforgotten Past
Part II

By Brianne E. Pryor

In loving honor of my siblings, Matthew, Kendal Lee, and Elijah Pryor. For their support, love, and everlasting friendship. God bless you.

PART II

Enjoy ♥

Love, Pop Pop & Nana

Forget the former things,
do not dwell on the past.
Isaiah 43:18

Previously

LooAnne felt as though Ricky had betrayed her. Not only was he not allowing her to be engaged to Kyle but he had sent him away without even telling her.
"That's not fair!" LooAnne cried.
"Don't raise your voice to me, young lady," Ricky scolded.
"I love him, Uncle Ricky, and you made him leave without even letting him see me again!"
"I didn't want you to have to say goodbye to him."
"Uncle Ricky, that's not true and we both know it!" LooAnne snapped angrily.
"LooAnne!"
"I know why you sent him away without telling me, you were afraid that I'd run away with him just as my mother ran away! What kind of person do you think I am anyway? How could you do this to me? No wonder my family was incapable of love, they had seen how much pain it causes! I wish that I had never left them! I wish I had never met you!"
Turning LooAnne ran upstairs without another word...

ONE

The Torching Flames

*And the Angel of the Lord appeared
to him in the midst of the bush. So he
looked and behold, the bush was
burning with fire, but the bush was not
consumed. Exodus 3:2*

January 26th, 1924. 3:30 pm. Decatur, Texas.
The cold wind outside was sharp, causing the Nash
Estate to creak and groan under the pressure. The sky
overcast with light gray clouds which passed without
shedding a drop of their water but gave the fields a
melancholy look, matching the inner atmosphere of the
house.
LooAnne felt sick inside. She dropped down on her bed
and buried her face in her pillow, her tears poring out
and rolling down to wet her long red hair. Just days ago
she had thought that things could not get any better, but
now she felt as though things could not get any worse.
Her uncle had not only forbidden her from marrying the
only man she had ever loved but now he had sent him
away without the least courtesy of allowing a goodbye.

Ricky's heart pained him. He could still hear his niece's words as if she were standing in the room repeating them to him. *"I wish I had never met you."*

How could he have been so stupid? How could he have acted so as to turn her against him? Because of his own selfish endeavors to keep her from running away with Kyle Denson he had hurt her in such a way that he feared she would never forgive him.

As he sat in the study, his ward came down the hall and poked her head in the doorway, her face bright with curiosity.

"Where's LooAnne?" she asked, cheerfully.

"Upstairs," Ricky answered without looking up.

"Oh." Amarie frowned. "Is something the matter, Uncle Ricky?" she asked.

"Nothing, Amarie."

"You look upset."

Ricky looked up at his ward and said, "Amarie, don't you need to be practicing your piano?"

"Yes," Amarie said though she made no move to do it.

"Well why don't you go take care of that then?"

Amarie sighed. "Yes sir." She shrugged and went into the upstairs parlor to practice.

LooAnne failed to come down for supper and Ricky refused to allow Amarie to get her. He hoped that if he left her alone for a while things might look better in the morning.

For a second time that week LooAnne cried herself to sleep, still fully dressed and wearing her laced up boots. She was so tired that she fell asleep almost immediately and dreamed that someone, though she could not quite tell who, was calling to her from what seemed like far away. She could hear them shouting her name and the masculine voice sounded extremely familiar but her sleep-laden mind was unable to place it.

In an instant it seemed LooAnne was awake! She did not know what had awakened her but decided that it was the smell of smoke from outside her open window. Just as she was about to get up to close it she heard the man that had been calling to her in what she had thought was her dream. It was Chris and he seemed to be standing at the bottom of the stairs. He was yelling, "Miss Nash! Miss Hearten! Get up!"

At the same moment Amarie came bursting into the bedroom in a panic, a cloud of smoke following behind her! Her eyes were wild and she screamed, "LooAnne get up! The house is on fire!"

Immediately LooAnne was fully aroused and her heart began to beat wildly within her, pumping adrenaline throughout her veins as she processed what was happening!

Amarie grabbed her arm and tugged, "We've gotta get out!" she wailed hysterically.

LooAnne leaped out of bed and ran into the hallway with Amarie. Smoke pored up the stairs and the girls soon began coughing and choking. They held their handkerchiefs over their mouths and ran down the stairs to where Chris stood. The girls were stunned by the roaring flames that leaped up the walls and seemed to poor over their heads! Chris quickly herded them towards the door where maids were also running to escape the fire that seemed to be rushing through the

11

house at a shocking speed.

It seemed like an eternity before they were out of the burning house. Workers were everywhere, rushing towards the house with buckets of water that they were heaving at the fire as it roared up the sides of the house! When LooAnne and Amarie were safely away LooAnne began looking around frantically for her uncle. Not seeing him she told Amarie to stay where she was and went after Chris who was helping put out the fire.

"Mr. Block!" LooAnne called over all of the turmoil. Chris turned questioning eyes on LooAnne. "Where's Uncle Ricky?"

Chris looked around and then said, "I'm sure, he's out here somewhere. I woke him up myself."

"Are you *absolutely* sure he came out?" LooAnne demanded.

A frightened look crossed Chris's face as he searched the area for Ricky. "No Miss Nash, I'm not. As soon as I knew he was awake I went to get you, I didn't see him come out myself."

A lump got caught in LooAnne's throat and her stomach began to turn with fear. Her uncle must still be inside the house that was now nearly engulfed in flames! LooAnne didn't take time to think, she ran towards the open door that was framed with hot fire!

"Miss Nash!" Chris called frantically. "Miss Nash! No!" LooAnne payed little attention to Chris's pleas, she leaped the porch steps and ran through the burning door and into the house! Chris turned and screamed frantically to the ranch hands to work faster!

The second LooAnne entered the burning house she was

taken aback by the intense heat and the thick smoke that immediately began burning her eyes so that they pored with hot tears. LooAnne started coughing and choking as she held her now almost blackened handkerchief over her mouth. Flames leaped up the walls all around her and burned in places on the floors and furniture! The smoke made it almost impossible to see anything and she was so disoriented that for a moment she began to panic, but then she thought of her uncle in the house somewhere, maybe dying from smoke inhalation or even the fire itself! This thought urged her on through the torched house, leaping and dodging blazes of roaring fire and ashes to Ricky's bedroom!

The closets and bed canopy were ablaze! Her eyes burning from the sickening smoke, LooAnne looked frantically for Ricky, praying that he was there and that he was alright! She found him laying in the floor, fully dressed, but he appeared to be unconscious! LooAnne dropped down next to him and began coughing uncontrollably. Her lungs burned as if they themselves were on fire. Sweat pored down her face and mixed with the stinging tears. Ricky lay motionless and LooAnne knew he was not going to regain consciousness until she could get him outside away from the smoke. She grabbed his arms and pulled him to the window. LooAnne tried the latch but it wouldn't budge. Repeated efforts to open the blackened panes were in vain. Knowing that there was nothing else that she could do LooAnne took a few steps back and heaved her shoulder at the window. It shattered into dozens of pieces that scattered about the floor. Smoke began poring out the broken window as LooAnne raised her foot and kicked out the extra slivers that still hung on the frame. She then grabbed her uncle and with all her strength she lifted him up to the window sill and pushed him out of the house, jumping out after him!

LooAnne drug Ricky away from the burning house and then staggered away from him, coughing and gasping for air. She turned away from the roaring fire to face the cold winter air. Her eyes still burned but the cold wind felt soothing and came as a rush of relief. LooAnne sank to her knees, still coughing from the smoke that burned her lungs. At that moment Chris, who was frantic with worry saw LooAnne and her uncle who still lay on the ground unconscious, and came running to aid them. He knelt next to Ricky who rolled to his side and began coughing. LooAnne took a deep breath and filled her lungs with the cold, pure air that blew in from the fields, bringing the smell of cattle and frozen ground. After regaining some of her strength she turned and crawled next to Chris. He looked at her with admiration showing on his face that was flooded with relief.

"Are you alright, Miss Nash?" he asked.

LooAnne nodded, unable to speak. Just then the Huckster, which Chris had sent the footman to town in, came speeding up, loaded with men to fight the fire. Everyone jumped out just as there was a loud cracking noise from within the wall of flames and the peek of the house sank down into the fire with an ear-splitting crash! The fire engulfed what was left of the great Nash estate house and destroyed it right before the eyes of the Nash's and their workers. The night was lit from the flames and shadows danced eerily across the fields and outbuildings.

The footman that had been sent to town had wisely brought back a doctor who examined Ricky. LooAnne stood to her feet and steadied herself by leaning against a nearby tree. She watched the house burn to the ground, the crackling fire reflecting in her dark brown eyes. LooAnne wiped the sooty sweat from her forehead as she stared at the house. It burned with a fire so big that it seemed to tower over her head, shooting soot and debris into the night sky. LooAnne suddenly felt tears rolling down her face, collecting black soot. Suddenly she was aware of Chris standing next to her. LooAnne looked over at him, he, too was watching the roaring fire with sad eyes. Chris turned to LooAnne and said, "You were amazing, Miss Nash."

LooAnne smiled wanly, her throat still too raw for her to talk.

Chris suddenly looked down at LooAnne's arm and said, "You need to have the doctor look at that burn, Miss Nash."

LooAnne looked down at her arm and saw that there was a nasty burn on it that was puffing up into a large blister. In the excitement of the moment she had not noticed her injury. Now that she saw her arm it began stinging with a sharp pain.

"I'm fine," LooAnne croaked in a hoarse whisper.
Chris frowned, "Are you sure, Miss Nash?"
LooAnne nodded, "I'll have it looked at later," she assured him.
Chris nodded in agreement and returned to fighting the

fire.

LooAnne continued watching. The flames seemed to burn on and on relentlessly. LooAnne had been watching for what seemed like ages to her, when she glanced in the direction of Ricky. Dr. Hall was no longer there, and Ricky was laying in the grass sitting up on his elbows watching the fire. LooAnne walked to his side and together they stared. He looked up at her from his position on the ground, his face black with soot and ashes. LooAnne didn't see her uncle looking at her for she was too engrossed in the fire. Ricky reached up and took hold of his niece's blackened hand. Pulling her down to his level he looked her in the eye and smiled a wan smile.

"You went back in," he whispered hoarsely, referring to LooAnne's heroic move to save his life.

LooAnne nodded. "You were still in there."

"That was little reason for you to risk your life, young lady."

"I couldn't just stand out here knowing that you were still in the house and I could save you," LooAnne pointed out.

Ricky shook his head, "I acted foolishly. I got dressed and was just about to get out when I realized that I couldn't leave the ring in there, but it took me a few minutes to find it."

"What ring?" LooAnne asked, perplexed.

Ricky reached into his pocket and pulled out a small ring with a skinny band and a tiny gold nugget on it.

"It's a Nash identification ring," he said. "Only my most trusted friends have one of these. I had them made so

the wearer could be identified by the guards." Ricky looked up at the consumed house. "But I suppose they won't be needing to get in here any more." Ricky laid the little golden ring in LooAnne's hand and said, "There's only six of them. This one was my sister's. She gave it to me the day she left. Now it's yours."
LooAnne turned the ring over in her hand, thinking that her mother had once wore it. "Thank you, Uncle Ricky," she whispered as she slipped the ring onto her sooty finger.
The two watched as men repeatedly dowsed the flames, causing clouds of steam to rise into the sky and disappear amongst the smoke. Chris came a short time later and told Ricky and LooAnne that the doctor would drive the family to town where they could reserve a room at the hotel. Ricky agreed and the doctor took, him, LooAnne, and Amarie to town in the Huckster. As they rounded the curb, LooAnne turned and looked back at the estate. Fire still shot upwards in a few places but most of the house was nothing but smoldering timbers.

TWO

Triple Creek Hall

But the Lord stood with me and strengthened me so that the message might be preached through me, and that all the gentiles might hear. Also I was delivered out of the mouth of the lion. And the Lord will deliver me from every evil work and preserve me for His heavenly kingdom. To Him be the glory, forever and ever. Amen! 2 Timothy 4:17 and 18

"Can I be of any assistance, sir?" Dr. Hall asked as Ricky helped LooAnne and Amarie exit the Huckster in front of the hotel.

"No thanks, Doc," Ricky said. "There's nothing any of us can really do until morning. Thank you though for all your help."

Dr. Hall nodded and walked down the road towards his house, leaving the Huckster with Ricky and the girls.

The trio made their way into the hotel lobby where they found the clerk sitting at the front desk sound asleep in his chair.

Ricky rang a bell that sat on the desk, causing the clerk

to jump and nearly topple out of his chair.

"What can I do..." when the man saw Ricky and the girls he frowned and squinted at them through his thin rimmed glasses.

"We'd like two rooms, please," Ricky said.

"Has there been an accident?" the clerk asked.

"Yes," Ricky answered, his voice raspy. "A fire. Now can we have those roo-"

"A fire? That's terrible, sir," the man interrupted. "You three look exhausted!"

"We are, and that's why we'd like to have two -"

"Have you seen the doctor, Mr. Nash?" he interrupted again.

"Yes, thank you, and now I'd like to go to sleep, could we -"

"Yes, you most certainly need your rest! Are you sure that the doc-"

"Excuse me for interrupting but the girls and I would like a room, please?"

"Oh yes, of course. Would the two rooms in the back hall be alright?"

Ricky nodded, "Perfect."

"Very good, sir." the man turned to the key box to retrieve the key but could not quite seem to find it.

"I seem to have misplaced the key to room 19," he said. "Would the two rooms in the front hall be alright?"

"I don't care which rooms just so long as they've got a bed and bath to wash off all of this soot."

"Well I'm afraid that room 7 doesn't have a functioning bathroom, how 'bout -"

"How 'bout I go down to the other side of town and stay

somewhere else?" Ricky snapped irritably.

"Rooms 1 and 2 are in good condition but the fee is two dollars more for front rooms."

"I own the hotel!" Ricky demanded.

The clerk jumped and began rubbing the back of his neck nervously, "Oh of – of course, sir. This way, sir" He turned and led way up the carpeted stairs. After unlocking the door to the girl's room the clerk handed the keys to Ricky and excused himself. "If there is anything else you need sir, just ring the front desk."

In a calmer voice Ricky replied, "We need night clothes. We'll need something to wear once we wash this filth off ourselves. If you could please attend to that I would be grateful."

"Yes, sir. Of course, sir. I'll bring them right up to you." The clerk ran down the hall and returned a mere minute later with enough clothing for each of them to manage until the morning. Ricky opened the door to the girl's room and told them to clean up and get some rest. He then went to his room, washed off all of the soot, and climbed into bed.

LooAnne and Amarie were silent for a long time after entering their room. They washed and dressed in the long cotton shirts and bathrobes the hotel had provided. LooAnne laid down and in seconds she was dreaming. She dreamed about the consuming fire that had destroyed the Nash Estate. She dreamed that she had been unable to get her uncle out the window, no matter how hard she struck it, it would not break. Just as the house fell down on them, consuming them, LooAnne awoke with a start!

The instant she saw the sunlight poring though the window and realized that it had been just a dream, LooAnne sighed with relief. She pulled the blankets closer around her and looked about the room. Amarie was still tucked under the covers, sound asleep. The window was fogged over and the room was cold. LooAnne could still smell the smoke even though there was none around. She rubbed her nose, trying to rid herself of the awful smell that seemed to haunt her even in her dreams, but the smoky aroma never faded. LooAnne got out from under the warm covers and went to the frosty window. She slid it open and stuck her head out into the cold, fresh air. Taking a deep breath she filled her lungs with the refreshing yet icy cold breeze. People mingled about down on the street and the smells of town soon reached LooAnne's nostrils. The bakery stood next to the hotel and the wonderful aroma of cakes, cookies, and breads filled the air. This made LooAnne's stomach growl with hunger and she wished that she could go across the street and buy a warm cinnamon role and a steaming cup of hot chocolate. "Shut that window, are you mad?" came Amarie's annoyed voice from where she was huddled under the quilt. "We'll freeze, LooAnne."

"But it smells so lovely out there," LooAnne said, finding her throat very raw and sore from all of the smoke that she had inhaled.

Amarie jumped out of bed and ran to LooAnne's side. She gingerly stuck her nose out into the cold morning and sniffed, then she smiled and said, "It sure does smell good. Makes me hungry."

LooAnne nodded, "Me too."

"Can we eat?" Amarie asked anxiously.

"We can't leave this room, we have nothing but these shirts and robes."

"What about breakfast then?" Amarie wined.

LooAnne put her hands on her hips and frowned disapprovingly, "The estate just burned last night and all you can think of is your stomach? You should be grateful for what you do have."

Amarie snorted, "As you said, the estate burned, what exactly *do* we have?"

"Our lives!" LooAnne pointed out. "We could have all very easily been killed last night."

Amarie dropped down on the bed and sighed, "I suppose your right."

LooAnne nodded, "I am. We got no choice now but to wait for Uncle Ricky."

Amarie grunted in displeasure. "I always thought that the life of the upper class was supposed to be carefree, but here we are, in a hotel, freezing our toes off with no clothes, no food, and no home. It's perfectly ridiculous!"

LooAnne nodded in agreement. "It is, but what would you expect? As I said we should be thankful we got out of there alive."

Before Amarie could respond she was interrupted by someone knocking on the door.

"Who's there?" LooAnne called.

"Chris Block, Miss Nash," came Chris's voice from outside the door.

LooAnne wasted no time in opening it, finding Chris standing in the corridor, his clothes, face, and hands still black with soot. His eyes were tired and he looked very dejected. "Good morning," he said hoarsely. "How do you ladies feel?"

"Better, thank you, and you?"

"Exhausted but well trained in fire extinguishing," Chris replied trying to find some humor in the awful circumstances.

"What does the house look like?" LooAnne asked, not sure that she actually wanted to know the answer.

Chris lowered his head and shook it sadly. "We managed to save some of the furniture but everything's been leveled. It burned to the ground I'm afraid. Here," Chris handed LooAnne a suitcase and said, "Mrs. Moore stopped by the tailor this morning and got you girl some things to wear."

LooAnne took the suitcase and nodded her thanks. "Have you seen Uncle Ricky this morning?" she asked.

"Yes, I just went by and gave him some clothes. He said to tell you that once he's changed he'll be right over. The townspeople who helped last night just got back early this morning so I was a might late with the duds but we all had to stay just to make sure that the fire was not going to flame up again."

"Thank you for bringing us something to wear, Mr. Block," LooAnne said gratefully, "we were just wondering what to do for clothes."

Chris smiled wanly. "I recon I'd better go get cleaned up, I'll see y'all later." The steward turned and strode down the corridor as LooAnne shut the door and laid the suitcase on the bed. Amarie came running over and pulled it open anxiously. Reaching inside she removed a blue dress new from the store and smelled of perfumes and fresh cotton. She buried her face in it and inhaled deeply. "Oh it smells so lovely, LooAnne."

LooAnne removed a green, pleated skirt with white lace trim and a matching green blouse with long, silk sleeves. The skirt was not as long as was the fashion but it was warm and deeper down in the suitcase was a full length wrapover coat with a warm fur collar. Amarie dug down into the suitcase and pulled out an all wool knitted cape that matched her blue dress, gasping when she saw it, "How lovely!"

LooAnne nodded, "Mrs. Moore certainly has beautiful taste."

"Hurry let's put them on! I want to see what they look like," Amarie urged.

LooAnne nodded in agreement and dug out some undergarments from the suitcase. Just as they finished changing there was yet another knock on the door.

"Who is it?" LooAnne called.

"It's me, my I come in?" came Ricky's voice from the hall.

LooAnne hurried to open the door and found her uncle standing in the hallway. He was wearing a new blue suit. His shirt caller was buttoned down and his gray vest was well hidden beneath his suit coat. Even his pocket square and his red cloves were neat and orderly, to the eye of the world he looked as though nothing had happened, it was the look behind his troubled brown eyes that LooAnne found so disconcerting.

"Good morning, my dear," Ricky said, his voice hoarse and deep. "How did you ladies sleep?"

"Well enough," LooAnne answered, "What about you?"
Ricky sighed, "Not at all I'm afraid."
LooAnne frowned, her repression laced with worry,
"Are you feeling alright?" she questioned.
"I'm fine," her uncle assured her. "Thanks to you,"
Ricky gave LooAnne a half smile, but his eyes were dull
and sad. "May I come in?"
LooAnne nodded and Ricky stepped in the room. When
he saw the girls he smiled slightly. "You ladies look very
lovely."
The girls smiled at his attempt to be pleasant. "Mrs.
More outdid herself this time." Amarie said as she
admired her reflection in the mirror.
"She most certainly did," Ricky agreed, "Now shall we
go get something to eat?"
"Yes, please," Amarie begged.
"We'll go next door to the bakery for some breakfast if
you like?"
Both the girls nodded and grabbed their coats that lay on
the bed then followed Ricky down to the hotel lobby.

THREE

Never Forgiven

*I said in my heart, "God shall
judge the righteous and the wicked,
for there is a time for every purpose
and for every work." Ecclesiastes 3:17*

*You shall not take vengeance or bear a
grudge against the sons of your own people,
but you shall love your neighbor as yourself;
I am the Lord. Leviticus 19:18*

When Ricky, LooAnne, and Amarie stepped out
onto the street they were immediately swarmed with
reporters and the bright flashes of two men with the
newest Kodak Exakta and flashbulbs. Questions were
thrown at them from every direction, each man wanting
a story to print in his paper.
"What happened last night Mr. Nash?"
"Do you know how the fire was started, sir?"
"Do you think it was arson?"
"Is it true that you were pulled from the estate
unconscious?"

"Were you expecting anything of this kind to happen?"
"Do you know of anyone who might want to hurt you?"
"Was it a spark from the fireplace?"
"Do you think it was the Luthers?
"Was anyone hurt?"
"Why do you think it spread so quickly?"
"Do you expect foul play?"

The trio were hunched together in the midst of the reporters who did not stop their onerous questioning until Ricky held up his hand for silence. Immediately the crowd quieted. Ricky cleared his sore throat and said calmly, "We are not yet sure what caused the fire nor will we be until we are able to inspect the damage."

The reporters scribbled Ricky's words down and the second he stopped talking a reporter asked, "Is it true that you were pulled from the estate unconscious?" Without even a glance at LooAnne or a twinge in his voice Ricky said, "Yes that's true."

"Who was it that saved you, sir?" asked another man.

"I couldn't say, I was unconscious."

"So you don't know who it was that saved your life, sir?"

"I was unconscious," Ricky repeated without directly saying yes or no.

"Do you have any idea why the cause might be arson?" Ricky's face took on surprised look at the thought of such a thing. "I've got no reason to believe that it wasn't started by natural causes," he answered.

"So you don't think it was arson?"

"I'm inclined to believe against it, yes."

"Were you awakened before you passed out or did you

not know what had happened until you regained consciousness?"

"My steward awakened me and while he was getting the girls I passed out from smoke inhalation. He naturally assumed that I had left immediately and took the girls outside."

"But you had not left immediately?" the reporter persisted.

Ricky shook his head, "No I did not."

"Why didn't you leave the second you found out?"

"I didn't realize the fire was as serious as it turned out to be. I was looking for and removing important family items."

"What do you plan to do now that the estate has burned?"

"I plan to survey the damage and then decide from there."

"Have you been back since last night?"

"No I have not."

"Do you-"

"If you gentlemen will excuse us we've got quite a few things that need tending," Ricky interrupted. He herded LooAnne and Amarie through the reporters and set a fast pace down the street away from them. They did not attempt to follow, instead they ran to file their stories, obviously content with what information they had.

Ricky stopped in front of the bakery and watched after them. "I suppose every word I just told them is going to be all over the country come morning."

"Why didn't you tell them that I was the one who pulled you from the house?" LooAnne asked.

"Because then they would have pestered you. The trick is to tell them some of what happened and not answer anything they don't ask. After you've answered a few questions then you leave them to their own conclusions. Whatever it is they print in their paper the truth will eventually come out."

"Can we hurry and get inside?" Amarie asked Ricky uneasily as she looked around at all the people who were staring so hard they were almost gawking.

Ricky nodded understandingly and led the girls into the bakery out of sight of the onlookers. Unfortunately due to the early hour there were quite a few people inside eating breakfast. They all looked up, laying questioning eyes on the Nashes, who tried their best to avert their gaze as they approached a small, circular table in the back.

The trio took a seat and were instantly approached by an elderly lady wearing a flower-covered apron and a kind smile.

"Good morning, Mr. Nash," she greeted, removing her note pad from her apron pocket. "How can I help you this morning?"

"I'd like a cup of black coffee, please." Ricky asked.

The lady nodded and turned to the girls who both ordered raisin muffins with hot chocolate. As she walked away to get their breakfasts LooAnne asked her uncle, "So will we be staying at the hotel again tonight?"

Ricky shook his head, "No, I think that we need a more comfortable atmosphere. We'll head down to Quinn Creek Manor after this and see if we can stay there until

29

more permanent plans can be made."

Amarie frowned thoughtfully, "What is Quinn Creek Manor?"

"It's a place I own on the other side of town. Very comfortable house with a pigeon farm in the back. There's only five acres but the house is pretty. My father used to use it as a boarding house back in the day."

"Do you think we'll be staying there indefinitely?" LooAnne questioned.

Ricky shook his head, "I honestly have no idea what our future holds at the moment. But where we live is irrelevant, we are all alive and that's what matters."

At that moment the elderly lady returned with Ricky, LooAnne, and Amarie's breakfast which they finished within a matter of minutes. Ricky took the last sip of his coffee slowly, enjoying the warmth it radiated throughout his exhausted body. He felt the weight of many things baring down on him, things he felt he had little control over. He would have to find them all a permanent home but the thought of leaving Decatur was appalling to Ricky. He had lived there his entire life, all the memories of his childhood and earlier years had been made in the small town. Ricky could not stand the thought of leaving it. With the house gone, Decatur was all he had left of his former years.

The bell over the front entrance rang as the door was opened and Chris entered. He made is way to the back corner where his employer and the girls were just finishing their breakfast.

"Ah Chris," Ricky greeted his steward, "Sit and have a cup of coffee with us."

"Thank you, sir, but I've had my breakfast," Chris declined politely. "I just came to tell you that the Sedan is outside. I'll be out there waiting for you when you're finished."

"We're ready now," Ricky said as he laid the money on the table and pocketed his wallet.

"I don't mean to rush you, sir," Chris objected.

"No no, the sooner we get a move on the better. You ready, girls?"

Both LooAnne and Amarie nodded and stood, following Ricky and Chris out the door to where the Sedan was parked. The foursome caught many curious stares before Chris opened the door for them and they climbed in the back seat. People had begun to gather on the sidewalk, watching as Chris cranked the vehicle and got in, driving in the direction of Quinn Creek Manor where the girls prayed they would be out of the public's eye.

It was not long before the tall, pointed roof of Triple Creek Hall came into view from above the other buildings. When it came fully into view LooAnne examined it closely, curious as to what the place she would call home for some time looked like. The house was two stories high and was a bright yellow with green shutters. It had a small front porch that framed the green door and a second story balcony where a maid stood beating out a rug that was hung over the railing, her cold breath shooting into the air. The bare oak tree that stood beside the house was swaying in the light winter breeze, it's topmost branches gently scraping the side of the house. It was in no way similar to the Nash Estate and LooAnne found herself somewhat disappointed.

Chris parked the Sedan in front of the little white fence that surrounded the yard and opened the doors for Ricky and the girls. Ricky exited the car, thanking Chris, and then made his way through the open gate to the front door. He knocked on it and a few seconds later it was opened by a short, middle aged woman with grayish-blond hair and a kind, gentle look on her fine-lined face. Her eyes widened when she saw Ricky and the girls.

"Why Mr. Nash," she exclaimed, surprised to see him standing there. "I haven't seen you in some time, sir. How are you?"

"I'm afraid we're not as well as we could be, Mrs. Munro. I'm sorry for the short notice but we need a place to stay."

"Yes, I just heard about the estate, I'm terribly sorry. Do you know what the damages are yet?"

Ricky shook his head. "My steward and I are going out there as soon as I get the girls settled in."

"Well come right in and make yourselves at home. I'll show you the rooms that would best suit y'all.

Mrs. Munro led the way through the beautifully furnished first floor to the stairs that curled in a spiral up to the second floor. The railing was made of mettle and the stairs were carpeted with a dark red carpet as was the entry hall. The second floor corridor was also carpeted with this same red and the hallway went all the way to the front of the house where the door to the balcony was. Lining the hall were four doors, one of which Mrs. Munro opened.

"I'm sorry that the rooms aren't perfectly clean but I'll get one of the maids to change the sheets and dust while you're gone, Mr. Nash." Mrs. Munro told Amarie that she could have this room, the next was LooAnne's and the last Ricky's. LooAnne's room had flowered wallpaper on the walls and a high posted bed with a white canopy over it. A dresser sat in the corner and a role-top desk in another. An armchair sat before the small fireplace with a little tea table to it's right. LooAnne went to the window of her room and pulled back the blue curtains. The window overlooked the back of the house where she saw the pigeon coop and a tall white fence to provide more privacy. She was glad that, although it was in the midst of town, the house was not open to much public surveillance and therefore would provide them with the solitude they all desired. It was a lovely place and very well kept, but it was not home nor could it ever be.

LooAnne then remembered that Ricky had said that he was going to the estate as soon as they were all settled. She wanted badly to go so she decided to ask Ricky if it was alright with him. She opened her door and peeked down the hall where she could see Ricky talking to Mrs. Munro just outside his bedroom door.

"I'm sorry about the short notice, Mrs. Munro," Ricky was saying.

"Oh, it's not a problem at all," she assured him with a wave of her hand. "I'll run downstairs and see if I can get you something to eat and maybe find some clothes for the girls."

LooAnne waited, watching from her room until Mrs. Munro went downstairs, then she walked down the hall and stuck her head in Ricky's open door, knocking on the door frame as she did. Ricky sat on the side of his bed loosening his tie.

He looked up when he heard his niece knock. "Yes dear?"

LooAnne went to the bedside and asked, "Is it alright if I go with you to the estate?"

Ricky frowned. "Are you sure that's a wise decision, my dear?"

LooAnne nodded, "I want to see it."

Ricky nodded understandingly, "It won't be pretty," he warned.

"I know, but I have to see it. It all happened so fast last night, I have to know that it wasn't a dream."

Ricky sighed and nodded, "I know the feeling," he admitted, "But as I said, the sight will not be a pretty one. I would think it to be quite terrifying actually."

LooAnne shrugged, "And when has that ever stopped me?"

Ricky smiled wanly. "It certainly didn't stop you last night when you realized I was still inside."

LooAnne let her shoulders droop and leaned against the bedpost. "Last night," she repeated. "It certainly doesn't seem like last night. It seems as if it's been days since it happened but at the same time it almost doesn't feel real."

Ricky nodded soberly. "I could not agree with you more. That was a brave thing you did, coming back into the house, I owe you my life."

LooAnne blushed and lowered her head. Ricky lifted her chin up to where he could look her in the eye and said, "I'm sorry, for how I handled the whole Kyle Denson incident. I was wrong."

LooAnne shook her head in disagreement, "Not nearly as wrong as I was. I can't believe that I was so disrespectful, I've got so much Luther in me I fear I'll never change."

Ricky frowned as though he had been taken aback by his niece's statement. "Change? My dear, I don't want you to entertain such a thought. If you want to subdue your impetuous temper I'll not argue with you, but don't ever try to get rid of the Luther inside you or you might end up getting rid of the real you."

"But what if the real me isn't what I want it to be? What if the real me is someone I've been hiding since I became a Nash? I sometimes feel as though I'm living a lie."

"But you aren't, LooAnne," Ricky assured her, trying desperately to form his words so that his niece would understand. "Your name does not define you. Whether you go by LooAnne Nash or Beth Luther it doesn't make you anyone different from who you are. The Lord put you into that situation for some reason, a reason that we will one day see."

"I know that, Uncle Ricky, but it's so hard to look back on it all positively. To know that I was taught to commit such horrors and that I was letting it happen right before my eyes, how can you see that and not be appalled?"

"LooAnne, the Luthers were smart people," Ricky stated. "But they used their wisdom for nothing but self gain and to harm others. You're not like them; you don't have the mindset and thoughtlessness of a criminal therefore you won't use that wisdom for the things they did, you'll use it for the good of others and that's what you were intended to do."

LooAnne pondered these thoughts carefully, never having heard anyone say it in such a way. Her uncle was right, that had been the whole reason she had left her family to begin with, because she was an outcast, disliked because she was different, because she knew that what they did was wrong.

LooAnne looked at her uncle and smiled gratefully, "Thank you, Uncle Ricky. I've never thought of it in such a way before."

Ricky returned his niece's smile and nodded, "You are very welcome, my dear. I hope that we can put our bickering behind us?"

LooAnne nodded in full agreement with the idea. "Now back to my original question; may I go with you to the estate?"

Ricky nodded solemnly, "You may, but I warn you, you'll not like it."

"I don't expect to, but at the same time I must see it."

"Well in that case let's be on our way." Ricky stood, straightened his tie, and followed LooAnne downstairs where Chris was waiting in the entry hall talking to Mrs. Munro.

"Are you ready, sir?" he asked.

"We are, Mr. Block. Mrs. Munro we'll be back within the next two hours."

"Lunch will be on the table waiting for you, sir," she smiled kindly.

Ricky thanked her and the threesome exited the house. They climbed into the Sedan and Chris drove through

town and down the country road towards the estate.
"How are the staff getting on?" Ricky asked his steward
as they drove.

"The hands are working at the ranch as they have
lodging in the bunch house. I sent the maids and butler
home to their families and those who had none are
staying at the hotel in town."

"You mean to say that the servant's quarters burned as
well?" Ricky asked, though he sounded none too
surprised.

"I'm afraid so, sir. Everything within ten feet of the
house burned, including the smoke and ice houses. The
bunk house and stables are well away so they escaped
without so much as a singe."

"For that we must be thankful I suppose, Mr. Block,"
Ricky mused, trying to make the best of the situation.
LooAnne, however, could feel a knot growing in the pit
of her stomach with each word Chris spoke. A part of
her refused to believe that such a tragedy could befall
her home, and yet as they grew nearer the nightmare
became reality. The roofs of the bunk house, barn and
stables came into view but in the spot where one would
normally see the third story of the Nash Estate was
nothing but bare, blue sky. As they rounded the corner
LooAnne tried to prepare herself for what she would
see, but in no way could her emotions have been ready
for the next moment. They took the turn at what seemed
like a sluggish pace, each moment baring it's own
weight. When they rounded the corner the trio looked
toward the empty space where the house had once stood.
It was nothing but level ground with three tall chimneys

that reached into the sky like bare trees on a winter day. At the base were the still smoldering beams.

LooAnne's hand flew to her mouth in shock and she could feel tears beginning to puddle in her eyes, though she refused to allow them to fall.

The sight of Ricky's lifelong home burned to the ground was too much for him to whiteness. He turned away from it, his expression laden with pain.

The sky over the sight looked bare and somehow lonely. The trees that had stood at the house's side were scorched and dying. One of the larger trees had succumb to the flames and had fallen, joining the smoldering beams. When the Sedan pulled up Ricky, Chris, and LooAnne slowly exited and stood in shock. For a moment the three remained silently looking at the heap of blackened wood, heartbroken at the sight of it. The smell of smoke was strong, almost overbearing.

Ricky slowly approached what was left of his home. He kicked a loose board that toppled over into the pile, breaking the silence with a crack as it fell. Ricky looked out over the heap and shook his head sorrowfully.

"What did you manage to save, Chris?" he asked, a catch in his deep voice.

"The ranch hands pulled out a good deal of things, they've got them in the bunk house."

Ricky nodded his approval and then said, "My mind is a muddle, Mr. Block. I would appreciate your opinion on the matter?"

Chris sighed, "I'm sure I don't now what to think, sir."

Ricky turned away from the remains of the house and faced his steward and niece. "Is it possible, and on top of that, wise to entertain the idea of rebuilding it?"

Chris raised his eyebrows at this new thought. "It would take quite some time, sir. Maybe even up to two years. Not to mention the price would be none too small."

Ricky sighed in contemplation, "So you would not advise it?"

"It's hardly up to me, sir. I understand why you would want to build it back and, if you don't mind me saying, you certainly have the means to. If that's what you want, then I don't advise against it."

Ricky nodded, "That's what I want but I fear I may be out of my mind. I abhor the thought of leaving here and that's what it would come to should I not have a place to live."

"Uncle Ricky, this is your home," LooAnne spoke up, "if you want to stay here then I think you should do all you can to do so."

Ricky smiled at his niece, "Thank you, LooAnne. In that case, the original blueprints to the estate are in the bank safely unburned. I'll get them for you, Chris, and you do whatever necessary to build it back."

"Consider it done, sir," Chris assured his employer.

LooAnne looked out over the ruin and shook her head dolefully. "We were all right here, how did it burn so quickly?"

Ricky shrugged, setting his gaze once again on the burned rubble. "I wish I knew, my dear. I assumed that it was started by a spark from the fireplace, but there could be a number of different explanations considering it burned so quickly." Ricky's frown suddenly deepened. "You know," he mused aloud, "until our encounter with those reporters this morning I had not thought of arson as a possibility, but I suppose we had better not rule anything out."

"Arson?" LooAnne and Chris exclaimed in unison. "Who would want to burn down the estate, sir?" Chris asked, astounded that such a thought had even entered Ricky's mind.

"I've no idea, Chris. And I'm not saying that it was anything more than a spark from the fireplace but we've got to keep the idea in mind."

Ricky squatted down next to the timbers and examined them, then he straitened and said, "If there was any evidence that this was no accident it's gone now."

Just as her uncle finished his statement LooAnne saw an object that contradicted him. "No it isn't," she exclaimed as she carefully walked to the edge of the debris and gingerly pulled a half burned can from the ashes. She held it up so that her uncle could see it. Ricky took it and squinted at the scorched label, it read:

Carter's Kerosene

"Well there's the answer to our question right here," Ricky stated, staring hard at the can which had contained a liquid used to ignite his house.

"Here's another one," Chris spoke up from where he stood next to the road. "And another one," he said as he picked up two identical cans to the one that Ricky held. "There's probably more," Ricky said as he heaved the can into the debris causing it to smash into peaces. "Whoever did this certainly did a thorough job." He

40

shook his head as though he were in shock, "Who in possession of all their senses would want to burn down a house with it's residents still inside?"

Suddenly there came an evil cackle from behind Ricky, Chris, and LooAnne, startling them and breaking the thoughtful silence that had fallen. The three whirled around to face the source of the laughter and the sight that met them took them all by surprise. There, standing on the other side of the burned, smoldering timbers, was a man of middle age, clothed in soiled overalls and a ratted wool coat. His hair was a tangle of blond and gray wisps and his face was streaked with dirt.

His satisfied, eccentric laugh sent chills down Chris and LooAnne's spines, but Ricky found himself too overcome with curiosity to feel anything else. He knew this man from somewhere, he was sure of it, but his mind was unable to place him. Ricky cocked his head in contemplation as he looked at the man, trying to figure out why the sight of him brought back memories from the past. And then he remembered! His expression changed and his eyes narrowed as his curiosity was instantly replaced by disgust.

The eccentric man stopped his laughing and looked Ricky in the eye, a satisfied smirk on his face. "Figured it out yet, Nash?" he asked.

Chris looked up at Ricky in bewilderment, his eyes asking for an answer as to how his employer knew this ratted man. LooAnne, however, felt the color rush from her face as she herself, realized who he was.

Ricky nodded slowly in answer to the man's question, his hard gaze fixed on him. "I figured it out. You never carried out your revenge thoroughly did you?"

The man shook his head, the smirk never leaving his face. "But after all these years I got my chance. You didn't think I was just gonna forget it did you?"

"Frankly that is exactly what I thought. I had gladly rid my mind of you until this very moment."

"I came to even up the score and from the looks o' your beautifully scorched house I recon I succeeded."

"I should have done away with you that very day!" Ricky exclaimed, a look of pure rage on his face, "And now I regret having been civil! You've burned down my home, you nearly got me and my niece killed, and now you're standing here boasting about it! I warn you right now, I've no intention of letting you escape this time, Devin Luther!"

FOUR

Honor and Pride

*Beloved, do not avenge yourselves,
but rather give place to wrath; for it
is written: "Vengeance is Mine, I will
repay," saith the Lord.
Romans 21:19-21*

*Do not be conformed to this world, but be
transformed by the renewal of your mind,
that by testing you my discern what is the
will of God, what is good and acceptable,
and perfect. Romans 12:2*

It was indeed Devin Luther! He was much older and his visage lined with age, but his large body was well built and he looked at Ricky as though he were amused by the threat.

LooAnne sank behind Chris so that Devin would not get a good look at her. The fear that he would recognize her coursed through her body though she did not let it show. Devin looked at Ricky and laughed again. "You talk big, Nash. Too bad that's all you are, talk."

It was Ricky's turn to look amused."Coming from the man who failed to overthrow me twice."

Devin scoffed. "That was when I was young and foolish."

"Your wisdom does little for you when you've already decided to fight someone you know is better," Ricky countered.

"Better eh? Wouldn't wanna prove it to me would ya, Nash?" Devin challenged.

"I would like nothing better then to take my anger out on the man who caused such heartbreak to my family," Ricky stated.

Devin grinned evilly, "Then let's not waist no time."

LooAnne's heart was racing inside her chest, she could not let her uncle engage in combat with this man when she knew too well who was the superior fighter. But LooAnne failed to find a way around it as her uncle was the most capable of the three of them, but surely they were not the only ones on the property, she thought. There had to be ranch hands near the stables if only she could run and get them before her uncle got hurt!

LooAnne saw no harm in trying so while Devin was distracted by his banter she took off towards the stable door, running as fast as her legs could take her

When she reached it, LooAnne whispered a prayer that there would be at least one young ranch hand inside that could help fight off Devin Luther, and much to her relief she saw none other than Sam Moore hovering over the open hood of the tractor.

"Mr. Moore!" LooAnne called as she ran towards him. Sam snapped to attention upon hearing LooAnne's

frantic summons. "Miss Nash, what's wrong?" he asked.
"It's a Luther!" she cried, "Please, you have to help my
uncle and Mr. Block!"
Sam's eyes widened, "Where are they?" he asked,
tightening his grip on the wrench in his hand.
"Out front!" LooAnne answered.
Sam wasted no time in running past LooAnne and out
the stable doors to aid Ricky and Chris. LooAnne
followed close behind him and the instant she exited the
stable her heart dropped at the sight that met her eyes.
Ricky had just fallen to the ground as he received a blow
to the face from Devin who was looming over him!
Chris lunged at Devin in a bold attempt to protect Ricky
but was flung aside as the enraged Luther went to punch
Ricky again! Before he could, however, Sam had arrived
at the scene and stuck him in the back of the head with
the wrench! Devin clutched his head in his hands and
staggered to the side, but he was not daunted for long!
Devin recovered after only a moment and in his heated
rage he threw yet another punch at Ricky only to have
Sam strike him again with the wrench! Devin fell to his
knees this time but did not stay there long, he stumbled
to his feet and with an angry exclamation the Luther
took off away from his opponents, leaving them
somewhat stunned!
Chris was instantly at his employer's side, helping Ricky
to his feet.
"Uncle Ricky are you okay?" LooAnne asked anxiously
as she saw blood dripping from her uncle's lip and nose.
"I'm fine, LooAnne," Ricky assured her as he held his
pocket square to his bleeding nostril.

45

"Are you sure, sir?" Chris asked, obviously shaken by the Luther encounter.

"I'm quite sure, Mr. Block," Ricky insisted. He then took notice of Sam Moore who was looking on anxiously. Ricky extended his hand to the foreman and said, "I don't know how to thank you, Sam."

The young man shook his head as he took his employer's hand, "It was my pleasure, sir. I'm glad I could help."

"So am I. Had it not been for you there's no telling what would have happened. I'll see that you're properly rewarded for your bravery."

"No need to do that, sir," Sam objected. "I assure you it was my pleasure."

"And I assure *you* that tweaking your paycheck will be mine," Ricky smiled.

Sam thanked Ricky profusely before returning to his work in the stables. LooAnne examined her uncle's bleeding nose and lip and her heart instantly began to ache. They could have easily been murdered by Devin, the older brother of LooAnne's own father! And it had been he who had burned down the estate! LooAnne had never been so ashamed in her life as the thought of what her family had done.

"I'm so sorry, Uncle Ricky," she apologized dismally.

Ricky raised his eye brows at his niece, "Sorry for what, LooAnne?"

"For Uncle Devin burning down your house and nearly killing you," she said as though it were obvious.

Ricky shook his head, "You have no reason to apologize for what that scoundrel does. He's not taken anything from me that can not be replaced."

LooAnne shook her head in bold disagreement, "Ever since the beginning of their existence my family has done nothing but torment you," she argued, feeling more and more enraged towards the Luthers as she thought of all they had committed with no greater intention than to harm her uncle. "They've burned down your house, they're the reason your nose is bleeding, the reason you've lost everything, and on top of all that they are the reason you lost your sister!"

Ricky found himself taken back by his niece's words. Never in the years he had known her had she brought up the subject of his sister, and it was this that caused him to realize how strongly she felt on the topic. Ricky laid his hand on his niece's shoulder gently before speaking, "LooAnne, out of all the Luthers in this world the only one that really hurt me was the one I loved. And it was because I loved her that my sister hurt me so badly. I can build another house, the wounds on my face will heal, but I will never get her back and that was her choice. The Luthers had little to do with it." Ricky gazed out over the fields in the direction of the Luther Estate as though he were remembering that night she left. "Amanda was my baby sister, I was bound and determined to protect her and the fact that I had failed added to the pain she caused by running away. But it's in the past now. All any of us can do is forgive her for her choice. Everything else that her family – that our family – has ever done is irrelevant, because they have failed to take anything from me that I could not replace."

LooAnne could feel a knot growing in her throat as she

took in her uncle's words. As per usual what he said had been the truth. She was not responsible for the actions of her deranged relatives, nor was it through fault of her own that she had been born into their potential corruption. She could only be thankful that she had not been one of those corrupted.

LooAnne forced back the tears that threatened to spill and looked her uncle in the eyes. "Thank you, Uncle Ricky. I'm sorry for getting so angry."

"LooAnne you need to cease these apologies. I assure you, you have nothing to be sorry for. It's all been dealt with and is behind us now."

This statement caused a new thought to form in LooAnne's mind. Though they were done for the present, it was not forever behind them. Devin would come back with a new ruse to achieve his revenge and should they be unprepared, he would succeed!

"He'll be back, Uncle Ricky," LooAnne warned. "He was defeated a third time and brought great disgrace to himself. He'll have to do something rash to earn back his reputation with the family!"

Ricky frowned thoughtfully, "Surely after having been beaten three times he will have given up."

"No!" LooAnne protested, "He'll never give up. To him it is better to die with a good reputation then to live in shame."

"You're saying he would give his life to get back at me?" Ricky asked although he knew very well what his niece was conveying.

LooAnne nodded her head grudgingly. "I'm afraid so, he'll not stop until he has avenged himself, and that would most certainly involve the death of someone." Ricky sighed and ran his hand through his graying hair. "Or more than one someones should he try something so bold as to burn down another of my estates. He could have easily killed everyone inside last night. Thank the Lord that he didn't."

"Maybe," Chris spoke up, "if you ask the sheriff, he'll go up with a posse and get Devin Luther? The Luthers haven't raided the town in some time, maybe they're getting older and weaker?"

Ricky shook his head. "I tried that once," he said, looking off into space as the memory was brought to life inside him, "taking advantage of the fact that people would stick their neck out for my sister just because she was the daughter of the great Rick Nash. I got seven innocent men killed to my selfish request, I have no intention of doing it again. One thing I don't understand though, why did the guards not see Devin when he was dowsing the house in kerosene?"

Chris knit his brow thoughtfully, "I'm not sure, sir, the thought had not entered my mind until now."

"They probably didn't see him," LooAnne suggested, "Luthers are rarely seen unless they wish to be."

"But he could have a hard time concealing the smell," Ricky pointed out.

"That's true, it would have been nearly impossible," LooAnne agreed.

"If the guards said nothing about it," Ricky mused.

"Then one of them, if not all of them, were in on it!" The trio looked at one another in dismay, this was the only logical explanation for the guard's actions.

"They helped us put out the fire," Chris said. "And they were among those pulling things from the estate. Surely had they been involved they wold have wanted as much damage to be done as possible."

Ricky thought for a moment trying to figure in his mind which one of his supposed loyal guards would stoop low enough as to burn down the estate. Suddenly Ricky recalled a scenario from the night before and his suspicions were confirmed! "I know who it was," he suddenly stated.

"Who?" LooAnne and Chris asked in the same breath.

"Stan Edwards and Elisha Morrison."

"Why them?" Chris wondered aloud.

"Because, Lyndon Mockle is normally stationed at the back door but last night he swapped with Elisha Morrison because Elisha said that he wanted a change of scenery just for one night. That put Elisha at one end of the house and Stan Edwards at the other. They could get in, with Devin Luther, and poor the kerosene on the inside, not the outside, and that would assure that the house was destroyed." Ricky shook his head hopelessly, his face taking on a forlorn expression. "If you can't trust a guard then who can you trust? I've never slept with the fear that someone would break in just because there were guards outside every door. I never imagined that one of the guards would turn on me, let alone two!"

LooAnne frowned deeply, "That just can't be," she mused. "Luthers pride themselves on working alone, no one but Luthers are allowed to work with Luthers. I think that maybe Devin threatened them in some way." Ricky looked at his niece dubiously, "Threatened them to such an extent that they would stand there while the house burned with us all inside?"

"Oh yes, people have been known to do horrible things just because of Luther threats. Devin probably told them that he would kidnap or hurt some of their loved ones. The guards are willing to give their lives to save the estate and you and I but not their family's lives."

Ricky gave this some thought and then said to Chris, "Next time you get a chance, I want you to talk to Stan Edwards and Elisha Morrison."

"Yes sir," Chris agreed.

Ricky turned towards the Huckster and said, "Let's get back to town so we can make arrangements to get this debris cleaned up."

He, Chris, and LooAnne got into the automobile and Chris drove in the direction of town.

The moment LooAnne entered her room at Triple Creek Hall she fell backwards onto her embroidered comforter, physically and emotionally exhausted after the encounter with Devin Luther. She closed her eyes and tried to imagine that she was lying in her own bed in her room at the Nash Estate, but it was not the same. The mattress was hard and the sheets rough. The house, although pleasant enough, was foreign to her with it's new sounds, smells, and people.

LooAnne remembered the sight of the destroyed estate, the burned pile of wood that had once been her home, her things among the scorched timbers, nothing but smoldering ashes. To make matters worse, it had been her own relation who had done it. LooAnne thought of Ricky, having to stand there and see the only home he had ever known burn like an enormous bonfire right before his eyes, to see all the memories he had accumulated over his forty-five years of living within its walls, laying in a hideous charred jumble. It pained LooAnne to think that her own relatives, her *family*, could commit such heinous crimes, and that she herself could be numbered among them as their blood-relative. Suddenly LooAnne remembered Kyle Denson. He would surely be sick with worry after hearing of the accident which by this time had spread throughout all the state of Texas. She decided to write Kyle a letter, to rehearse the tragic experience to him but assure him that she, her uncle, and Amarie were safe and unharmed, leaving out the blistered burn on her arm. LooAnne went to the roll-top desk looking for some paper and a pencil. Finding both she sat down at the desk and wrote to Kyle.

Dear Kyle,

I'm sure that you've heard the news of the estate. It burned before we could do anything but get out with our lives. I was sound asleep when Amarie awoke me and we ran to safety outside. The heat and smoke were terrible. Had we stayed even a moment longer inside I fear that we would not have escaped with our lives. There was no saving the house which was, by this point, completely engulfed in flames. It burned to the ground, nothing left but debris, but we're all safe and unharmed, thank the Lord. We're staying at Triple Creek Hall in downtown Decatur. Uncle Ricky plans to

*have the estate rebuilt and we hope to be in it
sometime next year, I hope and pray that it doesn't
take that long. It has only been a few hours and
already I feel extremely homesick.
I miss you so much and wish that you had been here
last night. Although I know that you are in pursuit of
your dream and I would never deny you that.
I love you so much, Kyle.*

Your's,

LooAnne

LooAnne folded the letter and slipped it into an
envelope which she also found in the desk. She wrote
down Kyle's address on the front then tucked it into her
skirt pocket as she went down the hall to her uncle's
room and knocked on the door.
"Come in," came Ricky's somewhat drowsy voice.
LooAnne opened the door and stepped into her uncle's
room. Ricky lay on his bed with his hands behind his
head and his eyes closed, looking extremely fatigued but
comfortable. LooAnne strode to the bedside and asked
quietly, "Did I awaken you?"
Ricky shook his head, his eyes remaining closed, "I
wasn't sleeping, just resting my eyes. What is it you
need?"
"May I have a stamp?" LooAnne asked discreetly, not
wanting her uncle to be displeased by the thought of her
sending a letter to Kyle Denson.
Ricky's brow raised at her question though he still did

not open his eyes, "A stamp?" he repeated. "What for?"

"I – I need to send a letter."

"I suppose I don't need to ask who it's for?" Ricky's voice was calm, giving off no indication of his feels towards this notion.

LooAnne looked down at the floor and said, "I have to tell him of the fire. He'll hear and be worried and -"

"You don't have to explain," Ricky said. He opened his eyes and smiled kindly at his niece. "The stamps are in my wallet on the bureau there." Ricky gestured to the piece of furniture across the room where his leather wallet lay.

LooAnne, however, made no move to get them, she stared at her uncle, searchingly. "You're not angry?" she asked.

Ricky shook his head. "Certainly not, my dear. I understand that you are no longer a child in need of my unyielding protection. You need to find a young suitor who will fall in love with you and you with him, and if you think that you have found him and that it is God's will then I'll not stand in your way. But I still do not advocate the idea of being tied to each other while he is away for so long. You may not know what feelings you will have for each other four years from now. Granted you may still be madly in love and grow old together with twenty children, but let's not get ahead of ourselves for the time being, eh?"

LooAnne smiled gratefully at her uncle, "You're perfectly right, Uncle Ricky. Thank you."

"Thank *you* for being patient with me, my dear," Ricky said. "It's hard on an old man to watch his little girl grow up."

LooAnne withdrew in mock hurt. "Uncle Ricky I am not a little girl, nor are you an old man."

Ricky chuckled, "As to the latter I fear neither of us can keep fooling ourselves, and you will always be my little girl."

FIVE

A Shocking Accusation

*They have also surrounded me with
words of hatred, and fought against
me with a cause. In return for my love
they are my accusers, but I give myself
to prayer. Psalm 109:3 and 4*

*Now Cain talked with Abel his
brother; and it came to pass,
when they were in the field, that
Cain rose up against Abel his brother
and killed him. Genesis 4:8*

Headlines:
Man Killed On Street By Unknown Shooter

**Twenty-one-year-old Andy Stacey was shot down by
an unknown shooter in broad daylight on March 7th
at seven fifteen AM. He and his brothers were
passing through Decatur, Texas on their way to
Austin when an unseen shooter shot and killed Andy**

Stacey. The shot was fired from an alley next to the drug store in downtown Decatur. After a long, futile search for the shooter it is concluded that this was just another attack on the town committed by the dastardly Luther family. The U.S. Marshal's office asks that everyone please take every precaution possible to protect themselves from the well-known, well hated Luthers.

Ricky frowned as he read the headlines in the morning paper. He sat at the table in the dining room of Triple Creek Hall eating breakfast with LooAnne and Amarie. It was a sunny, spring morning with a cool breeze hissing through the open window.
The sun had just appeared from behind the horizon and was casting it's early morning rays across the town. It had been a little over a year since the estate had burned and the reconstruction was well in progress. Chris had confronted the guards not long after discovering that they had somehow been involved in the scheme to destroy the estate and they had both admitted to allowing Devin Luther into the house after he had threatened them with their families' lives should they refuse to cooperate. Both guards were extremely despondent when faced with the question, each of them apologizing to the Nashes in person for what they had been forced into. They, however, found their employer extremely understanding, allowing both the guards to return to work as soon as the estate was rebuilt.
LooAnne's burn was now an ugly scar on her forearm, it had healed well but was a forever present reminder of

the day she and her uncle had nearly lost their lives. She always wore the ring that her uncle had almost died to save from the torched house. She loved it, not only for it's allure but because it had once been worn by her own mother.

Upon hearing her uncle's troubled sigh, LooAnne looked up from her plate, her brow furrowing when she saw Ricky's disquieted expression, "What's the matter, Uncle Ricky?" she asked. "You look upset."

Ricky nodded towards the paper in his hands and said, "This man that was killed, he's - "

Before Ricky could finish Mrs. Munro entered the dining room accompanied by a hansom young man who appeared to be quite unnerved. He was tall and had a bit of red hair that protruded from beneath his worn cap. His eyes showed his fatigue and looked as though he had shed a few tears.

Ricky looked up at the visitor and then in an instant he stood, taking the young man into his embrace. "It's good to see you, Red," he said as he pulled away and clapped the young man on the back. "I don't know how to express my sorrow for you all. He was a good kid."

The young man whom Ricky had addressed as 'Red' nodded, managing a strained smile. "He was, Ricky. I'm sorry to bother you during breakfast but I could think of no one else to go to."

"Of course you are always welcome here, you know that. I should hope that you and you're brothers and sister will stay here for as long as you need?"

Red nodded solemnly, "That's what I came to see you about actually. We won't be here long, only until the arrangements can be settled."

"You stay as long as you like, Red," Ricky insisted.

"I hate to impose on you," Red objected.

"Nonsense, it's a pleasure to host you after not seeing you in so long. Where are your siblings?"

Red's eyes turned downcast and his face instantly took on a pensive expression. "They're over at the undertaker's still, I told them I would be right back with your answer."

"Well my answer is yes," Ricky said, laying a reassuring hand on the young man's shoulder. "We would be pleased if you stayed for breakfast as well?"

Red shook his head but smiled gratefully, "Thank you but I'm afraid I can't. I gotta meet the others down at the undertaker's."

Ricky nodded understandingly, "Alright. As soon as you're ready feel free to come straight here and get settled in."

The young man smiled appreciatively, "We will, thank you again, Ricky."

"Don't mention it. I'll count on seeing you all for supper."

Red nodded, "We'll be here." The younger man turned and tipped his hat to LooAnne and Amarie before excusing himself and leaving the room abruptly.

Ricky returned to his seat, his face contorted in bemusement. He let himself drop into his chair and stared off into space.

LooAnne frowned at her uncle's bewildered expression before asking, "Who was that man, Uncle Ricky?"

This question seemed to snap Ricky out of his deep

thoughts. He faced his niece with somber eyes and said, "His name is Red Stacey, he's my cousin."

"Your cousin?" LooAnne repeated.

"Yes, I just now heard in the paper of his brother's most untimely death. Andy was shot by one of the Luthers while they were in town. They don't have any other place to go so they'll be staying here until they're done with the arrangements for Andy's funeral." Ricky picked up the paper and began reading the story more intently.

"They?" LooAnne asked.

"Red and his brothers and sister," Ricky clarified.

"Red sure is an strange name," Amarie commented.

Ricky cast Amarie a warning look from over the top of his paper. "If I were you I wouldn't bring up that subject to him or to any of his brothers."

"Does he not like his name?" Amarie asked curiously.

"No he does not, and non of the other boys do either."

"Whatever for?"

"It's quite a short story but one I do not have leave to tell you," Ricky answered. "Just call him Red and forget that is not his given name."

Amarie nodded, "Yes, sir."

"Is Red the oldest?" LooAnne asked.

"No, he's got one older brother. His parents passed away not long ago and the death of his brother must be a terrible blow to the family." Ricky looked at his watch and said, "You girls had better get a move on. Wouldn't want to be late for your tutorial."

LooAnne and Amarie finished eating and then left for their privet lessons. As they walked through town LooAnne's thoughts dwelt solely on Red Stacey. He had struck her as a queer kind of man, one of many untold secrets, like herself. His outward appearance was grungy and unkempt but his interactions with Ricky showed a very tender personality. LooAnne found that she could not keep her mind of this peculiar individual. She thought about him all through her lessons, her mind differing from one subject to the next with the thoughts of her uncle's cousin in the back of her mind. She looked forward to meeting his brothers and sister when she got back to the house.

At three o'clock the girls' daily lessons were accomplished and LooAnne and Amarie were picked up in the Sedan by Quinn Creek Manor's valet. When they arrived back at the house they saw the Huckster parked in front which meant that Chris was back from the estate. The majority of his time was spent there supervising the reconstruction which was going quickly with the added help of townsmen being payed high wages for their labor. The Nashes expected to be back in their home sometime within the next month.

When LooAnne and Amarie walked inside they were met with the sound of voices coming from the parlor. The girls removed their coats and handed them to the butler then went to the door of the parlor and peered inside.

Ricky was seated on the chesterfield sofa next to Red and another young man whom the girls did not recognize. Chris was standing in the corner leaning against the wall with his arms folded as he listened to the conversation. Seated comfortably on the settee just across from Ricky and Red was a man and a young woman about LooAnne's age, whom she noticed to have a much lighter complexion then her brothers. They were all very somber, serious looking men, their jet black hair adding to their humorless expressions.

Standing behind the settee was a man of like demeanor who looked to be the oldest of the siblings, he was busy giving Ricky a full account of his brother's death.

When Ricky saw LooAnne and Amarie standing in the doorway his face brightened from it's sorrowful expression and he stood. "Ah girls, come in."

As they entered the parlor Ricky introduced them to his cousins. "LooAnne, Amarie, these are my cousins, Alec, Red, Phil, Ty, Lee, and Theodora Stacey. Guys this is my niece, LooAnne Nash, and my ward, Amarie Hearten."

LooAnne and Amarie nodded in polite acknowledgment of the introduction and then listened closely as Alec Stacey, the oldest of the six, went on with the story of how Andy Stacey had been killed.

"We were on our way to the hotel when we heard a gun shot. At first we all thought that it was just some fella goofin' around but then we saw that Andy had been shot... and that he was dead. There was no sign of the shooter and the sheriff said that it was probably the Luthers."

Ricky nodded. "There's hardly a family in Decatur that hasn't been faced with the Luther's terrors. They're like a plague around here, but nonetheless, Decatur is growing and will soon be able to overcome the Luthers and they'll be nothing but a memory instead a shadow over us."

"It's been years, Ricky," Alec stated, "Why has no one done anything about them? After all they did to you and to this town I would imagine someone would be done with their shenanigans and put an end to it."

Ricky only shook his head despairingly, "You don't understand, Alec. We've tried, the sheriff has tried, but it has only resulted in the death of many innocent people. Law has been scarce out west. We must be patient until the time comes when we are strong enough to overthrow them. If we act too quickly the townspeople would be put in grave danger, and they would surely lose many loved ones."

"But you outnumber them!" Alec protested, "You're a whole town and they're just a family."

"People are afraid, Alec, even the sheriff and his deputies are afraid. They are afraid that they'll lose someone close to them, a husband, brother, or son, or even a wife or daughter should the Luthers come into town. You can't blame them for not wanting to fight."

Alec sighed in defeat, resolving not to pursue the subject any further. "Well, Ricky, thanks for letting us stay here until we get things taken care of. We really are beholden to you."

"You're more then welcome here, Alec. We should be moving in a couple of weeks though, thank the Lord. Not that this place has not fit our needs well but I miss the solitude of the country and the general feeling of home. I know the girls do as well."

"Whatever happened to the estate?" Red asked. "Did you figure out what caused the fire?"

Ricky nodded. "Venture a guess."

Red frowned, knowingly. "It wasn't the Luthers was it?" he asked.

Ricky nodded wistfully, "I'm afraid it was. More particularly Devin Luther."

The Staceys looked exasperated. "Why?" Red asked, appalled.

"I had beaten him in a fight many years ago when we were both very young," Ricky explained, "He came back to avenge himself on me. That's what I mean when I say that people are afraid that one of the Luthers will get away if we attack them. If they come back they'll do much worse. No matter the time or century they will come back and they will get revenge. Devin Luther burned the estate more than a year ago and it's been..." Ricky counted the years in his head..."it's been twenty six years since I last fought him. The best example there is of how long they hold their grudges."

"That's amazing," Theodora mused, shaking her head unbelievably.

Ricky nodded, "It is. So many years ago that it happened, it seems as though it has been a lifetime."

The day he had first fought Devin Luther was vivid in Ricky's mind. He recalled trying to get Susan to ride to town with him. She had refused and taken the shortcut through the field where Devin Luther had attacked her. Ricky remembered hearing her scream, riding after her, and diving off of Stingray's back, tackling his assailant to the ground where he had lain in the scorching sun unconscious. Devin had come back the next day to even the score and Ricky had beaten him again in every effort to save Susan from the hands of a savage man who sought to take her for his own.

It had been twenty six years since the day that he fought Devin for the first time. It barely seemed possible to Ricky that all of that time had passed.

While he talked further with his cousins LooAnne left to see if there were any letters for her from Kyle. She went to the study where Mrs. Munro was seated behind the desk scrutinizing some paperwork that sat before her. LooAnne knocked on the ajar door lightly before entering. The housekeeper looked up and smiled at LooAnne before reaching into the desk and handing LooAnne an envelope. "I assume that this is what you're looking for, Miss Nash?" she asked knowingly.

LooAnne grinned and took the letter. "Indeed it is. Thank you, Mrs. Munro."

"You're very welcome."

LooAnne retreated to the privacy of her room were she sat on the daybed and opened the letter from Kyle.

It read:

Dear Loo,

How are things in Decatur? I hear that the estate is going to be finished soon. I know you're very glad for that. Can't wait to get home and see you. My schoolwork keeps me mighty busy these days. School is going fine enough though I wish so much that I could be there with you, sitting on the barn gate watching the stars or riding through town and seeing people stare at us as though we were the queen and the slave out together. I guess that's what we really are. I have little time for reflection but on the clear nights I go outside and look at the moon wondering if you're looking at it too. I think about us so much out there, wondering what our lives will be like years from now when we're married with kids. I must admit this is the most contenting thought.

I miss you so much, LooAnne.

All my love.

Kyle.

LooAnne folded the letter and gently slid it into her skirt pocket with a contented sigh. She laid back on the daybed and stared up at the off-white ceiling, imagining that she was outside on the front balcony in the moonlight, looking up at the luminous sphere and knowing that Kyle was watching it too. She missed him terribly, never once was the thought of him absent from the back of her mind. She could only imagine what a wonderful reunion they would have when he returned. LooAnne's daydream was unexpectedly interrupted by a subtle knock on the door.

"Come in," She called, sitting up and running her hands through her mussed hair to straiten it.

Amarie came in with Theodora Stacey. She was a very lovely young woman with dark black hair that dropped down her back in a long ponytail. Her light green eyes were soft and calm and her long blue dress was well worn.

"LooAnne," Amarie said, "can Theodora sleep with you, all of the bedrooms are taken?"

"Of course," LooAnne agreed readily.

"Thank you, I'll leave you all to get acquainted." Amarie turned and went back downstairs leaving Theodora Stacey standing in the doorway. She looked up at LooAnne and smiled kindly. "Thank you for sharing your room," she said, her voice soft and somewhat timid.

"Oh, your more than welcome. It's not really my room anyway." LooAnne looked Theodora over and said, "You look to be about my age, how old are you?"

"Seventeen," She answered.

"Me too," LooAnne nodded. "I turned seventeen in January."

"My birthday's in December, on the twenty ninth."

"So you're a month older then me. Mine's on the twenty fifth."

"That's strange, you look your age, I look like a little girl, or at least so my brothers tell me."

LooAnne shook her head in protest as she looked at Theodora's mature figure and complexion, "You don't look like a little girl at all, I just look old."

Theodora laughed at this remark and LooAnne invited her to take a seat on the daybed.

"Oh no thank you, I should go down and find my brothers. I'm not sure if they need to do anything else about..." Theodora looked down sorrowfully at the thought of her lost brother, unable to finish her train of thought.

LooAnne's heart went out to the grieving girl, knowing all too well what it was like to lose someone.

"I'm terribly sorry about your brother," LooAnne condoled, feeling the ultimate guilt for what her family had done.

Theodora shook her head, tears gathering behind her eyes, "I just wish that we could go back to that moment before he was killed, maybe one of us could have done something to save him."

LooAnne arose from the daybed and gathered Theodora in her arms just as the young woman broke down into sobs. She cried into LooAnne's shoulder as though all her emotions had finally been allowed to free themselves from within her. LooAnne held her silently, allowing her to release all the sadness she had felt over the last few hours. LooAnne was inexperienced when it came to comforting someone but she could not leave Theodora alone to cope with the so recent death of her brother. All she had to do was let the grieving girl know she was not alone.

"Theodora!" came an alarmed cry from the doorway. Within seconds Ricky's young cousin was out of LooAnne's arms in the arms of Red Stacey whom LooAnne had not heard coming down the hall.

"Oh Red it's not fair!" she cried into her brother's chest. "What did Andy ever do to deserve that?"

Red's face was creased with sorrow and grief but he concealed this from his sister, trying to be strong for her. "Death happens to everyone, Dora, but it's not the end.

He's in a better place now with our Lord and there is no reason to shed tears over that."

"Of course there is!" Theodora sobbed. "He didn't get to live his life, he didn't get to grow old and marry and have children, and he is not here with us anymore!"

"Sh sh, it's okay," Red comforted, tightening his embrace on his sister's shoulders.

LooAnne's heart ached inside her as she watched the aftermath of her family's cruelty. It was not to her knowledge who had pulled the trigger but that was of no matter, she knew it had been one of her relatives. The very thought of the bereavement they had inflicted on the Staceys was almost unbearable. LooAnne had to do something to ease the pain.

"Theodora," LooAnne addressed gently, laying a comforting hand on the girl's shoulder, "you're brother's right. Andy is in a much better place now. He's watching you and will always be with you in your heart. Think of it, he's in heaven with your parents. He's seeing them right now after years of being without them! I know he's not here in flesh and blood but as long as you carry a love for him he can never truly leave you."

Theodora's tears had slowed almost to a stop. She sniffled and lifted her head from Red's chest, "Thank you, LooAnne," she smiled weakly. "I just wish there had been some way to prevent it. Any way at all."

LooAnne nodded, understanding wholeheartedly what she meant. "I do too, Theodora, believe me."

The tearful girl pulled away from her brother and wiped her dampened face with a handkerchief. "I'm sorry for making such a fool of myself, LooAnne," Theodora apologized. "I'm not usually one to cry in front of anyone."

"Oh no, you did absolutely nothing wrong," LooAnne assured her. "I'm not one to show my emotions myself but you can't keep it bottled up inside forever. You have every right to cry, especially over something so heartbreaking."

Theodora looked down at her hands and nodded, "Do you have any place where I can clean up before heading downstairs?"

LooAnne nodded and pointed Theodora in the direction of the upstairs lavatory. Once she had disappeared LooAnne turned to face Red who visibly sighed and ran his hand through his mussed red hair. "Thank you for that," he said gratefully.

"No need to thank me, Mr. Stacey," LooAnne insisted.

"Please, call me Red, a strange name I know but my real one ain't worth it's weight in gold."

LooAnne laughed at this, "You'll not tell me your real name then?"

Red shook his head, "Not til you prove yourself worthy of such knowledge."

Again LooAnne laughed but decided to let the matter go as her uncle had instructed. "I wish I could have done more for Theodora. I know what it's like to lose someone close to you."

"You've done quite enough I promise you. Our little family ain't necessarily made o' females so Theodora don't have a lot of ladies to talk to."

"I'm glad I could comfort her. She needs the company of another girl I'm sure."

Red nodded in agreement, "She does. Not having any sisters really takes it's toll on her, especially with us boys around all the time."

"You seem to be very good brothers," LooAnne complemented, thinking of the contrast between them and her own cruel brothers.

Red smiled, "Thanks, we try our best. I wish our mother was alive so that Theodora could have some companionship. She never really got to know her since she and our father both died in a house fire when she was only six. She doesn't really remember them all that well."

LooAnne shuddered, thinking of someone dying in the flames that she had encountered a year before. She remembered their rage that seemed to be roaring upon her and she couldn't imagine what it would be like to have been caught and doomed to such a death.

"I'm so sorry," she whispered sadly.

Red shrugged, "It was a long time ago. I wasn't close with either of them to be completely honest. My father didn't think very highly of me."

LooAnne frowned, her heart going out to this man, "I understand that feeling all too well myself. My father didn't think very highly of me either."

Red nodded, "I figured somethin' like that, since you're living with Ricky and all. I really am sorry."

LooAnne smiled but before she could say anything she and Red heard the doorbell ring.

"I wonder who that is?" LooAnne said as she got up and went to her window. She looked down at the front porch and saw Mrs. Munro letting three policemen into the the

71

house.

"It's the sheriff," LooAnne said, perplexed. "That's strange."

"Maybe they have some news about Andy's killer," Red said as he turned quickly to meet the men.

"Wait for me!" Theodora called as she ran from the lavatory, her flushed face now completely rinsed of tear stains.

LooAnne followed Red and his sister down the spiral staircase where they found the sheriff and two deputies in the parlor with Ricky, Chris, and the Stacey brothers.

"We were hoping that y'all were here," the sheriff said referring to the Staceys.

Red entered the room and asked, "Have you found the man who did it?"

Sheriff Low nodded his greetings to Red and said, "We think so, Mr. Stacey."

"Who is it?" Alec asked anxiously.

The sheriff awkwardly avoided the question and went on with his story. "One of the detectives found the murder weapon on the street not far from the scene of the shooting."

LooAnne frowned deeply, this was not like a Luther at all to leave one of his or her weapons lying around where it might be discovered. Unless the Luther had obtained an ulterior motive then it had to have been someone else!

"So it wasn't one of the Luthers then?" LooAnne asked, somewhat surprised.

The sheriff glanced at one of his deputies and then looked at LooAnne and said, "No, Miss Nash, it wasn't."

"Who was it then?" Lee Stacey asked impatiently.

"We traced the gun and found the owner," the sheriff went on.

"Who killed our brother?" Red demanded.

All eyes were fixed on the three lawmen as they all looked at each other, deep frowns creasing their faces.

"We found the man who sold the gun and he said that he sold it four years ago to *Rick Nash*!"

SIX

The Sheriff's Arrest

*Blessed are you when they revile
and persecute you, and say all kinds
of evil against you for My sake. Rejoice
and be exceedingly glad, for great is
your reward in heaven.*
Matthew 5:11

*For by your words you will be justified,
and by your words you will be condemned.*
Matthew 12:37

"**T**hat's ridiculous!" Chris bellowed as he stepped
forward in Ricky's defense.
"Absolutely and completely ridiculous!" LooAnne
backed him up.
Ricky got to his feet and laid a reassuring hand on Chris'
shoulder. He seemed very calm, giving the impression
he was in complete control of the situation. "Now let's
not get all excited. I'm sure this can be explained
without anyone loosing their temper." He turned to the
sheriff and said, "That couldn't have been my gun, Low.

All of my things were burned in the estate and that's a well-known fact."

"I don't know how you did it, but that was your gun, no question about it. The gun was a Colt 38 and I have a record that says it was sold to you on July 15th four years ago. Do you deny that you own one?"

Ricky frowned deeply. "I haven't seen my 38 since it was burned along with all of the other things that were in my house."

"So you did own one?" Sheriff Low pressured.

Ricky nodded. "I most certainly did. I have no intention of denying it, but the gun burned. Ask my insurance company. They'll tell you they payed for the gun, along with my other property, after it was destroyed."

"You can't prove that that gun was in the house at the time of the fire and neither can your insurance company," Low spat hatefully.

"Hold your peace, Low. I'm not on the whiteness stand," Ricky defended.

"Not yet, but you will be! Rick Nash you're under arrest for the murder of Andy Stacey."

Sheriff Low started towards Ricky but he held up his hand and said, "Don't be so hasty, Sheriff, I want to see the warrant. When I do then I'll go with you, but not before."

Low smiled slyly and pulled a piece of paper from his pocket and handed it to Ricky. He looked it over and, though he kept his face calm, his heart sank. The warrant was perfectly legal. He was actually going to be arrested for his own cousin's murder! Ricky sighed and handed the paper back to Sheriff Low who was still smiling. "Fine then," he relented. "You seem to be within your rights." Ricky turned to Chris and said, "Call Zeke and tell him I'm in need of his immediate assistance. When your done with that get out of town. Go strait to the estate whether it's done or not and stay there. Don't let the girls leave and double the guard. When this hits the papers there's no telling the uproar that could occur."

"Yes sir," Chris agreed, a slight catch in his voice. Ricky turned to leave with the sheriff but looked back at Chris and said, "I promise you it will all be fine. It's just a misunderstanding."

Chris nodded and Ricky cast LooAnne a look which she could not read before he was led away.

As the front door closed with a thud everyone stood frozen in a shocked, uncomfortable silence. LooAnne played her uncle's expression over and over in her mind, trying to find out what he was trying to tell her when he was taken out the door. He had looked dismayed, apologetic almost. As though he, himself was not as comforted by his words as she and Chris had been. *He was afraid,* LooAnne said to herself. *There is something more to this!*

At that moment Amarie came running down the stairs having seen Ricky be taken by the sheriff from the second floor.

"What happened?" she asked worriedly.

Before anyone could answer her question Alec said to Chris, "Under the circumstances we won't be staying, Mr. Block. Come on boys."

He started for the door with Phil, Ty, Lee, and a regretful

76

looking Theodora right behind him. Red paused and looked at Chris and then at LooAnne. He didn't know what to think anymore. His heart went out to LooAnne who just stood in the doorway to the parlor staring at him with a pleading look.

"Come on Red," Alec called from the front porch. "We can't be seen in the house of the man that killed our brother."

Red sighed and turned away, following his siblings. The door slammed shut and Amarie burst into tears and ran back up the stairs, leaving Chris and LooAnne standing in the entry hall still staring speechlessly at the door. LooAnne felt as though she had been hit in the stomach. She started to say something but the words became caught like a ball in her throat. Chris ran his hand though his graying hair and shook his head unknowingly. His eyes rested on LooAnne who's eyes were wide as they met her uncle's steward's.

"Mr. Block what will we do?" she asked.

Chris shook his head, "I don't know, Miss Nash," he said uncertainly. "But don't worry. As your uncle said, I'm sure it was just a misunderstanding."

LooAnne would have been inclined to think so too had it not been for the uneasy look on her uncle's face, almost begging her to whisper a prayer for him, which she did.

"I guess you'd better get packed." Chris said as he turned and went towards the study to find Mrs. Munro. LooAnne trudged up the stairs and went to her room. She pulled her suitcase from beneath the bed and placed it on the smooth quilt. She removed all of her clothes from the chest and folded them neatly into the suitcase, the whole time thinking about Ricky......in jail.

Once all her belongings were packed she went to help Amarie who she found lying on her bed, her eyes wet with tears and her face sullen.

"You need to pack, Amarie," LooAnne instructed gently.

"Why?" Amarie asked.

"Because we're going home."

"We are!" Amarie cried sitting up with a sudden rush of delight.

LooAnne nodded. "Once everyone hears that Uncle Ricky has been arrested it won't be safe here anymore." Amarie nodded and hastened to pack her things.

LooAnne left her to the task and went in search of Chris, finding him in the entry hall talking to Zeke Mason, Mr Nash's attorney.

"I'll go right away," Mr. Mason was saying. "Mr. Nash is right about you three leaving. It won't be safe after the news spreads."

"Won't the town be on Mr. Nash's side?" Chris said incredulously. "Surely they won't believe that he would commit such a heinous crime?"

"That's just it," Mr. Mason explained, "there will be a riot throughout town because of Mr. Nash's arrest. He has friends, employees, and business partners who will not look kindly on this scandal. That's why you all must leave."

LooAnne came up behind Chris and said, "Excuse me for interrupting, but if it's not safe for us here, than why would it be safe for Uncle Ricky?"

Zeke frowned. "He's safer locked away in that jail then

he would be out here where anyone could get to him."
"You don't think there's any chance he'll be convicted do you?" LooAnne asked hopefully.
"I don't think so. If the jury knows him well enough they won't convict him because there will always be a point of doubt in their mind. And if he is convicted I'm sure that there are people in this town devoted to him who will do whatever they can to keep him from facing punishment. He didn't do anything to them so they won't hurt him."
LooAnne frowned angrily at Ricky's lawyer. "He did nothing in the first place, Mr. Mason."
"That's not what the evidence says," Ricky's lawyer contradicted.
"Maybe not, but that's what the law says, a man is innocent until proven otherwise and Uncle Ricky hasn't been."
"In my opinion, Miss Nash, things aren't looking good for your uncle."
"If you don't believe him then how are you going to convince a jury contrary to what you think?" LooAnne snapped, repulsed by this man's obvious doubt.
"It's my job, Miss Nash," Mr. Mason stated arrogantly.
"And my uncle's life depends on whether or not you know how to do your job, Mr. Mason." With that said LooAnne excused herself and retreated back up the spiral staircase, knowing this to be the only way that she could refrain from scolding her uncle's lawyer any further.
Zeke Mason left soon after and made his way to the sheriff's office to see Ricky. Chris began loading the

Huckster with suitcases that the butler brought downstairs. By the end of the day they were at last ready to leave Quinn Creek Manor for the newly built Nash Estate.

Mrs. Munro walked the three to the door, expressing her sympathies and bidding them goodbye. Chris thanked her for everything she had done for them and then he, LooAnne, and Amarie left.

LooAnne had been looking forward to this moment for more than a year. They were finally going home, but they were going without Ricky. She found herself wishing they had never met the Staceys. It added to her pain when she thought of how Red had walked out on her after having so recently offering his friendship.

LooAnne leaned her head out the window where she could feel the cold wind in her freckled face, hoping that it would somehow blow away her troubled thoughts. The whole situation seemed like a terrible nightmare that she could not awaken from, a feeling she was all too familiar with.

It took about forty five minutes to reach the estate. When they came to the corner where LooAnne could see the barn and the bunk house there was no longer the empty space in the sky, the peek of the estate roof stood there just as it had before. When they rounded the curve there it was, their home standing just where it had been. Though it was not identical, there was almost no difference between this house and the former.

Chris pulled the Huckster up to the front door and the three stepped out. Many of the estate staff were outside working on the muddied lawn that surrounded the house. LooAnne stepped into the mud and looked up at the estate, despite the lawn it was a quite beautiful structure. LooAnne closed her eyes, inhaling the cent of wildflowers brought in by the warm spring breeze, and imagined that everything was as it had been a year and half ago. But when she opened her eyes again and saw the rutted, muddy lawn and the stumps where trees had once shaded the house – and the fact that Ricky was not standing there with her – she was brought back to reality. Everything was far from the same and LooAnne, along with Chris and Amarie, wondered if things were ever to be the same again.

The trio climbed the porch steps just as Kane Thompson opened the door for them.

LooAnne, and Amarie stepped inside, greeted by, Clark, the butler who make haste to unload their luggage from the automobile. As they walked into the living room they immediately noticed the blank slate of the interior. The furniture was stacked in the middle of the floor along with boxes and trunks that were stacked almost to the ceiling. Maids and a few ranch hands and footmen were in different rooms hard at work with paint cans and wallpaper. The floor was covered in ratted sheets that had paint splattered on them and some of the overturned furniture was also covered. The whole house smelled of paint and sawdust and new wood. Chris warned the girls not to leave and then he went to find Sam Moore. Amarie said that she was going to go look at her room and then disappeared down the hall. LooAnne saw Mrs. Moore in the kitchen unpacking stacked boxes of pots and pans.

"Mrs. Moore," LooAnne said as she entered the kitchen. "Hello Miss Nash, I didn't know that y'all were here."

"We just arrived. We're moving back in."

"Moving in!" Mrs. Moore exclaimed in surprise. "Oh my! We better work on your bedrooms then. They aren't near done."

"Oh that's alright," LooAnne assured the kind lady. "I can sleep anywhere."

"Oh no, we'll not have the lady of the house sleeping on the sofa. I'll get Sam to work on your bedroom right away."

LooAnne smiled thankfully at Mrs. Moore who continued, "Where is everyone else?"

"Amarie's upstairs and Mr. Block has gone to talk to Mr. Moore..." LooAnne started to tell the foreman's wife about Ricky but she decided to leave that to Chris. Instead she thought that maybe a little work would help her get her mind off of her uncle's arrest.

"Can I help you with anything?" she asked Mrs. Moore.

"Well the only room that is near finished is the study. Drake is in there now trying to clean up a bit. You could help him arrange things?"

"Alright I'll do that, thank you, Mrs. Moore."

LooAnne made her way through all of the clutter until she found the study. It had already been painted a dark shade of brown with white molding around the ceiling. The fireplace was dark and uncommonly clean having not yet been used. The things that were to go in the room were stacked in the middle of the floor. Drake Jenson, one of the ranch hands, was standing in the midst of the room looking at the mess in uncertainty as he rubbed the back of his head.

"Let me give you a hand, Drake," LooAnne said from behind him.

Drake turned around surprised and said, "I'd be mighty obliged, ma-am. I'm a field hand and I don't know the first thing 'bout decoratin'."

"Well you do the moving and I'll do the decorating."

"Sounds good to me."

LooAnne rolled up her sleeves and she and Drake began putting the study back together. They worked for about an hour before Chris came in and spoke. "Drake your needed out in the fields."

"Yes sir," Drake nodded to LooAnne then jogged past the steward who now turned to LooAnne and asked, "Would you like some supper, Miss Nash?"

LooAnne wiped the sweat from her forehead and smiled wanly at Chris. "No thank you, Mr. Block, I'm not all that hungry."

Chris nodded understandingly and left the room.

LooAnne sighed, feeling fatigue which had long since set in, she decided to go upstairs and examine the state of her bedroom. Turning the light off in the study she trudged up the stairs and opened her door. Like the study below it, the room was also painted a dark brown with white molding and as the study all of the furniture was piled away from the wet walls. LooAnne looked at it all and shook her head in absolute bewilderment. Her mind was spinning with all of the so recent events that had ended with the house in disarray and her uncle in jail soon to face a jury and a possible conviction. LooAnne sat down on the floor and leaned against the window, unable to believe that all this was anything but a terrible dream. She closed her eyes and once more imagined things to be as they once were, for the first time in her life they had been perfect, but she was so exhausted she fell fast asleep.

SEVEN

Guilty or Not Guilty?

*Do not eat the bread of a miser, nor
desire his delicacies; for as he thinks
in his heart so it he, "Eat and Drink"
he says to you but his heart is not with
you. The morsel you have eaten you will
vomit up, and waist your pleasant words.
Proverbs 23:6-8*

"That hearing was full of evidence against me.
What will happen at the trial?" Ricky asked Zeke
Mason, distress evident in his voice. He was sitting on
his cot in the jail cell at the sheriff's office with Zeke
Mason sitting next to him discussing the hearing that
had just taken place that morning. The trial had been set
for Tuesday of the next week and things were looking
grim.
LooAnne was standing just outside the cell leaning
against the bars with her arms crossed. She was listening
closely to the men's conversation, trying to gather every
bit of information she could. It was the first time in the
week that Ricky had been in jail that she had been

allowed to leave the estate for the hearing.

"I agree, the evidence is very convincing, Mr. Nash." Mr. Mason said.

"And what exactly does that mean for me?"

"The jury isn't likely to be fooled just because of you're social status."

"Fooled!" Ricky exclaimed as he got to his feet angrily. "If they aren't to be fooled then that means they'll let me go, because I did not kill Andy!"

"That isn't what the evidence says and that's what the jury is going to listen to."

"That's extremely relieving," Ricky grumbled sarcastically, running a hand through his hair in exasperation.

"Forgive me, Mr. Nash, but it's the truth," Mr. Mason said without the slightest hint of regret in his voice.

"It also happens to be the truth that I am innocent of this crime! Andy was a cousin to whom I was very close. Why should I want to kill him?"

"That, Mr. Nash, will be the key to an acquittal. Should the jury not have a motive there will be doubt in their minds, and just one sliver of doubt can sway the trial in favor of the defendant."

Ricky sighed and slumped back down on his cot. "I only pray that you're right, Zeke. Should they convict me of such a thing, not only would I lose my life but I lose my good name. It would ruin my family's reputation for generations to come."

LooAnne frowned upon hearing her uncle talk so. She could not bear to think of what would happen to him should he be convicted. He would most certainly be hung for the crime of another, and she would be without a family, again.

"How about putting up bail?" Ricky's question brought LooAnne out of her forbidding thoughts. "The thought of spending the next week in jail is very unappealing to me."

"Personally," Mr. Mason said, "I think it is preferable that you remain here. You have the means to easily flee the country if bail were posted so your remaining in jail gives the appearance of innocence. There is also the Stacey family to consider. The Stacey boys may stir up the town against you. Talk could very well get you killed before you ever see the jury."

Ricky furrowed his brow, "They would never do that to me, Zeke. They're my cousins. We're family."

Mr. Mason raised his eyebrows doubtfully, "And as I remember it was Devin Luther who burned down the estate and he is also family."

Anger flashed in Ricky's eyes and LooAnne felt her body stiffen somewhat but her uncle said nothing to contradict his lawyer, knowing that however uncalled for the comment had been, he was right. "Zeke, for the moment all I want to do is to get out of this cage."

"Mr. Nash you have no idea how the town will take this. It's been everywhere. Every paper in the country is covering this story. Daily updates are broadcast on the radio. It's growing into quite the scandal and it may not be safe out there where people could get their hands on you!"

"Zeke, I've lived in this county for forty five years, these people know that I would never kill anyone!"

"It's just for two weeks at the most. You can be proven innocent but it does you no good if you're dead!"

Ricky sighed, "Fine, I won't put up bail yet, but so help me if I even sort of get the idea that it would be better I'm out of here!"

"Well," Mr. Mason said as he stood and grabbed his coat and briefcase, "that's your decision. I have another client waiting for me across town. I'll be back tomorrow so we can go over our approach for the trial."

Ricky stood up and shook Zeke's hand. "Alright, thank you Zeke."

Mr. Mason nodded, "You're welcome."

Sheriff Low let him out of the cell and he left the office. Ricky sat back down and sighed deeply, shaking his head discouragingly.

"He thinks that you're guilty, Uncle Ricky," LooAnne stated.

"I know it, but he hasn't lost a case. He's one of the best in the state, LooAnne."

"How good can he be if he thinks you killed your own cousin?" LooAnne opposed. "Who in their right mind could think you would kill anyone?"

Ricky sighed and shook his head. "I don't know, LooAnne."

"Surely everyone in this town knows you too well too believe you capable of such an atrocious crime."

"I certainly hope so, but you heard what Zeke said, he doesn't think bail is advisable."

"He also thinks you killed your own cousin in cold blood for no reason."

"LooAnne he's the best. He has been a defense attorney

for five years. He's had multiple chances to prove his abilities."

"Multiple chances?" LooAnne repeated. "Uncle Ricky, he may have all the time in the world but you only have one chance. If he fails this time and you're convicted, it will not only cost you you're life, it may also cost me mine, because I will not allow you to die for something you didn't do when I have the power to stop it."
Turning, LooAnne left the sheriff's office without another word. Ricky watched her go, perplexed by her words. Should he be convicted he wondered how his niece would be able to stop his lawful execution.

LooAnne walked towards the bank which was where Chris and Amaire said they would meet her. Her stomach churned with the thought of her uncle facing the gallows. If Ricky was convicted she could and would save him, but if she failed in her search for the real killer they would have to spend the rest of their lives in hiding from the law. LooAnne had lived that life and her entire being loathed it, but if that's what it took to save her uncle, then that's what she was going to do.
LooAnne met Chris and Amarie at the bank where they were making a payment on the construction loan for the new estate. When her uncle's steward saw her he asked anxiously, "What did Mr. Mason say?"
LooAnne sighed audibly, "He thinks that Uncle Ricky will be convicted, but Uncle Ricky is convinced that since he's known as one of the best lawyers in the state he'd be making a terrible mistake by hiring a knew one."
Chris rolled his eyes slightly but did not attempt to

contradict his boss' decision. "Well, all we can do is pray for the best."

LooAnne nodded, she knew that all things were working together for good but she wondered what kind of trials she and her uncle would be put through before good was achieved.

And so the day of the trial grew nearer until it was finally upon them. People from all over Texas and some from surrounding states were gathered outside the courthouse in a huge throng. Chris, LooAnne, and Amarie were at the sheriff's office awaiting Sheriff Low's instructions. Zeke Mason was repeating what he expected to occur once the trial began. The sheriff was giving orders to his deputy and Chris was standing next to Ricky listening intently to the conversation.

As they spoke the office door was opened by one of the deputies who ushered in Robert Nash before closing the door against the pressing crowd. All the room's occupants stared at him in surprise as an awkward silence fell over the building. Robert wore a concerned look that told everyone he had heard of the murder supposedly committed by his elder brother.

"Robert!" Ricky exclaimed, breaking the momentary silence. "I didn't expect to see you here today."

Robert approached the cell and shook his brother's hand, he looked as though the entire arrangement had him a bit baffled. "Wh-what in the world happened, Ricky?" he asked almost disbelievingly.

"I was framed," Ricky stated.

"What are they going to do?" Robert asked.

Ricky shook his head, "We're not sure. The trial is about

to commence as we speak."

"But they can't convict you! They all know you too well! What motive would you have to kill our cousin?"

"That's exactly what we're hoping the jury will believe as well. Without a motive there is little chance of a conviction."

"I should hope so!" Robert exclaimed. "Who would even think of convicting you of murder?"

"A jury from another state," came Sheriff Low's mocking voice as he entered by the back door. He approached the cell and related some very disturbing news. "You're cousin, Red, has requested a jury from Colorado for you and your lawyer to plead with," he said derisively. "They're lookin' for a good conviction too."

Ricky's heart sank upon hearing this news. Now he was surely to be convicted, and worst of all, those who would send him to the gallows had been obtained by none other than Red Stacey himself.

"How could he betray me in such a way?" Ricky whispered sorrowfully.

LooAnne, too, felt the weight of Red's actions pressing on her. Now the chances of Ricky being convicted were much greater, and his own cousin was the instigator. Sheriff Low instructed Chris to take LooAnne and Amarie in through the main entrance, assuring them that he had deputies awaiting to escort them safely inside. Chris handed Ricky his coat and then he took the girls and Robert and they left in the Huckster. When they pulled up in front of the courthouse the crowd started pointing and whispering. The ranch hands of the Nash

Estate were among them and they immediately came to the Huckster to help the deputies who surrounded Chris, LooAnne, and Amarie as they exited the vehicle. They busted through the crowd and entered the courthouse with little trouble. They were then shown into the court room and were seated just behind the defendant's desk. The court room began filling up rapidly and was soon full of people whispering and yelling and moving about. The commotion softened as a side door opened and Ricky and Zeke were escorted by the lawmen to their table where they were seated. Soon the District Attorney entered and sat at the table just across the isle from Ricky and Zeke. He purposely kept his gaze from them, conferring with his companions quietly. After a moment a commanding voice rang out calling, "All rise for the honorable Judge Morton."

The whole courtroom rose and the hum of voices ceased. Judge Stanley Morton entered the room and took his seat at the bench. His face was hard as he looked over the courtroom with an air of authority before taking the gavel in his hand and striking the desk, "Court is now in session," he announced. "Bailiff read the docket."

"State vs. Nash. One charge of first degree murder."

The Judge looked at Ricky and Zeke and said, "Mr. Mason how does your client plead, guilty or not guilty?"

Zeke rose and said, "Not guilty, Your Honor," and then he sat back down.

Judge Morton turned to the apposing attorney, John Kelly, and said, "Mr. Kelly will you please proceed with your opening statement?"

John Kelly stood and strode boldly into the middle of the room in front of the bench. Turning he addressed the Judge and jury saying, "Your Honor, and good members of the jury, I intend to prove that Rick Nash is guilty of the willful murder of Andy Stacey. I am prepared to provide evidence against him that proves beyond a reasonable doubt that he is guilty of murdering a nineteen-year-old boy, his own cousin. His gun, the murder weapon, a Colt 38, which he claimed had burned in the Nash Estate, was found only a few blocks away, bluntly implying that he lied about it burning in his house. The gun had recently fired one bullet which was found in the body of Andy Stacey. I also have a witness that says he saw the defendant leaving the scene of the crime moments after the shooting took place!"

Upon hearing this, the crowd that was in the courtroom gave a low hum of surprised disapproval. Judge Morton slammed the gavel against the desk and called, "Order in the court, ladies and gentlemen."

The room fell silent once again and Mr. Kelly was asked to continue. He went on for the next hour, showing the court his evidence and accusing Ricky of murdering his cousin. Everyone listened quietly until Mr. Kelly finished and Zeke was asked to give his opening statement. He arose from his seat and instantly the whole courtroom boomed with applause. Zeke looked a bit startled, Ricky grinned triumphantly and leaned back in his chair, and Judge Morton immediately demanded for the court to come to order. Once everyone had stopped their clapping the Judge reminded them that they were guests in the courthouse and would be removed should another outburst occur in his courtroom. Zeke approached the bench and began his opening statement just as Mr. Kelly had, by addressing the Judge and the jury. Then he went on with defending Ricky, taking the accusations one at a time.

"It is a well-known fact throughout this state that the Nash Estate burned in January of last year. It is also widely known that when Mr. Nash was taken from the house that he was unconscious. I have whiteness' to prove this. How then, if he was unconscious, could he have possibly taken the gun from the house? Yes the gun did not burn in the Nash Estate, but my client did not lie when he said that it had because this is what he thought had happened. He had no idea that the gun had been saved and he has no idea who saved it. I intend to prove that my client is innocent of the charges against him."

As soon as Zeke finished Mr. Kelly was asked to call his witnesses. Standing up he said, "I would like to call Amarie Hearten as my first whiteness."

Amarie got up and went to the whiteness stand. After the bailiff had brought her the Bible and she had swore to "tell the truth, the whole truth and nothing but the truth", Mr. Kelly approached the stand and began with his questioning. "Miss Hearten," he said, "where were you the morning of March seventh when Andy Stacey was killed?"

"I was eating breakfast at Triple Creek Hall," Amarie answered.

"And who was there with you?"

"Um, LooAnne and Mr. Block."

"But not Mr. Nash?"

"No sir."

"Why wasn't he there? Isn't he normally?"

"Yes sir, most of the time."

"Then why wasn't he this particular day?"

"He had gone out."

"And where had he gone, or do you even know?"

"I don't know where he was. He had already gone when I woke up."

"And has he ever left without you knowing where he was going?"

"Um – u – not usually but it has happened, sir." Amarie wiggled nervously in her seat, knowing that with each question doubt was replaced by surety in the minds of the jurors.

Kelly turned to Zeke, having made his point, and said, "Your whiteness, Mr. Mason."

Zeke stood up and walked towards the stand. "Miss Hearten, was that the first time that you had awakened only to find that Mr. Nash had left on some matter?"

"Oh no sir, that's happened many times."

"I see, so the fact that he left is not unusual?"

"Not at all sir."

"So you were not surprised when you woke up and found him gone?"

"No sir."

Zeke nodded. "Thank you."

Amarie was excused and Mr. Kelly stood up to call his second whiteness. "I'd like to call LooAnne Nash to the stand."

After she was sworn in Kelly asked LooAnne, "Miss Nash, do you happen to know just where Mr. Nash had gone the morning of March seventh?"

LooAnne looked over at her uncle who was rubbing his forehead in exasperation. LooAnne looked back at Mr. Kelly and said, "No I don't."

"And isn't that rather strange that he didn't tell you where he was?"

"It's happened before. So no."

"And on those other occasions has he always told you later where he was?"

LooAnne bit her lip in vexation. "Yes sir."

Kelly now told Zeke that he was finished and then sat down. Zeke stood up and said to the Judge, "No further questions at this time, Your Honor. I would like to ask for an adjournment until tomorrow so that I should be better prepared for my witnesses?"

"The court's adjourned until tomorrow morning at ten o'clock." Judge Morton slammed the gavel once again and dismissed the court.

EIGHT

Secret Payoff

*...fracture for fracture, eye for eye,
and tooth for tooth; as he has caused
disfigurement to a man so shall
it be done to him. Leviticus 24:20*

*So then each of us will give an account
of himself to God. Therefor let us not pass
judgment on one another any longer, but
rather decide never to put a stumbling block
or hindrance in the way of a brother.
Romans 13:12 and 13*

All during the night and into the morning Zeke gathered his thoughts and mulled over his next move. He believed Ricky to be guilty but he was being paid to get him off. When the trial resumed the next morning Mr. Kelly called his next witnesses. They all seemed to be more and more convincing to the jury of Ricky's guilt. Finally Kelly called to the stand the man that had claimed to have seen Ricky run from the scene of the crime. The middle aged man took the stand wearing clothes suited to a difficult life.

Once he had been sworn in Kelly approached the stand and asked, "Would you please state you're name, sir?"

"Ollie Trenton," said the man in a low, hoarse voice.

"Mr. Trenton, would you please explain what you saw the morning Andy Stacey was murdered?"

"Well, I was walkin' down the street on that mornin' when I heard a gun shot. I looked across the street I seen Andy Stacey go down and looked to where I thought the shot had come from. Then I seen Mr. Nash running around a corner with a gun in his hand."

"And you're sure that you saw all of this?"

"Objection!" came Zeke's voice as he almost jumped to his feet. "Your Honor, it is a well-known fact that Mr. Trenton has just been released from a mental institution. I hardly believe that his testimony can be held as reliable."

Kelly faced the bench and said, "As Mr. Mason said, Your Honor, Mr. Trenton has just been released from a mental institution and has papers that prove that he is of sound mind."

"Objection overruled," Judge Morton announced. "Please continue Mr. Kelly."

Kelly turned to Zeke and said, "Your witness, Mr. Mason."

Zeke put his hands behind his back and casually walked to the whiteness stand. Eyeing the witness watchfully he said, "How can you be sure that the man you saw running away was Mr. Nash?"

"His picture's everywhere. Everyone knows what he

looks like, he's famous."

"You said yourself that he was running around a corner when you saw him, couldn't you have been mistaken?"

"No, it was Mr. Nash sure as day."

"How many times have you seen Mr. Nash in your lifetime?"

"Too many to count."

"And how long has it been since you were released from the mental hospital?"

"Objection!" Kelly called as he stood. "Your Honor, Mr. Mason is dwelling on facts with the deliberate attempt to harass the witness."

Zeke immediately came to his own defense, "It may in fact state whether or not Mr. Trenton actually saw who he says he saw, Your Honor."

"Objection overruled, please answer the question Mr. Trenton."

"It's been about a week," the whiteness answered.

"And why were you in this institution?"

"You're Honor, Mr. Mason insists upon asking personal questions that have no bearing on this case," Mr. Kelly called again.

"Objection sustained," Judge Morton stated.

"No further questions," Zeke said. He slumped down in his chair and sighed.

Kelly then called Ricky to the stands.

"Mr. Nash, where were you on March seventh at seven fifteen AM?"

"Walking towards the bank," Ricky answered plainly.

"What was your business at the bank?"

"I was going to check on a recent transaction."

"And what transaction would that be?"

"I had recently purchased a boat from a man in Key West, Florida. I payed with it via check and wanted to make certain the transaction was completed."

"Why didn't you tell your niece or your ward what you were doing and why did you choose to walk rather then have the valet drive you?"

"It was a beautiful morning and I enjoy the out of doors. As for not telling the girls, I purchased the ship for my ward's birthday which is in three months and wanted it to be a surprise."

LooAnne looked over at Amarie who clapped her hand over her mouth, almost unwilling to believe what she heard. Ricky bought her a boat just as he had LooAnne! Mingled emotions ran through Amarie's mind. She was overjoyed that Ricky had thought of her in such a way as to do something so wonderful for her, but at the same time she was distressed that in his attempts to please her he had been lacking an alibi that would certainly clear him of the charges.

Kelly grinned and said, "So that was the reason that you didn't tell Miss Nash or Miss Hearten, because it was a surprise?"

Ricky nodded in clarification, "That's right."

Kelly looking Ricky in the eye, "Mr. Nash can you explain how your gun happened to end up at the crime scene?"

Ricky's face hardened slightly but his attempt at hiding it was successful to all but his niece, who frowned along with him.

"No," Ricky stated in earnest.

"And can you explain why you were seen running from the scene of the crime?"

"Yes I can. The man that supposedly saw me is delusional."

Mr. Kelly grinned and continued, "Can you explain how Andy Stacey was murdered?"

"If I could I wouldn't be here now."

The lawyer turned to face the jury that was looking on intently. "Well I can tell you how Andy Stacey was killed and I can tell you why. Through this whole trial we've had everything but a motive, well now I have one." Kelly whirled on his heals and pointed an accusing finger at Ricky. "This man, the cousin of the victim, shot him down in cold blood because he was being blackmailed!"

The courtroom gasped and reporters bent farther over their notepads, writing every word! LooAnne saw her uncle stiffen. He glanced at her with the same worried expression she had seen when he was led away from Quinn Creek Manor. It was then that LooAnne realized that her uncle had, indeed, been hiding something, something truly terrible.

"Is that not true, Mr. Nash?" Kelly persisted.

Ricky's eyes burned with anger. He stared at Kelly and spat, "*Yes*, that's true."

"No further questions at this time." Kelly returned to his seat. Zeke was so stunned that he failed to rise with questions so Ricky was excused. He dropped down in his seat and looked at Zeke who was staring at him, baffled.

Kelly's last witness was Red.

"Mr. Stacey is it not true that your brother was blackmailing Mr. Nash?"

"Yes it is," Red said, glancing at LooAnne who was near tears.

"Would you please tell the court what Andy was holding over Mr. Nash that was bad enough for Mr. Nash to kill him?"

Red sighed audibly, as though what he were about to reveal was as difficult for him to say as it were for others to hear. "Ricky's sister, Amanda, ran away many years ago with a Luther. As I'm sure you all know she married him." Red continued solemnly, "Shortly before she was killed her two boys raided a small farm and killed the elderly couple that lived there. Andy was working at the farm as a hired hand and was somehow able to escape. He heard the two call each other by name and realized that they were the boys of Amanda Nash Luther. Andy needed money bad and went to Ricky and told him what he had seen and heard. He told Ricky that if he wasn't given a thousand dollars a month then he would tell the world what he knew. Ricky didn't wanna blur his sister's name no more then it already was so he agreed. Ever since then he's been payin' Andy regularly. The sad thing is all he had to do is ask Ricky and he'd o' given him the money he needed! But Andy was crafty and a bit wild ever since I can remember. Doin' things the right way never really appealed to him."

"Thank you Mr. Stacey. Your witness, Mr. Mason."

Ricky sat with his elbows on the desk and his face buried in his hands, not bothering to look up when he saw the flashes of cameras.

Zeke rose and spoke, "Your Honor I'd like to ask for an adjournment to review this new evidence."

There was a bang as the judge's gavel hit the desk. "Court's adjourned until tomorrow afternoon at one o'clock."

The jury was dismissed and everyone filed out of the courtroom. LooAnne watched the sheriff lead Ricky and Zeke out the side door. Ricky looked beaten and a bit bewildered. It pained LooAnne to see her uncle suffer so, and she hated the thought that it was all because of her own brothers. Her family had ruined her early years and now they were ruining this happy life. Ricky would surely be convicted now that the jury had a motive. LooAnne would have to risk her life and even her true identity to save him from a fate that seemed sealed. LooAnne's heart burned with mingled sadness, fear, and anger. She had thought for a moment, while talking with Red in her room on the day Ricky was arrested, that she had found a trustworthy friend in him. Now Red was almost as guilty for ruining her and her uncle's life as her own brothers were.

LooAnne did not see Ricky until they resumed the trial the next day. She couldn't bear to face him though she was unsure why. She assumed that it was because he was almost sure to be convicted and all because of her own brothers with the indirect assistance of Red Stacey. Upon the resumption of the trial it was Zeke's turn to call his witnesses, and his fist was LooAnne.

"Miss Nash you were present when Mr. Nash was pulled from the estate during the fire were you not?"

"Yes I was," LooAnne answered thinking of what an understatement that was since she herself was the one to pull him from the house.

"And was he unconscious at that time?" Zeke asked.

LooAnne nodded, "Yes he was."

"So he couldn't have taken the gun from the house then?"

"No sir."

"Did anyone else that you know of have any reason to take the gun from the house?"

"No."

Zeke nodded in satisfaction and turned to the district attorney. "Your witness Mr. Kelly."

Kelly stood and said, "Isn't it possible, Miss Nash that your uncle could have taken the gun from the house before the fire took place?"

"I suppose so but see no reason why he would."

"Obviously someone took the gun from the house before it burned and if Mr. Nash didn't then who do you suppose did?"

"Maybe the man who burned the house down?" LooAnne suggested.

"Maybe, but as you know, people were pulling things from the house as they exited so couldn't the gun have been pulled out?"

LooAnne shook her head, "No sir."

"And why not?"

"Because that particular gun was kept in a safe in the study and the only people who knew the combination were me and Uncle Ricky."

As he listened to what LooAnne was saying Ricky

suddenly realized what her scheme was. Without lying she was attempting to plant the idea that *she* had taken the gun from the safe herself!

Kelly raised his eyebrows. "So the safe wouldn't have burned and Mr. Nash could have come back later and gotten the gun?"

"No sir, the safe did burn because when we found what was left of it, it had been left open and the contents burned to pieces."

"So if your uncle was unconscious during the fire, and you claim that he didn't remove the gun beforehand, and the only other person who knew the combination was you, then it must have been you who took the gun from the safe?"

Ricky desperately nudged Zeke with his elbow. "Object, you idiot!" he hissed under his breath.

Zeke leaped to his feet and called, "Objection!"

Everyone turned questioning eyes on Zeke who stumbled over his words before finally saying, "I fail to see the point in all this, Your Honor. Miss Nash is not the one on trial. If she did in fact take the gun from the safe I still don't see how this can have any bearing on this case. The fact is that the gun was taken from the house. Who took it can have nothing to do with what happened a year later."

Kelly immediately leaped to defend his question. "Your Honor, finding out who took the gun from the house may help us in finding the murderer."

Judge Morton thought for a moment and then said, "Objection sustained. Mr. Kelly please remember that Mr. Mason holds the stand."

"Yes, Your Honor. No further questions."

Zeke's next whiteness was Red, he took the oath and then Zeke began. "Mr. Stacey, why didn't you come forward with the information about your brother blackmailing Mr. Nash until just yesterday? What proof do we have that any of what you said is true?"

"I knew that what he was doing was wrong but couldn't bring myself to see him go to jail. He was just an innocent boy and, I am sad to say, he was never really paid any mind."

"You couldn't stand to see your brother pay for his mistakes, but you can sit there and watch your cousin pay for the mistakes of someone else?"

"Objection!" Kelly called. "You're Honor Mr. Mason is harassing the whiteness."

"Objection sustained. Mr. Mason please try to refer only to matters that concern this court?"

"Yes Your Honor. Your witness, Mr. Kelly."

"No further questions at this time."

And so the trial went on and on, but every man or woman that Zeke called to the stand was just another that Kelly manipulated into saying something that added to the suspicion that Ricky was guilty. Finally Zeke made his closing statement and the jury was sent to confer with one another.

Chris, LooAnne, Amarie, and Robert, who had been staying in Decatur since the beginning of the trial, went home to the estate. The house was nearing completion but still LooAnne did not feel at home there, the house was missing something, something that to LooAnne was the most important part, and that part was to be convicted of murder in the first degree. Amarie dropped down on the living room couch and sighed, "I guess there's no doubt about it now, he'll be convicted for sure."

"You can't be certain, surely there's a chance," Robert said though he didn't even believe his own words.

Chris went to his room and wasn't seen for the rest of the evening. LooAnne went into the study and dropped down on the couch, staring into the dark fireplace. She looked at the fireplace and thought of how dark and lonely it seemed without a blaze roaring in it. LooAnne suddenly frowned thoughtfully. "Fire," she whispered to herself as she went over the killing of Ricky's cousin in her mind.

There was a pile of letters from Kyle that stuck out of the desk; LooAnne had yet to read them. Knowing that they were about Ricky's trial she couldn't bear to hear any more of it. She wished that Kyle would come home so that she would have someone there for her through all the fear and turmoil. She hadn't seen Kyle in a little more then a year and she longed for his company.

She wished that he was there to sit next to her in the courtroom, to comfort her on days when it all seemed hopeless as this one did. She wished he could have been there to hold her hand as Red Stacey told the secret of her brothers' ruthlessness, hurting the innocent name of her mother as he all but dug her uncle's grave.

Ricky's fate had been decided by the members of LooAnne's own family. Her brothers being the reason Andy had blackmailed Ricky, her father being the reason her brothers had grown into such barbarous men, and his brother, Devin Luther, being the reason the estate had been burned.

As her mind dwelt on the final of these reasons it gave her an idea. She bit her lip as she thought and suddenly she had it! LooAnne knew exactly what had happened! She knew how the safe had been opened and she knew who had killed Andy Stacey. She only had to figure out why he had done it, and how he had framed Ricky for it! "All because of the fire," she said under her breath as she slowly rose from her seat, her eyes darting back and forth across the room as her mind whirled with the idea. "No," she corrected herself, "all because of *me*! That's it!" LooAnne cried, elated that she finally knew what had happened and why, but her new hopes of saving Ricky were suddenly dashed as she realized that she could not prove a word of what she thought to the jury, especially after they had already heard all of the evidence that was piled up against Ricky. Nevertheless, there was still one way that she could save her uncle's life, and that was to get the real killer and force him to confess! LooAnne assumed that it would take the jury at least two days to decide on a verdict so she went to bed. She would need to get a good night's sleep for her next days exploit!

Early the next morning LooAnne arose from a peaceful sleep, dressed, and went downstairs for breakfast. Chris was standing in the living room talking with Mrs. Moore, both of them speaking in hushed voices. "What's the matter?" LooAnne asked hesitantly, afraid to hear the answer.

"The jury," Chris explained with a long face, "they've reached a verdict. We're to be at the courthouse at nine twenty."

LooAnne's heart instantly sank and she could feel the color in her face drain away. All of her plans for saving Ricky were ruined! He would surely be convicted and then she would have no time to find the real killer. Ricky would die for his cousin's murder!

"But it's only been a few hours!" LooAnne exclaimed.

"Apparently it didn't take them long to decide," Chris answered grimly. "Would you please go awaken Miss Hearten?"

LooAnne nodded solemnly and went back upstairs, her mind whiling with the thought of what was sure to happen. She resolved that no matter their upcoming circumstances, she would get her uncle out if it killed her!

At nine twenty exactly everyone was seated in the courthouse once more. Zeke seemed restless, Kelly appeared to be quite sure of himself, and Ricky looked extremely fatigued, as though he were ready to get it over with no matter what the outcome.

The Stacey brothers sat just across the isle from Chris, LooAnne, Amarie, and Robert. They kept their eyes downcast, all except Red, who occasionally glanced up at LooAnne, only to find her refusing to look at him. At that moment the quite hum and milling about in the courtroom was interrupted as they were asked to rise and Judge Morton entered the room and took his seat at the bench. Soon after the jury filed in.

Judge Morton eyed the room watchfully and then said, "Would the defendant please rise?"

Ricky and Zeke stood up and the entire room held their breaths, waiting for servel grueling moments for the Judge to continue. Judge Morton looked over at the jury and asked, "Has the jury reached a verdict?"

One of the members of the Colorado jury stood and said, "We have Your Honor."

There was a tense, almost painful silence as the man went on to read the verdict. LooAnne felt her stomach leap into her throat and she felt lightheaded as the color eased from her face.

"We the jury," he began, "find Rick William Nash – *guilty* of the first degree murder of Andy Stacey."

The courtroom erupted with shouts, and reporters ran out the door trying to be the first to file a story.

Ricky was immediately handcuffed by the sheriff's deputies, Zeke looking down regretfully. Ricky looked a bit startled and fearful, but he said nothing. Judge Morton demanded order in his courtroom, slamming the gavel down hard on the desk. Once order was restored he said, "It is now the duty of this court to pronounce sentence."

The silence was suddenly broken by the door slamming as LooAnne left the courtroom in a rage of emotion!

NINE

Apologies

The horse is prepared for the day
of battle, but deliverance is of the
Lord. Proverbs 21:31

And we know that all things work
together for good to those who love
God, to those who are called according
to His purpose. Romans 8:28

"**I** don't know where she is!" Chris exclaimed
desperately to Robert who was sitting on the sofa in the
living room, his face buried in his hands. It was a
quarter past eleven and they had just returned home only
to find that LooAnne was not there, nor had she ever
been.
"It is none of my concern," Robert snapped, his voice
cracking slightly as he attempted to swallow the knot in
his throat.
"I understand your feelings, Mr. Robert, but I've got to
find her! Something might have happened to her. She
might have run into a Luther or something!"
"She's older, they won't recognize her."

"That doesn't matter. They could still hurt her!"

"Look Chris, my only brother is gonna be hung for murder, I have better things to worry about besides a Luther offspring."

Chris narrowed his eyes at Robert, his ire aroused anew. "Now Mr. Robert, I'm not one to get angry, especially at my best friend's brother, but I happen to care what happens to Miss Nash, not just because she's my responsibility and the niece of a man that I hold in high esteem, but because in two days she's gonna be the richest seventeen-year-old in the state of Texas!"

Robert looked up at Chris questioningly, "What do you mean, Chris?"

"Go look in the desk in the study. The will of Rick William Nash, every penny he owns is soon to be the property of his niece."

Robert looked appalled as he straightened his posture and gasped, "Are you saying that Luther is to receive the entire fortune?"

Chris nodded stiffly. "That's why I must find her, that and I can't have Mr. Nash die thinking ill of me for losing the only thing he had left."

Before Robert could say anything the two heard familiar footsteps in the hall and seconds later LooAnne appeared in the living room. She paused for a moment, looking at Chris and Robert with dull, sad eyes which seemed to look deep within their souls. For a fraction of a second Chris saw Ricky's eyes in his niece, the same ones that had looked right through him when he had returned from Oklahoma after the death of Susan, William, and Cindy. At that moment he realized that

Ricky's life was bound up in LooAnne's heart.

"I'm so sorry, Miss Nash," he said, a catch in his voice. LooAnne locked eyes with Chris and said in a near whisper, "He's not dead yet, Mr. Block. Could I talk with you privately please?"

"Of course."

Chris followed LooAnne into the study were she turned and faced him. "I know what happened to Andy Stacey. I know how, I know why, and I know who."

Chris was taken aback and he knit his brow as he stared at LooAnne. "You do?"

LooAnne nodded. "I do, and I know how to save Uncle Ricky too."

"How?" Chris asked anxiously.

"First of all, you remember how we found out that Devin had threatened the guards and they had let him into the house?"

Chris nodded.

"Well that means that he was inside the house that he was about to burn to the ground. He could have taken all kinds of things from in here and we would never know it because we would assume that they were destroyed. You see what I mean, Mr. Block?"

Chris nodded, still slightly confused, "I suppose so but what exactly does the fire have to do with Andy being murdered?"

"It has everything to do with it," LooAnne stated. "The key to the whole thing is that Uncle Ricky didn't die in the fire. If he had then Andy Stacey wouldn't have been killed."

Chris took on a look of bewilderment. "I don't quite

follow you, Miss Nash."

"Devin Luther started the fire with the intention of getting back at Uncle Ricky. We thought that he was getting back at him by burning the house, but what he really wanted was for Uncle Ricky, and possibly the rest of us, to die in the fire. That was to be his revenge. But when no one died he had to think of another way to get back at him. That's why he came and bragged about it in front of us all hoping that Uncle Ricky would fight him and he could use some kind of hidden weapon to kill him, but he was knocked out before he could get a chance to carry out his plan. He decided to wait and he devised a fool proof scheme to rid himself of Uncle Ricky once and for all. I think Uncle Devin took Uncle Ricky's gun from the safe as insurance. If the fire did not work then he knew that he could get Uncle Ricky into plenty of trouble with it later. How he got the safe open I don't know, but ever since the fire he's waited for the perfect time to do this, and that time came when the Staceys arrived in town. Uncle Devin knew that Andy was blackmailing Uncle Ricky and that fed into his plan perfectly. He shot Andy with Uncle Ricky's gun and managed to escape undetected. Then he left the gun where it was sure to be found and left town, leaving Uncle Ricky to face the law with the evidence that Uncle Devin had planted. That was his new form of revenge, since he couldn't get Uncle Ricky all by himself, he used the law to help him."

"But how did he know that Andy was blackmailing Mr. Nash?" Chris asked.

"I don't know," LooAnne admitted, "and I don't know

how he got the gun out of the safe either, but some how he did. He must have!"

Chris looked elated at this new turn of events of but expression soon fell. "How can we prove it?"

"By making Devin confess!"

"How can we possibly do that?"

"*We* can't, Mr. Block, but *I* can, it takes a Luther to beat a Luther and I'm a Luther."

"But even if I was going to let you risk your life, which I'm not, you couldn't possibly get to Devin before the hanging," Chris objected.

"I know it, which is why I'm going to break Uncle Ricky out of jail first," LooAnne stated.

Chris stood in the mist of the room staring at LooAnne as though he could not believe what he was hearing.

"I'll put some things in that cave on the back of the property," LooAnne went on explaining, "and Uncle Ricky can hide there until I can get Devin to confess to Andy's murder."

"How in the world do you plan to do that, Miss Nash?"

"I can get him from the Luther Estate and bring him back to town. We'll worry about the confessing part once I've got him there."

"Forgive me, Miss. Nash, but this is absolutely ludicrous! You cannot be serious."

"I assure you I am, Mr. Block."

Chris momentarily stumbled over his words before replying, "Do you not know what will happen if you are caught?"

LooAnne's sure expression softened into a sad frown.

"If they catch me they catch me, but I won't stand here

when I know who killed Andy and can get Uncle Ricky free."

"But you'll get caught for sure, if not by the Luthers then by the sheriff or one of the deputies! Well-bread young ladies do NOT break men out of jail!"

LooAnne sighed, "It is not as though I've never done it before..." she trailed off and look down shamefully.

Chris' eyes widened, "You're broken someone out of jail before?" he exclaimed in amazement.

LooAnne nodded, still looking at her boots. "I have. I was eleven. One of my brothers had been caught trying to rob the general store and was jailed. My other brother and cousins needed someone small to climb in the back window and unlock the front door for them. That someone was me. I had been trained all my life to walk silently and I knew how to pick locks, fire a gun, run miles without having to stop, and I knew how to get out of touchy situations, but despite all that I was scared. I had never been taken to a jailbreak before much less been a crucial part of one. I followed all my training and did everything just as my older brother told me and it all worked out perfectly except..."

LooAnne rubbed her hand together nervously and shook her head, not wanting to continue.

"Except what, Miss Nash?" Chris asked, laying a reassuring hand on her shoulder.

LooAnne sighed deeply and said, "I was to unlock the door and let my brother and cousins in and then I was to run outside and back to the Luther Estate. Well I got curious once they had all rushed inside and stayed in the doorway watching. That was when I was grabbed from

116

behind by a deputy. I don't know where he came from but I instantly began pulling every trick I knew to get away from him. Unfortunately I was little and no match for him. I screamed for help and my cousin Stan came running and shot the deputy. He died instantly. Stan shoved his body off of me, grabbed my arm, and we ran like mad back to the Estate. I got into huge trouble for not obeying orders, but the worst of it was the nightmares of the man dying because of me. I still have them sometimes." LooAnne sighed, relieved to have finished her account.

"Miss Nash, I – I don't know what to say," Chris admitted, looking at LooAnne dolefully.

She shook her head and looked up at him, pushing those terrible memories to the back of her mind where they lived and let a wan smile take over her features. "No need to say anything, Mr. Block. It was quite a few years ago and because of it I know I will be able to save Uncle Ricky."

Chris shook his head, "I cannot condone this, Miss Nash. No matter your past I can't let you take this risk!"

"What do I have to lose, Mr. Block?" LooAnne questioned anxiously. "My uncle is the only family I have left, I won't lose him. Uncle Ricky once said that all things were working together for good. I've been trained as a criminal and used to think that that was nothing but a nightmare that I would have to carry with me for the rest of my life, but now I see that my knowledge is a blessing, not a curse. I can use it, it was meant for bad but now I'm going to get the chance to use it for good, to save Uncle Ricky's life! That's why I must

117

go. If they catch me and kill me that's just as well."
Chris thought a moment, racking his mind for something
to say that would deter LooAnne from her crazed
scheme to save her uncle, and then he had it. "What
about Kyle, Miss Nash?" Chris asked, knowing that he
was touching a nerve but seeing no other alternative.
LooAnne, however, did not get angry upon hearing the
steward's question. She felt a knot growing inside her
chest at the thought of what all this would do to Kyle
should she not come back, but in her heart she knew
what she had to do. "Mr. Block," LooAnne said in a
near whisper, "I by no means want to hurt Kyle. I want
to spend the rest of my life with him and the thought of
losing that is almost enough to stop me, but sometimes
you need to just stop your mind, put every thought
away. When your head is so full of feelings, opinions,
and ideas you can't use it anymore and you must follow
your heart, knowing that the Almighty will lead it where
He needs it. I've not gone off half cocked, Mr. Block. I
have done nothing but pray since the moment the sheriff
took Uncle Ricky away. I might not know for sure if this
is the Father's will, but I've followed my heart, knowing
that He will guide it no matter what happens."
Chris shook his head in amazement as he stared at
LooAnne, a girl who had been through so much and yet
refused to give up. He sighed helplessly and said, "Miss
Nash, I wish you all the luck and prayers in the world."
A smile spread it's way across LooAnne's face, "Thank
you Mr. Block."
Chris nodded and left the study, his hard stride being
heard as he walked down the hall towards his room.

LooAnne dropped down in the desk chair and stared out the window at the sky which was overcast with thick gray clouds. LooAnne thought of her life what seemed like many years ago and she recalled every moment well. It seemed against her better judgment to walk right back to it after she had risked so much to get away. For a moment she second thought herself, the whole notion seemed demented to her, but then she remembered what she had told Mr. Block only minutes before, sometimes it was better not to think once you had made your decision. LooAnne resolved to not let the doubt creep into her mind again, she was determined to save her uncle and she new that was the right thing to do.

She got up from the desk and went into her uncle's bedroom where she pulled his suitcase out of the closet and laid it on the bed. She then filled it with blankets, a flashlight, and food. She then took it to the stables where she found two of the ranch hands feeding horses.

"Sidney," LooAnne said, " would you saddle Papa's Girl please?"

The young ranch hand nodded, "Yes, Miss Nash."

Sidney saddled one of the mares and LooAnne hooked Ricky's suitcase to the saddle then rode toward the back pastures. She knew a spot not far up the mountain that had a secluded cave in the side of a ridge where Ricky could hide until it was safe. The sky was beginning to darken with gray storm clouds and a cool wind swirled through the fields, whipping LooAnne's hair around her face. She held tightly to the suitcase as she rode up the green hillside and through the thick trees, heavy with new leaves and budding flowers. Once she reached a clearing she could just barely see the dark hole in the side of the mountain through the trees. She rode to it and dismounted, pulling the suitcase with her. The cave was much bigger than it had seemed from further away. Inside the dark cave the floor was damp and cold. LooAnne laid her uncle's suitcase on the slightly muddy ground then left. It was way past noon when she returned to the estate but she wasn't in the least bit hungry for all of the excitement and worry had ruined her apatite. Chris met her in the hall and asked, "Miss Nash, where were you?" His face was tense with worry and she realized that he had been upset when unable to find her.

"I was at the cave on the south hill. Would you do me a favor?" she asked avoiding Chris' vexation.

"I suppose so," the steward agreed. "What is it?"

"Early tomorrow morning take some food and go to the cave. If all goes well tonight Uncle Ricky will be there. Be sure that you're not followed. The news of the jailbreak will travel fast and the Luthers will no doubt hear of it sooner than you think."

"Where will you be?"

"I'll go straight from the cave to the Luther Estate and Lord willing bring back Devin, but you can't let Uncle Ricky know that's where I am. He'll come after me and ruin everything."

"What do I tell him if he asks me?"

"Anything but the truth."

Chris looked at LooAnne skeptically, "So you want me to lie to my boss?"

LooAnne sighed, "Mr. Block you know what he'll do if

he finds out I've gone to the Luther Estate?"

Chris nodded his eyes downcast as he thought of his employer being killed by the cruelty of the Luthers.

"He'll get killed,' LooAnne voiced Chris' thoughts. "I know it's not your nature to lie, but it's the only way. If you tell him where I am he'll come after me and get himself killed, and get me killed, and get you killed because you'll go after him. I can't risk it, Mr. Block."

Chris nodded understandingly. Then he looked at LooAnne with worry in his soft brown eyes and asked, "But what if this all works and you get Mr. Nash safely to the cave but you don't come back from the Luther estate? Then what, Miss Nash?"

LooAnne turned her head and looked out the window just as the rain began to fall lightly over the fields. "I don't know, Mr. Block," she said honestly. "I do know that whatever happens, that's the way it's supposed to be. The Bible says that 'the horse is prepared for the day of battle, but deliverance is of the Lord', so I'll prepare myself as good as possible and let Him take care of the rest."

Chris shook his head. "You certainly are an amazing girl, Miss Nash, and despite my worry, I'm obliged to you for everything that you're doing for your uncle, and for me."

LooAnne smiled. "It's the least I can do, Mr. Block. He loved me when no one else did."

"And you saved him from his loneliness," Chris added. He excused himself and walked down the hall. LooAnne went into the study and sat at the desk to go over her plan in her mind. She had not been there long when her thoughts were interrupted by someone standing in the hallway.

"Excuse me, Miss Nash?" It was one of the guards. LooAnne looked up and said, "Yes Kane?"

"There's a Mr. Red Stacey at the door wantin' to talk to you. Should I let him in?"

LooAnne was taken aback but her anger was kindled against Red for what he had done to Ricky and she was not about to speak with him.

"No!" she almost yelled. "Tell him to get out. I don't want to see him much less speak to him!"

"Yes ma-am." Kane turned and left.

When LooAnne thought of Red her heart ached with sorrow for the friendship that could have been. She hated to think that he had turned on them both. Ricky's own cousin who he had helped all of his life and now, when he had been needed the most, he had walked out and brought in a jury that he knew would have Ricky convicted! LooAnne flung her arms on the desk and buried her face in them, trying not to let her emotions free. Just then she was startled by a soft voice that said, "LooAnne?"

LooAnne jerked up and looked at the doorway where Red Stacey stood looking at her regretfully.

"How did you get in!" she nearly screamed. "I told that guard-"

"I told him that it was urgent," Red interrupted. "That I needed to see you badly. He knew who I was so he let me in." Red approached the desk and reached into his pocket.

"That guard should be fired! You get out of here this

instant!"

Red pulled his hand from his pocket and held a small object before LooAnne. It was a Nash identification ring.

"When you refused to see me I showed this to the guard," Red explained.

LooAnne looked at the ring and then took a glance at the one on her finger and remembered her uncle's words, *"Only my most trusted friends have one of these,"* she looked up at Red and repeated in a whisper, "'My most trusted friends'. Some friend you turned out to be, Red Stacey!"

"I'm so sorry, LooAnne," Red apologized as he looked down at the ring in his palm. "I know now that he didn't do it."

"You know *now*?" LooAnne exclaimed angrily. "Now is too late! He's sentenced to be hung in twenty four hours, and all because of what you did!"

"I know, I know, and I'm so very sorry. Really I am! I realized during the reading of the verdict today that he was innocent and I've never felt so horrible before in my life. I wanna ask your forgiveness LooAnne, please?"

"My forgiveness? Red, I don't think I'm capable of forgiving you. If all doesn't go well you've ruined my life."

"I knew you'd hate me," Red sighed, looking down at his muddied boots.

"No," LooAnne shook her head, "I don't hate you, I could never do such a thing, but when it comes to forgiveness you ask too much of me. You have no idea what you've done and you'll never know. You can never understand. He's your cousin, Red Stacey! You should have stood by him in his time of trouble as he did for you!"

Red seemed shocked at this. He took a step back and gaped at LooAnne.

"Yes," she nodded, "I know. I know that he's been giving you money on top of what he was giving Andy for keeping his sister's name from being drug in the mud. You owe him a great deal and you repay him by getting him hung for a murder he didn't commit!"

"I thought he was guilty," Red tried to defend himself. "I thought he had betrayed me!"

"And if you thought that Alec or Phil or Ty or Lee or even Theodora were guilty or had betrayed you, you would try to get them hung too I suppose?"

"Of course not!"

"Then why did you do it to Uncle Ricky?"

Red looked at the floor, ashamed of what he now realized he *had* done to his cousin. "My brother had just been killed, LooAnne, I didn't know what I was doing. I wasn't thinkin' straight."

"I understand that, Red, but he's family. He helped you when you needed help. The least you could have done was leave well enough alone."

"You're right. No doubt I wouldn't have made the same mistake if it had been one of my brothers."

Red turned and started for the door, "I know it does no good to say so, LooAnne, but I really am sorry."

LooAnne looked down at the desk and remained silent. She had nothing she could say that would not hurt Red even more so she remained silent.

"Thanks for listening anyway, LooAnne," Red gently tucked the Nash identification ring into his jean pocket and sighed deeply. "I'd better be goin'."

TEN

Moonlight Escape

"My God has sent His angels to shut the lion's mouths so that they have not hurt me, because I was found innocent before Him; and also, O Kind, I have done nothing wrong before you.
Daniel 6:22

Direct my steps by Your word and let no iniquity have dominion over me.
Psalm 119:133

Red trudged out of the study, his head held in shame for what he had done to an innocent man. A man who had done so much for him, whom he loved. LooAnne slumped back in her chair and sighed miserably. She didn't know what to think about Red anymore. Her temper burned with anger towards him. She would not hate him but to forgive him was something she could not find within herself.
"'He is faithful and just to forgive us our sins,'" she

whispered out loud as the scripture appeared in her exhausted mind. She realized that inwardly she wanted to forgive Red for what he had done, to get the burden of a grudge off her shoulders. Then it donned on her, she might not get the chance to forgive him in person, to relieve his mind of all bitter feelings.

Jumping out of her chair LooAnne ran down the hallway, through the living room, and entry hall where she burst out the south entrance just in time to see Red riding away.

"Wait, Red!" she called but he was already to far to hear her. LooAnne watched him round the curve wishing that she had been more understanding, but there was no time for regrets. She had to free her uncle before daybreak. She went straight to her room and opened her wardrobe, but she did not take one of her normal day-dresses, instead she knelt next to some boxes and pulled one open. Inside, folded neatly, was her mother's green dress that LooAnne had been wearing when she had first met her uncle. The dress that had been too large for her previously now fit perfectly. She dressed quickly then secured her hair in a tight ponytail. After removing her boots she went downstairs to Chris' room at the front of the servant's quarters. He opened it almost immediately after her knock and looked surprised to see her standing there. "Yes Miss Nash?" he asked.

"I'm going to go get Uncle Ricky, Mr. Block. He'll be at the cave when you get there in the morning." She spoke with a confidence she did not yet feel.

Chris frowned deeply, "But what about you?"

"I won't be there in the morning, and I may not ever be

there again, but if I don't come back you know what happened."

Chris shook his head in distress, "Miss Nash, what will he do if you don't come back? He won't be able to cope with such a loss, nor will I!"

LooAnne looked directly at Chris, "I have no intention of failing him, Mr. Block. If I don't try he'll die and if I try and fail he'll die. So you see I have little to lose."

"Besides your own life, Miss Nash," Chris corrected, "and the happiness of a young man whom you love."

LooAnne nodded, "And what is my life compared to that of the great Rick Nash? As Uncle Robert was saying when I came in this morning, I am the offspring of a Luther, a child of the devil's tools. I am nothing compared to my uncle. My death will not wreak havoc throughout the country. As for Kyle, he'll find someone better, someone worth his undying love. So you see, Mr. Block, there is no argument which will dissuade me, I am determined."

By this point LooAnne could see small tears glistening in Chris' eyes. She smiled kindly at him, trying to reassure him but he only shook his head, "You may count on my never ending prayer until you return, Miss Nash. Needless to say I do not think this a wise move, but I seem to have little say in the matter."

LooAnne grinned slightly, "I'm a Luther, Mr. Block, and as such I do everything I do with no intention of stopping for anyone, not even Uncle Ricky, who will be most angry when he sees that I've broken into the jail."

Chris chuckled, "Indeed he will be, but let him be angry. You are the greater of the two, but please don't tell your

128

uncle I said so."

LooAnne laughed, "I won't. Thank you, Mr. Block."
Turning, she left Chris' room, not looking back as she
walked away. He watched her go remembering the day
that Ricky had come back to the estate with this same
little girl at his side; and now, Chris realized, that this
wasn't the same little girl, this was a woman with great
strength.

As LooAnne walked through the house towards the side
door she heard a familiar voice from behind her call,
"LooAnne, where are you going?"

Turning she saw Amarie coming down the hall, a
questioning look on her face.

"Out," LooAnne answered simply.

"At nine thirty at night?"

"Yes, I need some air. It's hot in here."

"Why in the world are you wearing that old torn dress?
And you have no shoes on?"

"I feel more comfortable this way," LooAnne insisted.

"LooAnne, you're lying to me," Amarie stated.

LooAnne sighed in defeat, "Yes I am and I'm sorry, but
you ask too many questions. I can't tell you where I'm
going and believe me it'll be better for the both of us.
Now listen carefully and do exactly as I tell you. If
anyone asks if you saw me leave, anyone at all, you tell
them that you were in bed. Alright?"

"LooAnne you're scaring me. What's going on? Does it
have something to do with Uncle Ricky?"

"Amarie the less you know about this whole thing the
better. Please just do as I said and don't ask any more
questions?" LooAnne begged.

Amarie looked skeptical, "Well – alright, but please be careful doing whatever it is that you're doing."

LooAnne smiled wanly at Amarie's concern for her, "I will," she assured, "Now you go to bed, and remember, you never saw me."

"I'll remember," Amarie promised.

LooAnne turned and disappeared into the entry hall.

Amarie did as she had been instructed and went to bed, remembering that she wasn't to tell a soul what she had seen, but wondering what was going on and if LooAnne was coming back?

The sky had cleared and the moon lit the night. The guard was surprised when LooAnne came outside dressed as she was. "Can I do something for you, ma-am?" he asked.

"Yes, if anyone asks tell them that I went out but came right back in," LooAnne strictly instructed.

"Um, yes ma-am," the guard agreed though rather questioningly.

LooAnne ran out into the night, the dampness from the previous rain causing mud to spew up her back and eek through her bare toes. The rain had failed to cool anything down so a sticky breeze blew throughout the fields. LooAnne passed up the barn and stables, not wanting to cause any noise by riding to town on horseback. She recalled her training from the Luthers, it had taken place at this same time of night and she remembered everything that she had been taught. Every little detail hung in her mind as though it were burned there like the scar on her arm from the estate fire. She remembered her family's harsh words, her brothers'

130

endless bullying, the dread she felt waking up every morning to the same endless day.

As she walked the memories of the Luthers began to flood her mind. She could picture herself with them, giving her all for fear of what might happen if she failed. LooAnne rubbed her forehead as if to wipe off the memory of the past. The thought of the Luthers gave her an empty feeling in the pit of her stomach that seemed to squeeze at her from all sides. LooAnne stopped walking and took a deep breath, turning her thoughts to her uncle rather than remembering her life with the Luthers. She did not know how long it would take to get Devin away from the Luther Estate or if she was even capable of doing it, but she wasn't going to take the chance that she would be detained longer then expected and return successful only to find that it was too late to save her uncle.

Soon LooAnne's feet were caked in mud, but she in no way felt uncomfortable. She was used to the cold mud and the hard ground that she had walked on barefooted for twelve years. The night was growing cooler and a light breeze was beginning to blow. LooAnne had been walking for about forty five minutes when the lights from town began to glow in the sky. LooAnne increased her speed and walked briskly down the road until she began to see houses at the sides of the street. As she moved further into town there were a few people making their way down the street. Some were closing their shops and others were just getting home from a long day at work. Several lights were still on in a few houses and stores. Streetlights lined the sidewalks and

131

shined brightly throughout town, illuminating everything but the dark corners.

LooAnne walked in the shadows of the buildings, not wanting to be seen on the streets at this hour by anyone who would question her reason for such a late excursion, unchaperoned.

The sheriff's office was in the middle of town right beside the courthouse and the Nash hotel stood across the street. When LooAnne saw the front porch of the hotel she knew she was close. She silently walked alongside the hotel wall to the front of the building and peered around the corner to look towards the sheriff's office, a long brick building that ran next to the courthouse. She stayed within the shadows of the hotel and watched the sheriff's office front windows. Carefully waiting for the light to be extinguished indicating that the deputy on duty was about to go to bed. She waited for no more then a half hour before the light went out. It was then she looked out into the dim light of the lamps, watchfully scanning the street for anyone who might be there to see her cross. Seeing no one on the street or looking out from any nearby buildings or homes, LooAnne darted out into the dimly lit street and then just as quickly ducked into the shadows against the cold brick of the jail wall. She quietly crept up the porch steps to the door which she assumed was locked. LooAnne removed a small tool from her dress pocket which she carefully inserted in the lock and working silently she began to pick the lock. Gently raking the lock back and forth until she heard a slight click. She pulled the small rod from the lock and dropped it back into her pocket, satisfied with her work. Then she slowly wrapped her fingers around the doorknob and turned it. The door opened without difficulty and LooAnne smiled in relief. But that was only the beginning, now came the hardest part, freeing her uncle without getting caught!

LooAnne quietly pulled open the door, wondering if it would screech as she did, but it opened without a sound and she was able to enter silently. The room was dark and empty, LooAnne assumed the deputy was sleeping in the back room where his bunk was located. LoAnne was faced with two identical doors, one leading to the back room and one that led to the cells. LooAnne took a ring of keys out of the desk and prayed she had the correct door as she gingerly unlocked it. The mechanism clicked loudly as it unlatched and for a moment LooAnne froze, staring at the door barely daring to breath for an agonizing moment. When everything remained still she proceeded to open the door which creaked softly as it swung on it's hinges. LooAnne looked through the doorway and down a hall with cells lined on either side. It was dark but as she entered the corridor she could just barely see her uncle laying on a cot in the nearest cell. She entered, not making the smallest sound, and went to the cell door. A streetlight shined brightly through the window right on Ricky who lay on his cot with his hands behind his head, staring absentmindedly at the ceiling, wrinkles of worry lining his face.

"Uncle Ricky," LooAnne whispered in a small, almost unintelligible voice.

Ricky jerked up a bit, startled at hearing his niece's voice. "LooAnne!" he whispered in amazement as he got to his feet and came to the door. "What in the world are you doing here? How did you get in?"

"I'm a Luther, I can break into a bank vault if need be and at the moment I'm breaking you out."

"You're doing what, young lady?" Ricky exclaimed, his voice showing his astonishment.

"I'm going to break you out," LooAnne repeated.

"No, LooAnne," he objected. "I won't spend my life running from the law. I can't do that!"

"You won't have to," was all LooAnne said.

"What do you mean I won't have to? How could I possibly avoid it?"

"Believe me you won't." LooAnne inserted the key in the lock and turned it then she swung the door open and looked up at her uncle, the bars no longer separating them. "Please, Uncle Ricky?" she begged. "I promise you that you won't run from the law the rest of your life. I'll see to it myself, now we must get out of here!"

"They'll know who did it, LooAnne. They will come straight to the estate and take me back and they'll discover that you broke me out and then we'll both be in trouble."

"You won't be at the estate. I have a place all ready for you to hide until it's safe. As for me getting into trouble with the law, they can't prove a thing and they'll never be able to. I won't leave without you so come with me now before the deputy wakes up!"

Ricky shook his head in uncertainty, "I don't know, LooAnne," he whispered.

"Please, Uncle Ricky?" LooAnne begged fervently, "I know what I'm doing. Trust me."

Ricky looked down into his niece's pleading eyes and realized how much she had risked to be here now, trying to save his life. "Alright," he whispered, "let's get out of here."

LooAnne smiled and took Ricky's hand, pulling him out of the cell. She then re-locked the cell door and the two slowly and silently crept down the hall of now empty cells and out into the office. LooAnne quietly shut the door with the barred window and locked it back as well. "What are you doing?" Ricky hissed impatiently as he stood at the front door.

"Making it look like you walked through the walls," LooAnne answered as she replaced the key ring in the desk, being careful not to make the slightest bit of noise. She and her uncle then fled into the night air, carefully creeping along the street, ducking in the shadows of buildings. Everything was quiet until Ricky heard three men conversing as they walked down the sidewalk towards the Nashs. He acted quickly, grabbing LooAnne and pulling her behind a building as the two plastered themselves against the wall! They held their breath as the trio walked by chatting merrily to one another. When they had disappeared around the corner Ricky and his niece let out a sigh of relief.

"I've lost my touch," LooAnne whispered as she looked up at her uncle. "I didn't even hear them. I certainly am glad you did."

"I almost didn't," Ricky whispered back, gulping down some of the cold air as his heart began to slow again.

The two ducked from the side of the building and continued down the road at a brisk pace, anxious to get out of town. When they finally reached the edge of town they slowed their pace and Ricky asked, "You said I wouldn't have to run the rest of my life. I hope that wasn't just a ruse to get me to leave with you?"

"Certainly not," LooAnne assured him. "In a matter of days we'll find out what the outcome of this whole thing is to be."

"And how will we do that?" Ricky questioned.

"We just will," LooAnne stated.

"How?" Ricky persisted.

"I can't tell you that," his niece said bluntly, "Trust me, we'll know."

Ricky sighed, tired of dwelling on the subject, "If you say so, LooAnne. You know," he continued as he looked off through a moonlit field, a look of deep contemplation in his dark, tired eyes, "I saw what the life of a millionaire was growing up with my father. I knew that it wasn't an easy life but had no idea that millionaires could ever be convicted of murder in their own hometown when they were completely innocent of the crime."

"It was Red's fault," LooAnne said. "He came to the estate earlier and tried to apologize though. I'm ashamed to admit I didn't listen to him. I told him to get out and never come back." LooAnne sighed regretfully, "I was angry at him for not being loyal to his own cousin, but I finally realized, too late, that I wasn't being loyal myself."

Ricky put his arm around his niece's shoulders. "Don't

dwell on something you can't change. You won't always be able to go back and fix things. Some things that are said are just going to remain said, but this isn't one of those things. You'll have another opportunity to forgive Red for what he did."

LooAnne nodded soberly not wanting her uncle to know that might have been her only chance.

Ricky interrupted her thoughts, "When did you and Red become so well acquainted?"

"That day you were arrested. Theodora came upstairs and broke down over her brother's death. While I was comforting her Red came in and we talked for a while... until the sheriff came." LooAnne sighed dejectedly, "I couldn't believe it when Red and his brothers walked out without a word and then he turned on you completely. He made up his mind that you were guilty the moment Sheriff Low spoke your name. They all did. I couldn't believe they would be so quick to have their own cousin pay, with his life, for something he hadn't done."

Ricky sighed and let his hand drop form his niece's shoulders. It was then that LooAnne took a good look at him. He was dirty and unshaven. Thin from the terrible jail food or his lack of apatite for it. He looked more than tired. He looked exhausted from all he had endured over the last few weeks.

"He was grieving," Ricky interrupted LooAnne's thoughts. "When a man grieves his mind is not the same. He dwells on nothing but his loss and is desperate to somehow relieve the pain he feels. Red thought that by making someone pay, not particularly the killer, but someone, for the death of his brother, it would ease his grief. He found out the hard way, as everyone does, that there is no cure for the loss of someone close to you. You never truly get over it, but with time and prayer, you learn to keep going. You learn to move on but to never forget."

LooAnne found herself greatly moved by her uncle's speech. For years she had denied, almost forgotten, that her mother or father ever existed. She had pushed them to the back of her mind and the back of her heart where she was not forced to go through the pain of losing them. She denied their existence. She denied her need for them and their love for her. She even denied her love for them.

This realization struck her as her uncle spoke. She had handled her grief in quite a different way and yet it suddenly seemed worse to her.

LooAnne stopped walking and looked down at the muddied road, feeling a knot begin to grow in her throat. "LooAnne are you okay?" Ricky asked, stopping alongside her.

LooAnne could not choose this time to get emotional. She could not delay them with the chance that the law was not far behind. She could not cry in front of her uncle, especially over his lost sister.

LooAnne looked up at her uncle and smiled tiredly, "I'm fine, Uncle Ricky, just a bit sleepy."

Ricky looked at her skeptically, "Are you sure? I didn't mean to upset you."

"No no, you didn't upset me," LooAnne assured him, for it had not been her uncle's words that caused her pain but her own wondering, painful memories.

"I'm just sorry that Andy's dead is all, and on top of that you had to be blamed for it."

"I'm sorry too, my dear," Ricky sighed as they once again began walking. "Not only because my reputation's been tainted, I liked Andy, he was my cousin. He didn't mean to be wild and boisterous. He was just never taught different. Aunt Roberta and Uncle David were killed when Andy was very young. He never really had anyone to teach him except his brothers and they – well – they were just never really interested in spending what little time they had on their kid brother."

"What about Theodora? Wasn't she younger then Andy?"

Ricky nodded, "I think that was part of the reason Andy was neglected so. Theodora was a girl, something those boys knew nothing about and had no experience with. They paid her every attention. Did all they could to protect her and make sure they didn't fail her in any way. Andy was an afterthought. They thought he would grow to be like the rest of them, but he didn't. He was always wild and never really cared anything his older brothers were doing. He was always off somewhere else doing something silly, or even against the law on occasion."

LooAnne could see that thinking on the subject was causing Ricky pain so she did not ask him all of the questions that loomed in her mind, and they continued on through the wet summer night in silence.

ELLEVEN

A Den of Luthers

"Did we not cast three men bound into the midst of the fire?" They answered and said to the king, "True O King." "Look!" he answered, "I see four men loose, walking in the midst of the fire; and the forth is like the Son of God." Daniel 3:24 and 25

Direct my steps by Your word and let no iniquity have dominion over me. Psalms 119:133

When Ricky and LooAnne reached the Nash property LooAnne stepped off the road. "The cave is this way. I don't think going by the estate is wise just in case we're seen."
Ricky nodded in silent agreement and followed LooAnne passed the trees and brush that lined the road and then through the wet fields. The cave was quite far and in the dark it took them more than half an hour to reach it. As the two approached the dark hole in the side of the mountain they saw a small light glowing!

"Did you leave a light in the cave?" Ricky asked as the two paused just outside the clearing, staring at the small light that flickered from within the dark hole.

LooAnne shook her head, "No I didn't. There must be someone there."

"Do you know who it could be?" Ricky asked.

LooAnne shook her head apprehensively, "I wish I did." She thought a moment then said, "Wait, I might know who it is."

"Who?"

"Mr. Block," LooAnne answered. "He's the only one that knew I was bringing you here. I told him to come once the sun came up but maybe he got worried for our safety and came early," LooAnne whispered. "Wait here, I'll be right back."

LooAnne started towards the cave but Ricky grabbed her arm and held her back, "You can't just walk right up to the cave entrance!"

"I don't intend to. I'm just going to get a little closer so I can see."

"What if it's not Mr. Block?"

"That's what I intend to find out. Don't worry, whoever it is they won't hear me."

"Be careful, LooAnne," Ricky warned as he released her.

"I will." LooAnne proceeded forward, using her bare feet to feel what was under them so as not to step on a stick or a pile of dry leaves. Staying well inside the trees she made her way closer to the cave and the glowing light that flickered inside. The light was not strong enough to reveal anything inside making it necessary for

LooAnne to get closer. Without a sound she crept up to the cave's side, moving inch by inch towards it until she reached it's mouth. LooAnne drew in a slow breath before silently peeking into the cave to see who stood behind the light. She instantly smiled and sighed in relief upon seeing that their visitor was, indeed, her uncle's steward.

"Mr. Block!" she called in a whisper.

For a moment there was silence and then a familiar voice called, "Miss Nash?" He stepped from the cave into the moonlight and looked around frantically for LooAnne.

"I'm here," she said, stepping from her crouched position alongside the cave. When Chris saw her he asked anxiously, "Did everything go alright? Where's Mr. Nash?"

"I'm here, Chris," Ricky said as he stepped out of the concealment of the woods and approached the cave. Chris sighed with relief when he saw his employer emerge from the trees. "You don't know how glad I am to see you, sir," Chris said as he shook hands with Ricky. "I know that I wasn't supposed to be here until morning but I couldn't wait. I had to check on Miss Nash."

Ricky smiled and said rather proudly, "I've never seen a Luther at work before, but when they are working with you it's quite remarkable."

"That part was easy," LooAnne said modestly. "Uncle Ricky, you should have enough supplies in the cave to last until Mr. Block comes back in the morning with more food. Now you must stay here until you hear from me. Whatever you do, don't leave, and be sure to stay on your guard for anyone who might hear of your escape and come after you. Particularly Devin."

"I'm getting the impression," Ricky said to his niece, "that you're going somewhere. Am I right?"

"At the moment I'm going to go home and get a good night's rest."

"And then?" Ricky questioned, knowing that there was more to his niece's scheme then a good night's rest.

"I'm going to find out who really killed Andy Stacey. Meanwhile you stay here and rely on Mr. Block for your food and information."

"Where are you going to be?" Ricky persisted.

"Trying to figure out who the real killer is."

"I see, and when you figure it out what are you going to do?"

"I'm going to take my information to the sheriff so that you can be cleared of the charges."

"What if you never find the real killer?" Ricky asked.

"I will."

"What if you can't prove that he did it?"

"Then you'll hear about it and if you want to give yourself up then you can. I won't stop you."

Ricky sighed. "Alright, but you be careful and promise me that you won't take any unnecessary risks."

"I promise that I won't take any unnecessary risks," LooAnne said, thinking to herself how perfectly necessary her risks were.

"Alright then." Ricky looked at the cave and shook his head in disbelief, "I'm nearly the richest man in the whole country and I'm living in a cave eating canned beans."

"At least you're not facing sure death here in this cave," LooAnne said, her conscience aching with all the lies she had bluntly told her uncle.

Ricky shrugged, "I suppose you're right. Thank you for getting me out, dear. I must admit they had me scared."

"I'm glad I was there to get you out," LooAnne smiled, "and at the moment I'm exhausted. If you don't mind I'm going back to the house and get some sleep. Plus I need to be there in case that deputy finds out you escaped earlier then I expect and comes calling wondering where you are."

Ricky nodded in agreement, "You'd better go with her Chris, wouldn't want you to be away from the house in the same circumstances."

Chris nodded and said to LooAnne, "You go ahead, I'll be there in just a few minutes."

"Alright, Mr. Block." LooAnne looked up at her uncle for a moment, wondering if she would ever see him again, and how the whole situation would end. Then she turned and ran towards the house, the dark trees swallowing her up. Ricky and Chris watched her go in silence. When she was out of sight Ricky turned to his steward and said, "Alright, Chris, where is she really going?"

Chris was startled at his employer's sudden question. "What makes you think she's going somewhere other then the house, sir?"

"The way she looked at me before she left, and the look on your face as she was running off. Now tell me where she's going."

"I can't. I told her that I wouldn't."

"Well that makes absolutely no difference. You tell me and you do it right now."

"But sir, I-"

"I'm not interested in any of your explanations, Chris, if you don't tell me I'm going to go after her and make *her* tell me."

"She's going to find the real killer," Chris insisted.

"That's what she said but I don't happen to believe a word of it. Now if you're not telling me then that must mean she's going somewhere that I don't want her to be so you'd better tell me and you'd better do it now!" Ricky demanded.

Chris sighed in exasperation. "She knows who killed Andy Stacey, sir, and she's gone to get him and bring him to town so that he'll confess."

"And who is it that killed Andy?" Ricky asked.

"It's a long story, sir," Chris said attempting to stall for time.

"I didn't ask for the story, Chris, I simply want to know who killed my cousin!"

Chris rubbed the back of his neck nervously. "It was – it was..."

"It was Devin Luther wasn't it?" Ricky interrupted. "Well wasn't it?"

Chris sighed and nodded, "Yes sir, it was. Miss Nash has gone to the Luther Estate to get him and bring him back. She believes a confession is the only thing -"

"She went to the Luther Estate!" Ricky cried in horror. "To bring back a Luther!"

"Yes sir," Chris nodded.

145

"What's the child thinking, Chris! Doesn't she know that she'll be killed?"

"She's the only one who can get him here and have you cleared of the murder, sir."

"Then I don't want to be cleared! She can never get there and get Devin out without someone seeing her and killing her, or worse! Why didn't you stop her?" Ricky yelled, mixed emotions booming in his voice.

"Because I think she can do it. I'm sure of it."

Ricky looked at Chris and said, "We'll wait here until morning and then we're going to town for some much needed assistance."

"Assistance, sir?" Chris asked.

"Yes, Chris. We cannot fight this fight alone anymore."

Meanwhile LooAnne had crossed the creek at the bottom of the hill on her way towards the Luther property. She knew the only way to avoid being killed was to remain unseen, but she wondered how exactly she was supposed to accomplish this when she was sure that they had guards posted in every direction, waiting for a trespasser to come within range of their weapon. After another half hour of walking LooAnne made her way up a small hill on the very back of her uncle's property. At the top of the hill was a fence marking the property line that separated the Nash's from the Luther's. LooAnne walked to it and laid her hand between the barbs, gripping the thin wire as she scanned the other side. It was like a jungle, a jungle that she knew was full of angry beasts ready to devour her in one swoop of their viscous claws! She hadn't been this far back on the property since she had run away five years before. She had never wanted to see the Luther property again. She had been too afraid until this point to get this close to it. LooAnne turned her head and looked over her shoulder at her uncle's land. It was a place of safety and yet she was going to leave it. She was going to cross the fence into Luther territory where she was not sure if she would ever leave. LooAnne took one last look at the Nash property and then she lifted the middle wire and slipped through the fence, setting her foot on Luther ground! For a few moments LooAnne was unable to move any further. It had been five years of happiness since she had stepped on this soil. The last time she was too young to be scared. She had naively left with only the ragged and dirty clothes on her back and the painful memories in her head. LooAnne looked in the direction of the old Luther house, remembering how the fence line had looked to her five years ago. She had run to it as though the other side was calling to her to come and be rid of the pain forever. How silly that sounded to her now. How childish and yet vivid the whole thing was. Realizing she was wasting time LooAnne shook her head to clear her mind of the past and began to move. She started towards the Luther Estate just as thick clouds moved overhead and covered the moon plunging everything into a sudden darkness...

While LooAnne's progress was slowed because of the failing light she was glad that at least there was very little chance of anyone seeing her until morning. She continued in the direction she knew by heart, trying her best to move silently. It was about midnight when she spotted the black shadows created by the trees surrounding the Luther house, where she hoped for the right moment to nab Devin. The wind was beginning to blow harder and the pine branches rocked overhead, smashing into each other and knocking their green leaves and small twigs to the ground. LooAnne pulled her shawl tighter and carefully made her way up the side of the hill. She occasionally paused so she could check her positioning. She must be certain she avoided the spots from where the Luther guards were sure to be watching.

As LooAnne moved closer she squinted her eyes, wondering when she would see the house. One step more and suddenly there it was! A black wall against the night sky. LooAnne froze in her tracks, looking at the house for the first since she was a child. It stood exactly as it had before. Silhouetted in the moonlight, it creaked and groaned under the pressure of the wind. LooAnne remembered when she was twelve running down this hill away from her life as it had been. She remembered stopping almost exactly where she now stood and looking back at the Luther Estate wondering if they would come after her and bring her back to it all. LooAnne decided to spend the rest of the night in this spot. Before the sunrise she hoped to find out exactly where Devin was and wait for the right moment to nab him. LooAnne found a soft, slightly damp spot beneath a pine with low slung branches. She laid down amongst the fallen needles and looked up into the darkened branches that swayed in the wind causing a sharp rustle throughout the woods. LooAnne laid so that she faced the house just in case someone came outside. She wasn't the least bit tired but knew that she needed to rest after having not slept the entire night. LooAnne pulled a branch over her as a disguise and then she laid back and rested her head against the cold, wet needles. She tried her best to sleep but with every noise she jumped. Adrenalin pumped into her vanes and caused her heart to race. Only a few minutes passed before LooAnne realized that she could not go on this way. She could not relax and come morning she would be too tired and stiff to think clearly. She knew she had to calm herself down somehow. LooAnne closed her eyes and took a deep breath, filling her lungs with the fresh night air. She breathed steadily and thought of how she longed to be back home with her uncle, sleeping in her own warm bed, without worry.

As she laid under the pine tree, whispering a prayer into the night, weariness suddenly came upon her and she closed her eyes. In the next moment she drifted into a light sleep.

TWELVE

The Luther Family

The Lord is on my side; I will not fear,
what can man do to me?
Proverbs 118:6

To the choirmaster. Of the sons of Korah.
According to Alamoth. A song. God is our
refuge and strength, a very present help
in trouble. Psalm 46:1

LooAnne didn't realize that she had fallen asleep
until she awakened early the next morning. The sky was
a clear, crisp blue and the sun was already above the
mountain peek. It was already hot and sticky after the
previous day's rain and LooAnne felt little beads of
sweat beginning to run down the back of her neck. She
slowly crawled from under the branch and peered up at
the Luther Estate that stood at the top of the hill,
seeming to tower over her and cast it's intimidating
shadow across the trees.
LooAnne listened carefully for sign of movement but
hearing no one she made her way, quietly and carefully
up the hillside, the house slowly growing bigger and

bigger as she approached it. Suddenly she heard something that made her duck behind a large tree! It was the familiar voice of her aunt, Bessie Luther! She was saying in a loud, crackled voice, "Stanley! Stanley where's your father!"

LooAnne caught her breath, Stanley was Devin's son! *"Perhaps the Luthers are playing into my hand?"* LooAnne thought hopefully.

"How should I know?" came Stanley's voice from down the hill by the creek.

"Don't you go talkin' to me like that, young man!" Bessie commanded. "I wanna know where your father is now!"

"I dunno," Stanley said but his voice was closer now.

"He needs to go to town to get me supplies."

"How come ya always send Pa to town but the rest o' us gotta stay cooped up here ev'r day o' our lives?"

"Devin knows how to get things out o' people better then any o' the rest o' ya."

"But can't I be his bodyguard then?"

"Don't be stupid, Stan. You couldn't guard Bigfoot his self."

"But Ted always gets to go."

"Ted ain't goin',"

"Then who is?"

"Will."

"Will?" Stanley yelled in exasperation, "Will don't guard, do you 'member the last time -"

"All the more reason that he orda go, he needs t' learn to how to keep himself in check. Now you head on and fetch the twain of 'em."

"Fine," Stanley sighed angrily, stomping off.

LooAnne caught her breath, Will Luther was her older brother! He had a reputation as one of the cruelest most vile Luthers in the clan! How could she possibly get Devin with her brother right there watching him the entire time? LooAnne prayed that somehow things would change and Devin wouldn't go to town. If he did LooAnne would be forced to wait for his return and that would delay her arrival back to the cave. Chris would think she had been killed and might even tell Ricky which would lead to her uncle giving himself up to be hung for Andy's murder! LooAnne could not let that happen! If Devin was accompanied into town then her mission might fail miserably!

At that moment LooAnne heard Devin call from the creek bed, "What do ya want, Bessie?"

"Go to town and get some supplies. Take Will with ya."

"Look old woman, I got things I'm doin'. Things more important then your silly junk that you think you can cook. You want somethin' to eat then go shoot a squirrel."

"Have you forgotten who's in charge, Devin?"

"Are you kiddin'? Even if I could forget you wouldn't let me. Now I don't care if you're in charge or not, I ain't goin' to town."

"You are or you ain't getting no supper."

There was a pause before Devin answered, "Fine, but I better get me a good supper; and I ain't takin' Will neither, he'll just get me in trouble like always."

"You're not goin' by yourself are ya?"

"I don't get caught no how. Who needs a bodyguard

when the whole town fears him?"

Bessie huffed. "Apparently Rick Nash don't fear ya the way he's been lickin' your hide at every turn."

"You keep your mouth shut, woman!" Devin snapped. "You know darn well that I took care o' Mr. Nash. He's gonna be hung early tomorrow mornin' and there ain't nothin' nobody can do about it."

"You think that town's gonna let anyone lay a hand on their beloved money bags?"

"There ain't nothin' they can do about it."

"You've seen a lynchin' before, Devin, you know that they can do that. If a town can break a fella outta jail to lynch him then they can break him out to save him. Rick Nash ain't gonna hang for no murder, whether he did the killin' or not."

"You just keep right on thinkin' that, Bessie."

With that Devin turned and walked towards the road. LooAnne smiled to herself. Now that Will wasn't going along she would have ample chance to apprehend Devin. She rose up from her spot and slowly crept down the side of the hill away from the Luther Estate. She knew of a shortcut she used to take to the road to spy on her brothers so she could see what they were really doing when they said that they were training for a raid or going hunting. When she got far enough away from the Luther house she began to run so that she would be sure to reach the road before Devin. As she ran it was as though she were a little girl again. She remembered the times she had run to the road to watch her brothers ambush people. They would rob them of their money and little trinkets then sometimes let them be on their way and other times leave then laying on the roadside. LooAnne recalled so much of her childhood as she ran through the woods. She could see herself in every direction she looked, doing things alone or with one of her family, mainly training or getting into trouble. LooAnne looked ahead of her and tried to concentrate on Devin and not on the past, but she could not seem to bring herself to clear her thoughts of the place she had once called home.

Finally she caught sight of the road from within the trees and the momentary thoughts of her childhood vanished. LooAnne ran ahead and cautiously peered out of the woods to make sure there was no one about. Seeing it was clear LooAnne turned and found a small vine hanging from a tree. She yanked it down and ran across the dusty road to a small tree where she wrapped the long vine several times around it and then laid a log next to the sapling so as to keep the vine from unwinding. She then stretched it across the road and buried the vine just barely under the surface to conceal it. LooAnne ducked inside the trees and gripped the vine tightly, waiting for Devin to arrive. After about five minutes he appeared walking along silently as Luthers generally did. LooAnne held her breath and waited for just the right moment and then she yanked on the vine with all her strength. The vine sprung out from under the dirt catching Devin at the shins. There was no time to catch himself before he tripped and went sprawling on the ground! LooAnne acted fast, grabbing a large stick she ran out onto the road and before he knew what was happening she struck Devin over the head, knocking him out cold!

LooAnne stepped back, blowing some stray hairs out of her eyes she smiled slightly, realizing that her plan was working. She had Devin Luther, the man that could clear her uncle!

Now all she needed to do was get him to town and be prepared should he awaken! That was when an idea donned on her! LooAnne knelt next to her relative and searched his pockets finding two knifes along with a gun that was tucked in his belt. LooAnne smiled and decided that in stead of breaking her back dragging Devin to town as she had first planned, she would simply wait until he came too again and then use his own gun to force him to walk to town himself. LooAnne sat down against a large tree on the side of the road a few feet away from Devin and waited patiently for him to awaken.

The sun gradually rose high into the sky, scorching the earth below it. Sweat ran down LooAnne's forehead and soaked into the collar of her dress, collecting the dust that floated about, kicked up by the morning wind. Her stomach began to growl with hunger but she ignored it. For over an hour she waited until Devin finally began to stir. LooAnne pointed the gun right at him and watched as he slowly regained consciousness. The moment he realized where he was and that he had been unconscious he sat up, but closed his eyes tightly for a moment, waiting for his throbbing head to cease it's spinning. When it did he looked around him and saw LooAnne who had stood up and was covering him watchfully with his own gun. Devin momentarily squinted at her questioningly through the intense sun and then he narrowed his eyes angrily and asked in a gruff Texas drawl, "Who're you?"

"That's none of your business," LooAnne informed him, relieved that he did not immediately recognize her. "Get on your feet," she demanded.

"Ha!" Devin scoffed. "I don't think you know who you're dealin' with, girl."

"I know very well who I'm dealing with. Now you get on your feet and start walking towards town."

"Why should I?" Devin countered.

"Because I've got a gun pointed at you and I'm not afraid to use it if you don't get going. Now move!"

Devin stood up and slowly staggered in LooAnne's direction. She lifted the gun until the barrel was level with Devin's eyes and yelled, "You stay back there! Don't get close to me. The only thing that you're getting close to is town."

"Did you hit me over the head?" Devin demanded having recovered fully now.

"That's for me to know and for you to find out," LooAnne informed him.

A satisfied smirk came over Devin's face, "I've already found it out, found out who you are too!"

LooAnne instantly felt her stomach begin to turn with fear, though she did not show it outwardly. She held her breath as Devin continued.

"You're that girl that was at the ruins of the Nash Estate that last time I fought with Rick Nash. You must be his niece."

LooAnne let out an unnoticeable breath but she eyed her

father's brother carefully and said, "Fine then, I am LooAnne Nash."

Devin huffed in amusement, "What exactly are you tryin' to do?"

"I'm trying to bring you back to town," LooAnne informed him.

"That's a stupid move, Miss Nash," Devin warned. "Once my kin figure out what you done they'll come after us to get me back, and you'll come out on the short end o' the deal if you know what I mean."

"I know what you mean, but I'm not going to listen to your threats. Now you get going towards town and don't stop unless I tell you to stop."

Devin eyed the gun then glanced up at the hot sun. He looked back at LooAnne and wordlessly started for town with LooAnne following behind him at a distance.

They were quite a ways from town and the heat was excruciating. After waking nearly three miles LooAnne's throat began to grow dry and scratchy, sweat pored down her face and drenched her shirt. Her arms grew red from sunburn. She tried to walk in the shade but most of the road was too far away from trees to provide much protection from the scorching Texas sun.

LooAnne began to grow lightheaded and her feet stumbled along the road as if she herself was not controlling them. Finally she stopped at the top of a hill and said hoarsely, "Hold it, Luther."

Devin stopped and looked back at her questioningly.

"Down the hill," she commanded, gesturing with the weapon.

"I thought we were going to town?" Devin asked, he too

157

was a bit hoarse.

"We're going down the hill to find some water, now move."

"How do you know there's any water down there?" Devin countered.

"There's always water at the bottom of a hill," LooAnne retorted, refusing to allow him to get the best of her as she knew he would try.

"Not when it ain't rained in a week there ain't. That stream down there is dry as the Nash Estate was when I burned it to the ground," Devin smirked.

LooAnne narrowed her eyes at Devin and said, "I didn't ask your opinion, now make your way down that hill! You need water just as much as I do and you know it."

Devin turned and slowly began descending the hill through the thick underbrush. As they went Devin glanced back at LooAnne and realized that she was weakening from dehydration. When they reached the bottom there was a creek that was low but not completely dry. LooAnne looked over at her cousin and said, "Now you get something to drink and then step back against that tree."

Devin knelt next to the little creek and dipped his cupped hand into the cool water, the whole time watching LooAnne who was standing a few feet away from him rubbing the sweat from her brow. After taking a few handfuls of water into his mouth he straitened and backed up against the tree as he had been instructed. LooAnne carefully knelt next to the creek, pointing the gun at Devin as she drank. Devin eyed her watchfully then, in a sudden moment, he made a swift move towards LooAnne and kicked the gun from her hand! It went flying in the other direction and LooAnne toppled over backwards!

Devin immediately made a mad dash for the gun and grabbed it just as LooAnne put her hand on it! She froze and looked up at her cousin, worry showing in her brown eyes. Devin smiled in satisfaction and said triumphantly, "Now who has the gun, Miss Nash?"

LooAnne remained silent, staring at Devin with a hard, piercing stare, but inwardly she was trembling with fear! "Seems to me, Miss Nash that you just lost the fight," Devin bragged. "Now get up!"

LooAnne got to her feet and watched Devin carefully, trying to be ready to run if she got the chance which she knew in her heart was not likely to come.

Devin's grin faded and his face took on a look of hatred as he scrutinized his foe. "Now you tell me what this is all about," he demanded.

"You don't know?" LooAnne said, almost amazed that he even had to ask.

"I got a fair idea but I wanna hear it from you, out with it!"

"You killed Andy Stacey and framed my uncle for it," LooAnne stated bluntly.

"That's what I thought you were gonna say. You want me to confess to keep Rick Nash from hangin'."

LooAnne nodded stiffly.

Devin huffed in amusement, "How exactly were you gonna get me to say a thing that would make them think any better o' that man?"

LooAnne remained silent.

159

"I thought so," Devin sneered. "You got some nerve comin' up here and trying to overtake a Luther! I hope you don't think I was gettin' soft after that little bout I had with your uncle the other day? We surely wouldn't want anyone thinkin' that."

LooAnne held her breath, wondering what Devin was going to do to her to prove his authority. He pointed the gun at her face and said, "You know, I otta kill you right here and now, but the way I figure it that wouldn't be no fun. Someone needs to teach you that we Luthers ain't to be messed with." Devin smiled an evil smile. "Up the hill, girl!"

LooAnne looked at the hill that led to the road, not wanting to obey him as she knew where that would lead. "Move!" Devin yelled irritably as he shoved her in the direction of the road.

LooAnne stumbled but caught herself and slowly began ascending the small hill. When she reached the road she stopped and looked at Devin, wondering what his next move would be. He looked at her and grinned mischievously. "Get movin'."

"Where are we going?" LooAnne asked.

"Back home," was his terrifying reply.

LooAnne was not about to go back to the Luther Estate. Deciding that she had nothing to lose, LooAnne reacted instinctively. In the space of a few seconds she stepped back, raised her bare foot, and kicked the gun from Devin's hand just as he had done to her! Then she turned and ran down the road in the direction of town, praying that she could somehow get away.

With an angry exclamation Devin picked up his gun and

took off in pursuit of his prisoner! LooAnne ran down the dusty road as fast as her feet would carry her. She knew that her enraged uncle was close behind her and the fear of getting caught again kept her going on through the heat. The hot air seemed to clog her throat as she panted and wheezed, seeming as though she was running through a an ocean of heat.

She could hear him not far behind her but as time elapsed her distance grew! LoOAnne was sure she could loose the man if her body would keep this pace but as she reached the bottom of the hill she stubbed her toe on a rock and fell hard to the ground! Before she could get back up Devin had her in his iron grip! He yanked her to her feet and shook her roughly, "Don't you ever try that again, girl! Understand!"

LooAnne was out of breath and her mouth was dry and scratchy but she looked Devin straight in the eye, her gaze unwavering, and said through broken breaths, "Y-you can't – h-hold me for long. M-my family – w-will come for me. Y-you're no match for them!"

Devin grit his teeth and backhanded LooAnne across the face, sending her weakened body to the ground! "You think you're so smart, girl! Well I got news for ya, I'm takin' you back to the Luther Estate and you'll spend the rest o' your short life wishin' you had never been born!"

LooAnne's cheek throbbed painfully and she could feel a bruise starting to form but she had often felt that sting and it was nothing compared to what could happen should she let herself be taken back.

"You've forgotten that my uncle will fight for me!" she countered. "He won't stop until he's found me and you've payed for all you've done!"

"HA!" Devin laughed mockingly, "You're uncle might be a brave fella but there ain't nothin' he can do when he's dead!"

This suddenly gave LooAnne an idea. She was not sure that it would work but she had nothing to lose. She had to stall for time!

"Maybe you will take me back to the Luther Estate," she began, "and maybe I won't live long after getting there, but there's one thing that you're wrong about! Uncle Ricky won't hang for Andy's murder."

Devin snorted, "Last I heard he was sentenced to be hung in the morin'. How do you reckon he'll get himself outta that one?"

LooAnne smirked knowingly, "He's not there for anyone to hang. I broke him out last night. He's safe away from the law, the town, and you savage Luthers!"

Devin frowned for a moment, unsure as to whether or not he should believe such a far-fetched story, then he smiled and said, "Yeah sure. Tryin' to pull a fast one are we? Well it ain't gonna work, and you watch how you speak to me!"

"I'm not trying to pull a fast one on anybody," LooAnne insisted, "It's true, every word of it. Uncle Ricky's not in jail and he'll always be free to overpower you because I've foiled your revenge once and for all!"

Devin thought a moment and said, "Well then why don't you tell me where he is?"

"That's the catch to the whole thing," LooAnne said. "As long as I have information you're in need of you can't kill me."

"Don't you forget who your dealin' with, girl," Devin threatened, "If I wanna know something you know, then I got ways to get it out o' ya."

"Alright, so maybe you do. The only problem is, I'm a girl and fall apart physically very easily, so though you can throw me around a bit there's only so far you can go and I'm ready to go just as far as you can."

Devin smiled an evil smile, "As much as I would love to thrash you around a might, I got a better idea. If you don't tell me where your uncle is, I'll be at the train station here in the next few days waitin' for a certain young Kyle Denson to come home for your funeral, which will take place sometime in the next week. I know that he'll be here 'cause he's in love with ya!"

LooAnne felt her heart sink as she stared at Devin, not knowing how to counter his new threat.

"You look surprised my dear little Nash," Devin continued. "Don't be, we Luthers know everything that happens in your no-account town."

LooAnne, though worried, had to hold in a grin upon hearing this. Obviously the Luthers did not know that the great Rick Nash's niece was a Luther herself, and they did not happen to know that Ricky had been broken out of jail either.

"Say something!" Devin commanded harshly. "Tell me where your uncle is, NOW!"

Though she had withdrawn slightly, LooAnne answered Devin calmly, "The way I see it, if I tell you, you'll kill me, you'll go after Uncle Ricky, and more than likely kill him. Then when Kyle comes you'll shoot him just to spite me. So I won't tell you where Uncle Ricky is and you won't be able to kill me because I know a valuable piece of information. You won't be able to kill Uncle Ricky because you won't know where he is. Finally, you won't shoot Kyle just to spite me because he won't be coming since I'm not dead."

LooAnne was so amazed that she had thought of this and told it right to the face of a Luther that she had to smile.

Devin grit his teeth and yanked LooAnne to her feet! Pulling her face close to his he said, "You tell me where Rick Nash is or I'll bring the whole Luther clan down on the town!"

"That's no great loss to me," LooAnne lied smoothly. Devin shook her angrily, "Listen girl, you tell me right now or else!"

"Or else what?" LooAnne countered bravely.

"Or else I'll beat it out o' ya!"

LooAnne took a deep breath, her throat parched and aching. "I don't care, Luther, nor shall I ever care!" Devin growled and pushed LooAnne back away from him. He pulled a knife that she had overlooked from his boot and swung it at her but she dodged it just in time. Turning to run Devin stuck his foot under hers and she went tumbling to the ground! She rolled over on her back and stared up at her father's brother with anger in her eyes, but inwardly she feared for her life!

Devin knelt next to her, holding the knife tightly in one hand and gripping her arm with the other. He looked her square in the eye and said, "You tell me where he is or I'll cut your throat!"

"Killing me will do you no good!" LooAnne screamed

as she struggled against the enraged man. "You cannot be so daft as to think that I will disclose Uncle Ricky's location to you if I'm dead!"

Devin tightened his grip on her thrashing frame and pressed the blade harder against her neck, threatening to draw blood!

"Maybe not, but like I said, 'til you tell me what I wanna know I can make you wish you was never born!"

"You do what you like with me!" LooAnne exclaimed, feeling the sharp pain against her throat. "I'll not tell you! Not now or ever!"

Devin was now beyond enraged! He raised his hand and struck LooAnne's already bruised cheek, causing her head to snap to the side, but not dwindling the fight inside her!

"Kill me just as you did Andy Stacey and have done with it!" LooAnne screamed in his face, her throat and cheek burning. "You'll pay for what you did whether it be by the hand of the law or the hand of the Almighty!"

Devin let out a psychotic laugh, "No one but you will ever know that I killed that Stacey kid, and you'll be dead!"

Devin withdrew the knife from LooAnne's neck and raised it in the air, ready to plunge it into her flesh!

LooAnne closed her eyes, preparing for the moment that was to come....

THIRTEEN

Death's Taste

*Thus says the Lord; "Let not the wise
man glory in his wisdom, let not the rich
man glory in his riches; but let him who
glories glory in this, that he understands
and knows Me, that I am the Lord,
exercising loving kindness, judgment,
and righteousness in the earth, for in these
things I delight," says the Lord.
Jeremiah 9:23 and 24*

"No! Stop!"
LooAnne's world seemed to move in slow motion as the
familiar voice reached her ears. She was holding her
breath, waiting for the blade of Devin's knife to come in
contact with her skin, but when she heard those two
words she was suddenly filled with hope!
Her eyes shot open just as Devin was thrown away from
her and she felt the familiar embrace of her uncle! Men
were shouting; LooAnne could hear Devin's angry
exclamations as he was subdued by Ricky's companions.
There seemed to be people surrounding her and Ricky.

LooAnne could hear the distinctive voice of Chris Block, but she tuned them all out and held on tightly to her uncle, burying her face into his shirt.

"Oh LooAnne!" Ricky exclaimed as he held her, "Are you alright? How badly are you hurt?"

LooAnne took a deep breath and shook her head, her throat still burning. "I'm fine," she croaked.

"He nearly killed you, LooAnne Marie Nash! You are not fine," Ricky corrected. He pulled away from her slightly and looked over her sweaty face, hunting for any sign of injury. When he found her red and bruising cheek his eyes widened and his face flushed with anger! "Devin Luther did this!" he exclaimed in rage. Ricky leaped to his feet and started for Devin who was struggling against a deputy and two Nash Estate ranch hands.

LooAnne reached out to grab her uncle and restrain him but she was not fast enough. Ricky lunged at Devin, his fist raised, and brought it down on his enemy's face, striking him so hard that he fell away from the restricting arms of the other men and landed with a painful thud on the road behind him.

"Sir, please!" Chris objected as he took hold of his employer's arm and drug him back. Ricky shook Chris off easily and went to hit Devin again but LooAnne, who was now on her feet, stepped in front of her uncle and held him back. "Uncle Ricky, it's alright!" she insisted. "I'm perfectly fine and he'll pay for his crimes! There's no need to beat him senseless!"

"No need?" Ricky repeated. "He burned down my house, killed my cousin, and assaulted my niece, and

167

you say there is no need for me to beat him within an inch of his life!"

"He's going to pay for it, Uncle Ricky," LooAnne reassured and she held him away from Devin. "Please don't do anything that will get you put in jail again," she hissed quietly to him so that only he and Chris heard. Ricky looked at his niece and then over her shoulder at Devin Luther. He nodded and stepped back, recomposing himself.

The men grabbed Devin and held him as Sheriff Low cuffed his hands behind his back. It was then that LooAnne realized Red and his brothers were there as well, looking on at the situation with regretful faces. As she watched Devin being handcuffed by the authorities the realization of what had just happened began to sink in. Her parched throat ached and her head pounded with dehydration. Her neck stung from where Devin had punctured the skin ever so slightly and her bruised cheek was throbbing. LooAnne felt her legs growing weak and just as they were about to give out from beneath her she felt her uncle pull her into another hug and ease her to the ground.

"Chris, bring some water!" Ricky called to his steward. Within seconds Chris was by their side with a tin of water which LooAnne gladly accepted. The instant it was on her lips she gulped it down thirstily.

"Slowly, slowly," her uncle's soothing voice commanded.

LooAnne pulled the tin away and sighed heavily, leaning into her uncle's side.

"Better?" he questioned worriedly.

LooAnne nodded and sat up slightly, only one thought weighing on her mind. She looked up at her uncle and asked hoarsely, "Did – did they hear his confession?" Ricky nodded, smiling fondly at his niece, "They did. You've done it, LooAnne. You saved my life."
LooAnne felt relief overwhelm her! Her uncle was finally free. He was finally going to come home! Ricky pulled LooAnne into one last hug, holding her tightly. "I don't know what to say, my dear," he admitted. "There aren't words enough to thank you for all you've done."
LooAnne shook her head, laying it against her uncle's chest. "You don't have to say anything, Uncle Ricky. Had it not been for the Lord's enabling I would have never even tried such a-"
"Harebrained scheme?" Ricky interrupted.
LooAnne gasped in mock offense, "It was not harebrained! A bit risky perhaps but it worked didn't it?" Ricky shook his head in admiration for his niece. "You have no idea the worry you caused me, young lady. I almost witnessed that man kill you! But I'm more thankful then I can express that we can now put all this behind us, and I owe all that to you."
LooAnne hugged her uncle tightly before pulling away, "I'm just glad we're both alive. For a moment I was almost certain that we would end up killed, me by Devin and you by the law."
Ricky nodded soberly, "So was I. But it's all over and done with now. Neither of us need to worry about Devin Luther anymore."
Both LooAnne and Ricky glanced over at Devin who was still struggling against the men who held him. He

169

caught LooAnne's glace and grit his teeth in anger as he tried to lunge for her but was held fast by the angered ranch hands and deputies. Realizing that resistance was futile, Devin narrowed his eyes at LooAnne and spat at her feet, a growl rippling up his throat.

LooAnne looked at her relative and only smiled, "You might need a lesson in manors, but being rude is all you can do to me now. I win."

LooAnne then felt a hand on her shoulder and she turned to look up into her uncle's face. He looked down at her and smiled his thanks. LooAnne put her arm around Ricky's waist and laid her head on his side.

"I reckon I was wrong, Mr. Nash," the sheriff said as he strode forward. "I hope you won't hold it against me?"

Ricky smiled, "Of course not, Low. I understand you were just doing your job. Does this mean that I'm cleared of all the charges?"

Sheriff Low nodded vigorously, "Yes, sir, Mr. Nash. You're free to go."

Ricky squeezed LooAnne's shoulder and then felt Chris's hand on his. He smiled at his steward who's face was overcome with relief, then he looked at Devin Luther smiling triumphantly. Devin hissed at Ricky, "You think you're so smart, Nash, well I know better! By capturin' me you're niece has brought the whole Luther clan down on the town! They'll come after me and smash Decatur and every man, woman, and child in it! You've just won this battle but you can't possibly win the war that's about to take place in your little town!"

Ricky huffed, "We'll see about that, Luther. It's about time the people of Decatur realized that we out number you ten to one, and despite your toughness we might know a thing or two ourselves." Ricky looked down at LooAnne and smiled. "Though I doubt there's another person in all of Texas as brave and as smart as my niece."

LooAnne smiled and hugged her uncle tightly. At that moment she didn't care about the Luthers. To her the most important part of the whole thing was over. Her uncle was free to go home for the first time since the estate burned to the ground.

LooAnne looked behind her uncle and saw Red Stacey standing with his brothers watching silently. When he caught her eye he smiled a pleading smile that asked LooAnne to forgive him. LooAnne smiled back and nodded. Red's face lit up as bright at the sun which still beat down overhead, and LooAnne felt another weight lifted from her. She had been given another chance to forgive Red, a chance which she was sure was not to come again.

With this thought lightening her heart she turned to her uncle and asked the question that had been dwelling in her mind.

"How did you do it?" she asked. "How did you get the sheriff and deputies to follow you here when you were supposed to be in jail?"

Ricky smiled, "I find that people will do anything for a mob of angry ranch hands, providing they have guns of course."

LooAnne grinned, "And how did you find out where I was and what I was doing?" she looked accusingly at Chris who cleared his throat and said, "You just can't keep secrets from him, Miss Nash."

With that Ricky and LooAnne broke into laughter, releasing some of the stress from the previous weeks. Their laughter was so relieving that Chris was soon laughing with them. The ranch hands, the Stacey brothers, and the lawmen looked on smiling.

After a moment of light banter Sheriff Low stepped forward and said to Ricky, "Excuse me, sir, but there's one thing I just don't get." Everyone turned questioning eyes on the sheriff as he continued, "How did the gun get outta your house?"

This was a question that had everyone in a quandary, how indeed? If the house had burned with the safe open then how could the gun have escaped the blaze?

It was at this that Devin laughed menacingly, "Still got y'all stumped don't I?" he sneered.

"How did you do it?" LooAnne demanded.

Devin looked at her and snorted. "If you're so smart why don't ya figure it out?"

Ricky put his arm around his niece's shoulders reassuringly. "Don't worry, my dear. He confessed, that's all that matters. The details will most likely come out in his trial."

"That's very true, Miss Nash," Sheriff Low agreed as he glared at Devin. "We'll find out how you did it, don't you worry about that!"

"Ha!" Devin exclaimed defiantly. "You'll never get me to trial! My family will come for me just as sure as we're standin' here!"

"And we'll be ready for them," Ricky insisted.

"Do you really think we can hold 'em off?" Sheriff Low

asked.

Ricky smiled knowingly and said, "We can do better then that, Low, today's the day that the Luther clan meats their Maker!"

The group turned and began the thirty minute walk toward town. The ranch hands took charge of Devin who went along without a struggle, believing his detainment to be of short duration. As they walked Ricky looked down at his niece and said, "You're being rather quiet, LooAnne, are you sure you're alright?"

LooAnne sighed, "He's right you know."

"Who, dear?"

"Uncle Devin. He's right about it being my fault that the town will be attacked. I must admit that it never occurred to me."

Ricky shook his head, "It's about time that town saw they can take the Luthers, and it's going to take a Luther to show them."

LooAnne sighed, "I wish there had been some other way to get Devin here without putting the whole town in danger."

"Personally I'm glad that things worked out the way they did. Just think, this may be the end of a lifelong enemy of Decatur. Maybe by this time next year people will have forgotten about the Luthers."

LooAnne grinned slightly, "You can't fool me, Uncle Ricky. I know that anyone who ever had any dealings with a Luther will never forget it. Like you and Uncle Robert, you'll never forget your sister running away, and people in town will never forget the possessions and loved ones that were taken from them either."

173

"We might not be able to forget," Ricky agreed, "but we can forgive and move on. However hard that is in reality we can't hang on to sadness our entire lives, that would hardly make life worth living. I understand now why my sister ran away and how it has all worked out for the good of many people. However much she hurt me, I've forgiven her for leaving. My life would be completely different right now if she hadn't."

LooAnne smiled knowingly at her uncle's grin. "I don't really think that I was worth all the trouble she caused you."

Ricky squeezed LooAnne's shoulders and smiled, "You were worth every bit of it."

LooAnne grinned bashfully at Ricky, but said nothing. Just then Red Stacey approached them from behind. He smiled at LooAnne, looked at his cousin and said, "I'm real sorry about the whole thing, Ricky. I shoulda known from the beginning that you had nothing to do with Andy's murder. I hope you'll forgive me?"

"Certainly, Red. I don't blame you a bit. The way it looked anyone would've come to the same conclusion."

"That's just it, though, no one did except the jury and the judge. The whole town was in an uproar the day you were convicted. They were ready to brake you out themselves and they would have if LooAnne hadn't beet 'em to it. Me and my brothers were the only ones that thought you were guilty, and now the whole town is going to pay for our mistake."

"Don't beat yourself up about it, Red. As for the town, they're not going to be fighting because of your mistake. They're going to avenge their loved ones, to rid

174

themselves of a people who have haunted them for decades."

"I hope they won't hold it against me."

Ricky frowned as though this thought had not occurred to him, "Come to think of it, so do I."

LooAnne looked up at her uncle questioningly, "You think they might?"

"Well they certainly aren't going to be too happy, and out of all the people in town we'll more than likely find someone who blames Red for any Luther attack."

"Then we'll more then likely find someone who blames me for it too," LooAnne pointed out.

Ricky shook his head. "Not in a million years they won't. They'll find ways to avoid the thought of it being your fault from entering they're mind."

"Why?" LooAnne asked.

"Because you're my niece and they respect me therefore they respect you too."

LooAnne knit her brow thoughtfully and said, "Red's your cousin, shouldn't they respect him for the same reason they do me?"

Ricky frowned and scratched his thin beard that had grown since he had been jailed. "That does make good since, LooAnne. That gives me an idea as a matter of fact." Ricky looked down at his niece and raised his eyebrows, "I think I know how to keep the town out of Red's hair."

"How?" LooAnne and Red asked in unison.

"You'll see," was all Ricky said though he wore a knowing grin on his face.

When the group reached town they were surprised to find a mob of people in front of the sheriff's office yelling for the deputy to come out and face them! Deputy Stale was standing at the open window trying to quiet the mob so that he could speak.

Suddenly someone yelled, "Let Rick Nash go!"

"Yeah!" the rest of the crowd screamed in agreement.

"He's not here!" the deputy insisted desperately.

"How can he not be there?" someone yelled.

"I don't know! He and Sheriff Low disappeared during the night."

"What kinda stunt are you tryin' to pull, Stale!"

"It's not a stunt. He ain't here!"

"He's telling the truth," Ricky called. "I'm here."

The mob of people turned towards the group, "It's Mr. Nash!"

Ricky was soon swarmed by townspeople, bombarding him with questions. "How did you get away?" "Where were you?" "Are you still under arrest?"

Ricky held up his hand for silence and the yelling immediately ceased. He stepped onto the sheriff office porch and loudly addressed the crowd. "Alright, I need you all to listen carefully to what I'm going to say."

Ricky gestured towards Devin, "Devin Luther was the one that killed Andy Stacey, and my niece has gotten him to confess. This means that I've been cleared of all the charges."

Ricky was immediately interrupted by cheering and shouts of joy from the people. Once again he held up his hand and the crowd fell silent. "As you can see we've captured Devin on the road between the Luther Estate and town. The Luthers do not yet know that we have him, but as you all are aware, some of you better then others, the Luthers will come to take Devin back as soon as they hear he is in custody. That means a raid on the town!"

There was a worried hum of voices throughout the crowd and someone shouted, "Let him go back to the Luther Estate!"

Devin smiled in satisfaction at Ricky who ignored him and continued, "That is an option; however, it is not the best one in my opinion. We can send Devin back and avoid a raid, or we can keep him here and fight the Luther clan."

A murmur of disapproval went up from the crowd and many people shook their heads in disagreement with the idea of fighting the Luthers.

"Let him go, Mr. Nash!" someone called from the midst of the crowd. "We've got families to protect."

"And you think that letting Devin Luther go to come and shoot us down another day is a good form of protection? We'll release him if that's the decision of the town, but he'll be back. He'll come back and to do to us just as he and all the other Luthers have done for years."

"Are you sayin' you wanna fight the Luthers?" a man in front called.

Ricky nodded, "That's exactly what I'm saying. Every one of you have had dealings with one or more of that family and you've lost plenty to them. They come down here and parade around town taking whatever they want and doing whatever they please just because we're too scared to do anything about them. They rob your homes and steal your money and your belongings. They take off with your daughters and sons, your mothers and fathers, wives and husbands, and brothers and -" Ricky paused for a moment before finishing, remembering Amanda. "And your sisters," he finished. "Everyone of you have lost something or someone to the Luthers, and today could mark the end of it all if we just realize that we're bigger then they are. You and your children could walk around town without the fear that a Luther will jump you just as Devin did my cousin. You've lost family in the past and you'll lose family in the future if we all don't stand up to them and show them what we're made of. They might be great at what they do and they might be able to protect themselves with little trouble, but we outnumber them ten to one. As I see it there isn't room enough in this town for us and the Luthers. So we either wipe them out or we get wiped out ourselves, but I won't stay in the same town with them any longer!"

The crowd looked at one another and whispered among themselves before a man spoke up, "Someones bound to get killed if we have a war with the Luthers."

Another person called and said, "None of this would o' happened if Red Stacey hadn't had you convicted of that murder!"

"Yeah!" the crowd shouted together and all eyes fell on Red who looked at the ground shamefully.

"Now wait just a minute!" Ricky commanded. "It just so happens that I am just as much to blame as Red is."

Everyone turned and looked at Ricky questioningly.

"Together we went and got Devin Luther which is the reason that the Luthers are coming now. It's my fault as well as Red's so I suggest if you intend to get revenge for this situation you find ourselves in you get it on the both of us!"

The crowd remained silent and Ricky nodded, "Now I know you all blame Red for that jury from Colorado, and I understand why you would like to get back at him for it, but the fact is he's apologized for his mistake. I have forgiven him. I've already lost one cousin and I don't intend to lose another to an angry mob, especially one that's full of people I know, friends of my family." The crowd remained silent but did turn away from Red, who smiled his thanks to his cousin. Ricky smiled back at him and then addressed the crowd again, "This is your town," he began, "and if you don't want to fight the Luthers today then we'll let Devin go, but things won't change. We'll still be held within their grasp as we are now and as we have been. Unless we end the war today, one way or another, we'll end up fighting a long fight over the next few years. By the time it ends I promise you that a lot more people will have been killed. Either way we will fight the Luthers just as we've been doing for the last twenty years. Years that we've lost too many people to count. I'm offering you a way out, whether the Luthers win or we win, it's a way to finally rid ourselves of the shadow that hangs over us. Law is still scarce out west, us and our fathers before us knew that well when we decided to make it our home and with that comes the need to protect ourselves and our families, and that's what I intend to do. We either fight or I'm going to pack up my home and business interests and leave Decatur. I won't live under the Luther shadow any longer, but the rest is up to you. Do we fight or do we run like the cowards that we're proving ourselves to be?"

There was a hum of voices throughout the crowd, no one seemed to know what they wanted to do about the Luthers. Red realized that people were still vacillating so he stepped forward and called, "We'll fight with you, Ricky!"

All of the ranch hands, joined by Chris and the other Stacey brothers, cheered in agreement. The townspeople looked at one another and then someone yelled, "I'm with ya too, Mr. Nash!"

Half the crowd nodded and added their offer to be of assistance, but just as they did a man called and said, "What are we gonna get if we help you?"

Many people gasped at this ill-suited question. Ricky however raised his eyebrows and said, "You'll get a safe place to live that's free of the Luthers."

"You mean we don't get paid to fight this battle?"

"Not from me you don't," Ricky informed them.

"Why not? You can afford it."

"Yes, and I can also afford to fight this fight with one fewer man, especially when his heart isn't in it."

The man fell silent and suddenly an enormous cheer went up from the crowd and a man yelled, "We'll fight them doggone Luthers if it costs us every little thing we got!"

"Yeah!" the crowd yelled in agreement.

"And not only will we fight 'em, we'll beat 'em like dogs!"

"Yeah!" the crowd cheered again.

Ricky smiled, "I'm glad that you see things my way, and

I know that if it be the Lord's will we will fight and we will win!"

The crowd cheered with loud applause and shouts of determination. Ricky held up his hand for silence once more. "Now," he began, "I want all the townspeople to arm themselves and meet here at the square within half an hour. We don't have a lot of time to get ready for this war and we don't want to be caught sleeping. I need everyone to help spread the word. Tell as many as you can to get here as quickly as possible. We'll punch into the broadcast and make a radio announcement as well."

The crowd began to scatter in different directions to do as Ricky had instructed. Ricky stepped down from the porch where he stood and joined LooAnne and Chris who had remained at the corner of the Sheriff's Office.

"You were wonderful, Uncle Ricky," LooAnne exclaimed.

"Yes indeed, sir," Chris agreed. "I never thought they'd do it."

"They wouldn't have if Red hadn't encouraged them. Where is Red?"

"He and his brothers went to help the townspeople. The ranch hands went with them. Harry said you're welcome to his studio. He's gonna meet you over there."

"Good." Ricky turned to LooAnne and said, "You go to the estate and tell Robert to come to town and warn the guards to watch for any trouble there. When you get home you stay there and don't even dream about coming back to town, understand?"

"But Uncle Ricky, I'm the only one that knows how to fight Luthers. You need me here!" LooAnne objected.

"That might be but it's too risky and I have no intention of having you here where the Luthers might recognize you, now get on back home."

"I thought you were loosening your grip on me?" LooAnne countered.

"Not all the way I'm not. I can't stand here and let you fight. You're a young lady, not a man."

"That might be but I can't leave when I know *how* to fight them. That's not fair to me or the townspeople. I've got a right to be here with the Luthers and I've got a right to be here with the Nashes.

"LooAnne, I almost watched you be killed less than an hour ago. I can't take the chance that something will happen to you now."

"And I won't take the chance that I'll go home and you'll never come back!"

Ricky sighed and looked at Chris who shrugged. He then turned to LooAnne and said, "This is something that I need you to do for me, LooAnne. I know how you feel but I won't be any help to anyone if I have to worry about you the entire time."

"Uncle Ricky, I'm not a child. Out of all the people in town I'm the one that you don't have to worry about."

"Nevertheless, you're the one I *will* worry about. Not to mention you need to get someone to look at that bruise on your face. You've done more than anyone could have ever asked of you and now it's time for you to recover."

"But I know what I'm doing and I'm the only one that does. Some people might think they do but believe me they have no idea. None of you know what you're up against. I do and I'm willing to stay and help. You

182

should jump at the chance to have someone actually want to fight the Luthers."

"Ordinarily I would but not if the person who wants to fight is my niece."

"But -"

"No more argument," Ricky ordered. "Now get back to the estate and tell Robert what's happening."

LooAnne sighed, turned without a word, and started in the direction of the Nash Estate. Ricky watched her go for a moment, satisfied that she would be safe at home, and thankful beyond anyone's understanding that she was still alive to be protected.

"Um, excuse me for saying so, sir," Chris spoke up, "but are you sure that was the right thing to do?"

Ricky frowned at his steward and said, "Don't question my decisions, Chris."

Chris nodded as though this was the answer he had expected, "Yes sir."

"Come on," Ricky started towards the Sheriff's Office. Chris shook his head in exasperation and followed his employer down the street.

FOURTEEN

Midnight War

*For sin shall not have dominion
over you, for you are not under
the law but under grace. Romans 6:14*

*Let a man meet a bear robbed
of her cubs rather then a fool in
his folly. Proverbs 17:15*

LooAnne ran almost the entire way to the estate,
feeling replenished with energy now that she was safely
away from Devin and her uncle was free.
Once she reached the estate she ran past the guard and
into the house, finding Robert and Amarie in the living
room. Robert was pacing the floor worriedly and Amarie
was standing in the dining room doorway watching him
with a look of uncertainty on her face.
"LooAnne!" she cried when she saw her friend enter the
room.
Robert stopped his frantic back and forth and the two
ran to LooAnne's side.
"Where were you?" he demanded. "Where's Mr. Block?
What's happened to Ricky?"

"Uncle Ricky's been cleared of the charges," LooAnne told her uncle.

A relieved yet confused look crossed Robert's face, "How?" he asked.

"It's a long story and there's no time to tell it. The town is holding Devin Luther for Andy Stacey's murder and the Luthers are bound to know it by now. The town is expecting an attack within the next few hours." Turning to look directly at Robert she added, "Uncle Ricky wants you to come immediately."

Robert looked taken aback but his face soon enlightened with vigor, "It's about time those Luthers got what's coming to them!" He ran into the study and came back with one of Ricky's rifles. "We'll teach them a lesson they'll never forget!" Robert stormed out the door and went straight for the barn to get the Nash's sedan.

Amarie looked at LooAnne, a bit confused, "How did Uncle Ricky get Devin to confess?"

LooAnne shrugged, "He's amazing isn't he?" she smiled.

Amarie nodded, "He certainly is. But how did he get out of jail to get Devin? And what in the world happened to your face?"

LooAnne reached up and rubbed her cheek lightly, accepting the throbbing pain that she caused as she did so. Just one of many bruises that her family had inflicted on her, and now, with the goodness of Providence, maybe the last.

"He tried to kill me," LooAnne answered, solemnly.

"Who?" Amarie exclaimed.

"Devin Luther."

"Did he know who you were?" Amarie asked, horrified

at the very thought.

LooAnne shook her head, finding herself lost in a trance of mixed thoughts. "He didn't," she whispered as reality hit her. "He didn't recognize me!" she exclaimed, feeling yet another weight being lifted from her heart. A broad smile crossed LooAnne's face and she threw her arms around Amarie in merriment! "Oh Amarie he didn't recognize me! I'm finally free of them!"

Amarie was quite shocked at LooAnne's outburst but was soon smiling and laughing along with her, enjoying the carefree moment which neither of them had experienced in a long while.

Amarie then pulled away from LooAnne's embrace and asked, "Shouldn't we be doing something? About the Luthers I mean?"

LooAnne sighed in dejection and shook her head. "As much as I hate it, Uncle Ricky said for us to stay here and wait." LooAnne dropped down onto the couch, letting her tired limbs relax for a moment. "It's going to be a very long wait."

"What do you mean?" Amarie asked, cocking her head at LooAnne.

"I mean that it's going to drive me crazy sitting here not knowing what's happening."

"Why don't you eat something?" Amarie suggested. "You've got to be starving."

"I must admit that I'm not in the least bit hungry. My appetite seems to have left me." LooAnne got to her feet and said, "I think I'm going to go write a letter to Kyle. It's been so long since I have and I need to relate all that's happened the last few days." She turned and strode down the hall to the study where she sat down at her uncle's desk and pulled a piece of paper from the drawer. She laid it before her but found herself only staring at the white sheet. She stared at the stark white paper completely blank herself as to what she should put on it. The words which usually flowed onto the paper as fast as they flowed into her mind were not there. She didn't know what to write and suddenly the need to write was as absent as the words themselves. Instead her mind turned once again to her father's family. The Luthers would soon be consuming the town just as the roaring fire had consumed the Nash Estate. LooAnne could picture her friends perishing my the hands of her ruthless family. She could see the entire town burning with the same flames as the estate had. She could see the Luthers taking over and cheering victoriously, and she could only imagine what they might do to her uncle should they capture him.

LooAnne couldn't take it anymore, she pushed away from the desk chair and ran through the house to the kitchen where she found Amarie with Mrs. Sam Moore.

"Amar," LooAnne said, "I'm going to town, I can't just sit here while they fight my fight."

"But Uncle Ricky said-"

"I know what Uncle Ricky said, but if I stay here and something happens that I might have prevented I'll never forgive myself. I'll be back, Lord willing, and if I'm not, you know why."

"But LooAnne you can't!" Amarie objected. "Something might happen to you!"

"Something will happen to me if I stay here, I'll go

insane. Now don't you leave this house for anything."

"Don't worry, I won't, and that's a promise I intend to keep."

"Good, I'll be back." LooAnne turned and ran towards the southern entrance. She darted right past the guard so that he had no time to ask questions and ran for the stables. She went straight to Double Dutch's stall where she and her golden coated filly were. She led her mare out, leaving the one month old filly whinnying in the stall. LooAnne threw her saddle on her mount's back and fastened the strap then she took hold of the rains and pulled herself up onto Dutch's back. She squeezed the horse's sides and Double Dutch took off out of the stables. LooAnne rode to the gate and unlatched it then sped through and galloped down the road towards town. It was now almost four in the afternoon but the sun still shown brightly in the sky. LooAnne assumed that the Luthers would not attack until after dark so she decided to stay hidden until then. This time she needed to remain hidden from both the Luthers and her uncle.

When she approached town she could see that everyone was in a panic. Several women ran about the street dragging children behind them. Men hustled in and out of stores and houses carrying weapons and boxes of ammunition. Many people were boarding up their windows and doors with long planks of scrap wood. There were even some pieces of furniture placed on porches to slow suspected intruders. LooAnne rode to the back of the livery stable and left Double Dutch there. She then started for the town square. When she approached the sheriff's office she heard her uncle's voice and soon caught sight of him standing where he had before on the sheriff's office porch. The street in front of him and down the way was jammed full of men, women, and children who were all listening carefully to Ricky's instructions.

"I need all women and children to go down to the other end of town and stay inside. That way the Luthers will have to come through us to get to you. Lord willing they won't make it. Then I need every man to double check his firearm, be sure it's cleaned and loaded before you use it. I want us all here in the middle of town. We don't need to be spread out so that they can take us out a couple at a time. We need to stick together right here in the square. Now I need five men to volunteer to take the women down to the other end of town and stay there with them just in case they need anything."

The crowd looked at one another and then five men stepped forward, all of whom had wives and children. "Alright," Ricky continued, "You all move as far as you can to the other side of town and barricade yourselves in the strongest building."

The three men nodded and began walking down the street with the women and children in the direction of the eastern end of town. Ricky turned back to the crowd and said, "We need this to be our battle field. No one goes passed the crossroads at that end..." Ricky pointed down the road in the western direction. "...and no one goes past the drugstore at that end," Ricky pointed again but this time in the opposite direction. "Devin Luther is in the jailhouse and he's being guarded by the sheriff, the deputy, the Staceys, and my ranch hands, anyone

189

who wishes to join them may, just so long as you understand that that's the Luther family's destination. The whole reason they're coming in the first place is to rescue Devin Luther, but while they're here the only thing stopping them from taking the town is us. We can't loose this fight, gentlemen. We lose this fight and we lose our loved ones and our town! Now get to your posts!"

The crowd scattered in all directions, running into buildings that stood in the designated area.

By nightfall the whole town was in a dead, eerie silence. LooAnne had watched from up high in an oak tree, concealed by the thick leaves that swayed gently in a light breeze. The moon shown high in the dark sky surrounded by many small stars that seemed to pop out of no where just to take their place next to the full moon which gave the silent town a haunting look.

LooAnne knew better than to climb out of the tree for she knew that the Luthers were watching. She could feel their stares from the dark corners of town. Though she couldn't see them she knew that they were there, watching and waiting for the signal to attack. Everything was so quiet and still that LooAnne barely dared to breathe. She feared that the Luthers would see her and she feared of what they would do to the town. A chill ran down LooAnne's spine and she tried not to dwell on the worst. She had defeated destiny before and she knew she could do it again.

At that moment LooAnne heard something move in one of the buildings and looked down towards the street. She could see the dark outline of a man emerge from within the shadows of the building and then he stepped out into the light of a streetlamp and in a split second he took off across the street, aiming for the building on the other side! Just as he reached the middle of the street the silence was broken by multiple gunshots! The man that was running dropped to the ground, not moving! Just the first of what would be many Luther victims. There had been so many shots that no one, not even LooAnne, could tell from where they had come. Suddenly another person came running from the same building and grabbed the man that had been shot. He started dragging him back to the cover of the store but just as he was about to reach it another round of shots echoed through the night and the second man went down! LooAnne looked around almost frantically. She had to find out where those shots were coming from, but her efforts were in vain, there was no way she could tell where the Luthers were in the dark. Suddenly two more men made an attempt at getting the ones who had been shot. LooAnne watched in a stunned silence as the men ran out into the light of the streetlamp and likewise were taken down by a series of gunshots. LooAnne shuttered at the sight of the men laying in street. That they had even tried to save the men that had been killed previously just proved to her that these men did not know who they were dealing with.

LooAnne knew that the Luthers were thinking the same thing. The townspeople were proving to their foe they were even more ignorant when it came to skirmishes then they had originally thought them to be. LooAnne knew that she had to take action before all the men in town were killed by their own foolish endeavors. She carefully began climbing from the tree until she knew she was close enough to the ground and then she jumped the rest of the way, dropping in the dark shadows of the tree. LooAnne was contemplating her next move when she heard what sounded like a small explosion coming from the back of the building that the men had run from! She looked up and saw that flames were roaring up the back of the store! LooAnne knew exactly what the Luthers were doing, they were going to burn out the rest of the men and shoot them as they ran into the street! She had to prevent it but was in a quandary as to how. The fire was too big to extinguish by herself and without the right equipment, her only alternative was to get as many men out of the building alive as possible! Ducking within the shadows of the buildings LooAnne ran down the street to the burning store and burst through the back door just as a shot was fired at her back! LooAnne expected to feel a bullet pierce her skin but instead all she felt were her knees as they hit the floor inside the store, the door closing with a slam behind her!

There were about a dozen men inside and they were all desperately throwing sacks of flour onto the fire that was leaping from one object to the next! When LooAnne came bursting in the door they whirled around, aiming their weapons at her in fear that she was one of their foe. When they realized it wasn't a Luther the man closest to her rushed to help her to her feet exclaiming, "Miss Nash! What're you doin' here?"

"I know a way out without getting killed," LooAnne

192

said.

"How?" the townsmen cried anxiously.

LooAnne pushed past their staring eyes and climbed up onto the counter to push a small square in the ceiling, it moved aside and revealed a trapdoor leading to the attic space. "Come on!" LooAnne motioned to the awaiting men.

"But how can we get out from up there?" One asked.

"I'll show you, hurry!"

One of the men stepped up onto the counter and lifted LooAnne into the attic then he stuck his shoulders in and pulled himself up through the hole followed by the others. The room was small and the men had to duck to avoid the ceiling but they were able to stand. LooAnne ran to a small window and unlatched it then she tried to pull it up but the window was rusted and refused to open. Smoke pored up through the hole and swirled around the room threatening to choke them all.

One of the men instantly ran to aid LooAnne in raising the window. After a few attempts it broke free and flew up.

LooAnne was about to step out onto a small balcony when the man that stood next to her held her back, "Wait, Miss Nash," he said, "Better let one of us go first."

LooAnne stepped aside and the man climbed out onto the balcony and looked around, not seeing anyone he said, "Okay, it's clear."

The rest of the men ran to the window but LooAnne blocked their path by sticking her head out and asking, "Can you get down?"

The man swung his leg over the railing and leaped to the ground. LooAnne told the others that they should not all go out onto the balcony at once just in case the Luthers were waiting to blow this area just as they had the back of the store. The men nodded and quickly left the attic one at a time, each of them able to either jump or lower themselves to the ground. LooAnne went second to last, she climbed over the railing and held on tightly to the bottom of it, then let her feet go so that they were closer to the ground and finally she released her grip on the railing and dropped, landing nicely on her feet. She immediately took a deep, refreshing breath to clear her lungs of the smoke she had inhaled.

All of the men except one had scattered in different directions so as not to be caught standing together in case of a Luther attack. When the last man dropped he turned to LooAnne and said, "Thank you, Miss Nash. You saved our lives, but you gotta get outta town before them rotten Luthers start shootin' it up. You could get hurt!"

"I'll leave just as soon as the Luthers are gone." LooAnne didn't give the man a chance to argue, she ran into the shadows of the neighboring building and disappeared into the night.

She knew that the Luthers would try and burn the other men out of hiding. Somehow they needed to get out of the building or face almost certain death. LooAnne racked her brain to figure out how to save these innocent men before it was too late. She decided to find a way to get across the street but before she could take another step LooAnne heard gunshots coming from the front of the burning building! LooAnne ducked low within the shadows and ran alongside the general store until she could see out into the street. A man had apparently tried to run from the building on the other side to aid the men in the burning store and now he was laying in the light of a streetlamp just feet from the first four who had tried to do the same.

LooAnne squinted, trying to see who the man was. When her eyes adjusted to the light she let out a gasp; it was Robert Nash and he lay motionless in the abandoned street!

FIFTEEN

By the Light of the Streetlamp

*"But as for you, you meant evil against
me; but God meant it for good in order
to bring it about as it is this day, to save
many people alive."*
Genesis 50:20

*Then the king was deeply moved, and went
up to the chamber over the gate, and wept.
And as he went he said thus, "O Absalom -
my son my son Absalom – if only I had died in
your place. O Absalom, my son my son."*
2 Samuel 18:33

As LooAnne looked out into the street at the man
everyone believed to be her father, uncertain if he was
dead or alive, she knew she had to help him. Her only
dilemma was that she knew what had happened to the
others when they tried to rescue their friend from the
same predicament. "But I'm a Luther," LooAnne
whispered to herself. "And I can do it. *I have to.*"
LooAnne looked into the dark corners of the street and

beyond into the trees attempting to locate any Luthers who would surely shoot down anyone who came for the brother of Rick Nash. Just as she was about to run into the street someone grabbed her shoulder from behind! LooAnne's heart leaped as she whirled around, fear striking her, as she came face to face with who restrained her.

"Red Stacey!" LooAnne exclaimed in a whisper. "You scared me to death!"

"LooAnne what do you think your doin'?" Red demanded, his handsome features hidden in the darkness of the shadows.

"I've got to save him!" LooAnne whispered being careful not to call Robert uncle.

"You'll get killed!"

"Not with you here I won't."

"What do you mean?"

"I mean you have a gun. You get out there onto the front porch of this building and shoot in all directions as fast as you can. While you're distracting them I'll run out and drag him over here."

"How're you gonna do that? He's way heavier then you are."

"I'll be able to do it. Just cover me and everything will be fine."

"It's too dangerous, LooAnne," Red whispered dubiously.

"Please, Red, he's gonna die!" LooAnne begged desperately.

Red looked out into the street where Robert Nash lay, then he looked back at LooAnne. "Can you shoot a gun?" he asked.

"Yes," LooAnne nodded.

"Then you cover me and I'll run out there and get Robert."

"I can't ask you to do that," LooAnne objected.

"And I can't *let* you. Now we do it my way or we don't do it at all."

LooAnne let out a relenting sigh. "Alright, give me the gun."

Red handed over his rifle and LooAnne slowly crept down the side of the building and onto the porch being careful not to emerge from within the shadow of the roof. She stepped toward the front of the porch where she could see the dark corners of town and then she braced the gun against her shoulder, took a deep breath and broke the silence as she called, "Go!" and immediately began firing as fast as she could! Red darted out of the shadows of the building straight for Robert! Gunshots joined LooAnne's causing an enormous racket. Bullets whizzed off the ground at Red's feet but he ignored them and grabbed Robert just as men ran out of the building across the street and began firing into the dark corners! LooAnne watched in awe at the sight of all the townsmen covering Red as he drug his cousin out of the street and laid him on the porch next to LooAnne. Once Red had pulled Robert safely off the street all of the men assisting him ran onto the porch to take cover. In an instant the gunfire ceased and everything was plunged into silence one again. The only sound was the heavy breathing of the townsmen that crowded the porch and the crackle of the building next to them still burning rapidly, illuminating the town around it. The fire danced in everyone's eyes as they scanned their surroundings for the Luther clan.

LooAnne knelt next to Robert and took his pulse, it was weak but regular. He was unconscious and had a bullet in his side. At that moment someone knelt next to LooAnne and asked, "Is he alive?"

LooAnne looked over her shoulder at the man's face that was lit by the flames that flanked them. It was Ricky, his expression creased with worry for his brother. LooAnne nodded, "He's alive, but he needs that bullet out."

Ricky nodded and turned away, melting into the crowd, when he reappeared he had the doctor with him. Immediately he began examining Robert. LooAnne stood up and looked at her uncle who was staring at her, no expression at all on his face. But this lasted only a moment and he looked out over the town then back at his niece and asked in a whisper, "Can *you* see the Luthers?"

LooAnne turned and fixed her eyes on the town that was covered in shadows from the fire and streetlamps. After a moment of looking she turned back to her uncle and said, "I can only guess, and that guess isn't a very good one." Looking back at the town she said, "I think there's at least one over behind that building down at the crossroads."

"What makes you think that?"

"Because that's where you told the men not to go, so that's a safe place for the Luthers to hide."

"You mean they heard every word I said?"

LooAnne nodded. "They were watching, and I think

199

they'll make a go for Devin any time now. They've scared us, and they think they have us on the run."

Ricky nodded. "There has got to be a way we can get down to the Sheriff's office without getting killed."

LooAnne thought a moment then said, "I don't think you can right now. You'd better wait until they make their whereabouts known."

"Will they do that?" Ricky asked dubiously.

"They will if they want Devin before morning, and I know that once the sun comes up their game is over. They won't be able to hide in the shadows any longer."

"So we wait until morning?"

"You won't have to, they'll make their move before the least bit of light shows. If we can just stay safe until then, we've got them, but they'll do everything they can to take us out before they go for Devin."

Ricky nodded, "Alright then, what should we do?"

LooAnne smiled at this question, she knew that her uncle was angry that she had disobeyed him but he was willing to let her stay now that he realized how much they needed her. "I think that you should spread out a little, don't stay too close together or they'll get you all at one time. Send men off in groups of five or six. Tell them to be extremely cautious, and not to step out into the light for any reason whatsoever. If they see a Luther they need to make sure they understand that that Luther has a bodyguard watching his every move. If they even look like they're going to try to nab him the bodyguard will have them all in the blink of an eye. Also I think that you should shoot out the streetlamps so that there are no dark corners. Better everything be dark then just certain areas. The eye will look at the lighted spots first and completely miss the darkness which is what the Luthers are counting on."

Ricky nodded, having noted everything his niece had said, and turned to the men, but before he could say a word gunfire echoed through town!

Everyone turned in the direction of the gunshots only to find they were looking directly at the Sheriff's office. Gunfire was being exchanged between the men that were barricaded inside the office and someone hiding behind the bank next to the Nash Hotel, both of which sat across the street. Suddenly more bullets came whizzing towards the sheriff's office from the shadows of Roger's Antiques. The Luthers were making their move!

Ricky's mind raced. He knew they had to get there, that this was the chance the town had been waiting for to confront the Luthers. But was it safe to step out from their hiding place? Would they be shot down the second they were exposed to the light? Ricky knew of only one way to find out. He clenched his jaw tightly and stepped out into the light of a streetlamp! LooAnne caught her breath as her eyes were glued to Ricky in fear, but no one fired at him, all the attention was focused on the sheriff's office. LooAnne went to his side and said, "We need to get behind them!"

Ricky nodded. "You get to the other end of town with the rest of the women and children."

"But-"

"Do not argue with me, LooAnne Marie Nash."

LooAnne sighed, not wishing to be a victim of her

uncle's wrath, "Yes sir." Turning to the eastern direction of town she ran down the street, the darkness swallowing her up. Ricky watched her until she was no longer visible then he turned back to the firefight.

The Luthers were continuing to pour bullets into the sheriff's office at an alarming rate. Ricky watched for a moment then called, "Luther! I wanna talk!"

The firing ceased and all was plunged into silence. Ricky walked up to the sheriff's office, a knot in his stomach. He knew that he could be shot down at any moment, alive one second and dead the next, but the only sound was that of the cracking fire as it's shadows leaped across the street. Ricky stood in front of the Sheriff's Office, waiting for the Luthers' reply and feeling their stares and those of the townsmen.

"What is it Nash?" came the unfamiliar voice of a man from directly across the street just inside the shadows of the bank.

Ricky could hear the men inside the sheriff's office unlatching the door so that he could run in should the Luthers resume their firing. He turned in the direction of the voice across the street and said, "I want to see the person to whom I'm speaking, Luther."

There was a moment of stillness and just as Ricky was beginning to think the man was going to open fire on him someone stepped out into the light of a streetlamp. It was a man who appeared to be in his mid forties. He wore faded, old jeans that were torn at the knees, and a dirt-covered undershirt. His feet were shod with heavy boots and his huge hands held tightly to his rifle. All in all he looked like a castaway from a deserted island.

"Alright, Nash," he said, his gruff voice, hard and thick, "What do ya want?"

"I would like to make you an offer, Luther."

"What kinda offer?" the man asked.

"It's more like a bribe," Ricky admitted. "I'll give you four thousand dollars an acre for your land, and you take your clan, minus Devin, and get out and never return."

The man thought a moment then said, "You give me twelve thousand dollars an acre *and* Devin and then I'll think it over."

Ricky shook his head, "I'm keeping the man that tried to get me hung for murder, no negotiation."

Suddenly Devin's voice called from inside, "Don't listen to him, Don! It's a trap!"

Don Luther raised his gun and narrowed his eyes, "What're you tryin' to pull, Nash?"

"Nothing," Ricky assured him. "I've long wanted that land that boarders mine, I'm giving you the chance to make a lot of money and get you out of my way at the same time." He shrugged his head in the direction of the jail and continued, "You also get the opportunity to rid yourself of a useless man."

"What do ya mean useless?"

"From what I've seen Devin is nothing but a bur under your saddle. He can't beat me at any fight, even though he's tried numerous times. He gets himself caught because he's too proud to have a bodyguard with him, and now he's the reason that all this is happening. If I were you I'd be jumping at the chance to be shed of him."

Don was quiet for several minutes then replied, "I see

only one way to solve all o' this, Nash. You give me fifteen thousand dollars for my property, and then you and Devin fight to the death. He wins he comes with me, you win and he won't be able to come with me."

Ricky laughed out loud, "And then you'll have your men shoot me and you'll run back home with the money."

Don Luther raised his eyebrows in amusement, "Now would I do somethin' like that?"

Ricky nodded stiffly, "Yes, Luther, you would. Therefore, I fight Devin first, and then we'll get the money from the bank just to be sure that I stay alive."

"And what if Devin wins? How am I gonna get my money then?"

"If Devin wins you and your family will take the town and all it's money anyway."

Don knit his brow as he thought. "Fine then, it's a deal..." Don sneered, "... but only because your Jason's brother-in-law."

Ricky furrowed his eyebrows angrily. "A fact that I am sure does not play into this."

"Not denying your own kin are you, Mr. Nash?" Don taunted. "Your sister sure was a looker."

Ricky grit his teeth, resisting the urge to lunge at this man who mocked his pain. Ricky turned and called into the sheriff's office, "Bring Devin out here!"

Not a minute later two deputies came out with a handcuffed Devin Luther who wore a smirk on his lined face.

Ricky looked him in the eye, "Did you hear?"

"I heard," Devin smirked. "You're gonna rue the day that you ever agreed to fight a Luther."

Ricky huffed, "We'll see about that."

Devin nodded, "We sure will."

Don stepped out into the street with a man, woman, and two younger men about LooAnne's age behind him, all of whom were holding some kind of firearm. "Okay, Nash," Don said, "whenever you're ready."

Ricky turned to the deputies and said, "Turn him loose, boys."

One of the deputies removed his keys from his pocket and unlocked the handcuffs from Devin's wrists.

He smiled a stealing grin at Ricky as he rubbed his raw wrists and made his way to his cousin's side.

"You're a fool Rick Nash," he accused. "There ain't no way you can stop us."

"Even if I don't succeed in killing you, Devin Luther, these townsmen are tried of being pushed around. Years of torment is built up within them and it's going to be avenged tonight."

Devin snorted as if this statement were amusing. "You think you're so smart, Nash. Well I got the upper hand."

It was that moment that another, younger man, emerged from behind the sheriff's office with a struggling LooAnne held tightly in his grip!

Ricky's heart dropped as he watched his niece struggle in the arms of yet another Luther! A small stream of blood dripped down the side of her head as if she had been truck with something and yet she still fought with all her might to free herself, knowing as well as her uncle that this could be the end.

"Okay, Nash," the young Luther commanded, "here's how it's gonna be: You and your men are gonna stand down right this minute or Miss Nash dies!"

Ricky saw no other recourse but to comply and signaled for all the men to drop their guns. As they did Luthers began popping out of the darkness to take their place behind the man that held LooAnne in his iron grip! There were at least sixteen of them, men and women, and they all held a weapon, ready to kill anyone who made a move to defeat them.

Ricky locked eyes with his niece for only a moment, not finding the fear he expected to see, but a small glint, as though she were truly were not afraid.

"Now then," Devin spoke, drawing Ricky's attention, "You're gonna give us everything we want and there ain't gonna be no backtalk about it or I'm gonna have my nephew kill your niece!" He wore a satisfied smirk that scared Ricky and caused his anger to arouse but he had no intention of letting the Luthers know his fear. He narrowed his eyes and said, "What is it you want, Luther?"

"We want the money that's in the bank and we want a safe exit from this no-account town. And we want *you*, Nash!"

There was a round of gasps from the crowd and Chris looked at his employer pleadingly. Ricky ignored the worried townspeople and said, "Alright Luther." Then he turned to Chris and said in an undertone, "Go to the bank, take Ross with you so that he can open the safe. Bring back every cent that's in it."

"But, Mr. Nash-"

"Don't argue with me, Chris, just do as I tell you," Ricky snapped, his voice cold and full of emotion.

Chris nodded, "Yes sir." he was just about to go when LooAnne called, "Wait just a minute, Mr. Block."

Chris stopped and looked at Ricky then at LooAnne who said, "There will be no need for that. The Luthers are leaving town...NOW!"

Just as LooAnne finished her sentence she elbowed her captor in the ribs and to everyone's surprise he released her and doubled over! Moaning with pain he sunk to his knees, gripping his side! LooAnne dropped to the ground as all of the angered townsmen picked up their guns and fired on the Luthers, avenging their loved ones!

LooAnne looked away as a few of them were able to dart behind the buildings but the rest died where they stood, Devin and Don among them. LooAnne's family, such as they were, perished before her. She had not realized what emotion that would cause, the cringing of her soul as she witnessed her tormentors die on the streets. No matter how they had hurt her, they were still her family, and each one she had known well.

The night soon turned quiet again as all the townsmen slowly walked forward, guns ready, but the Luthers were either lying dead or running scared.

LooAnne remained on the ground. She watched in silence as the men examined the bodies, her head still bleeding from where she had been struck by a Luther hidden in wait for her.

Ricky knelt next to his niece, his eyes wide and his breath quick as adrenalin pulsed throughout his body. "Are you alright, LooAnne?" his voice was obviously strained as he laid a concerned hand on her shoulder.

LooAnne nodded slowly, her eyes still trained on the bodies of her family. Gradually she looked up at Ricky and said very quietly, "I know they deserved it, but they're my flesh and blood. They were all I knew for so long. I wish that somehow it could have been different."

Ricky squeezed her shoulder in an attempt to comfort her. "So do I, LooAnne. I wish so many things could have been different. But who knows what our path would look like now if they had been."

"Perhaps rockier," LooAnne answered grimly.

"Yes," Ricky agreed. "But our lives, especially yours, are falling into place and farther along we'll understand why these things have to be the way they are."

LooAnne smiled wanly at her uncle. "I've dreamed of this day for so long that I hardly know what to make of it. The Luthers are actually gone."

Ricky smiled. "Thank you for disobeying me, I wouldn't be here now if you hadn't. Not to say that I approve of such things in the future though."

A smile broke on LooAnne's soiled face, "I'm glad you're not mad."

Ricky gave his niece a sly look, "Did I say that?" he asked.

LooAnne smiled but winced as the pain in her head began to set in.

"Are you alright?" Ricky asked, concern creasing his face.

LooAnne nodded ever so slightly. "He jumped out behind me when I was on my way to the other end of town. I fought him so hard he hit be with something intending to knock me out but he didn't, only dazed me enough to get me here."

"I'll get you to the doctor. Can you stand?"

LooAnne nodded and with Ricky's help she was able to stand steadily on her own feet.

Ricky and LooAnne began a slow walk away from the Luther massacre. "I saw you save those men from the general store," Ricky commented as they walked. "How did you know about that attic? And what caused that man so much pain when you elbowed him?"

"Well, to begin with," LooAnne said, "you own the general store and I saw the blueprints when you had those repairs done last fall to stop the leaks. That man that had me, when he was about eighteen he had an accident with his knife during training and the wound never healed completely, or properly, and it's bothered him ever since. I knew that if I hit him where he had been stabbed it would cause him so much pain he would let me go."

"I'm glad you remembered who he was," Ricky said. LooAnne looked down at the ground with a sigh. "I should remember, he was my brother."

"Your brother!" Ricky exclaimed, looking down at his niece in shock.

LooAnne nodded, staring straight ahead, recalling the now faded memories of her four brothers. "Will and Oliver are the older twins, me and Ben are the younger twins, Cullen was in the middle."

"I'd never known about him," Ricky said gravely. LooAnne shook her head, "He wasn't our brother by blood, he was kidnapped when he was very young and raised as a Luther. He never knew that he wasn't actually one of us. My mother told only me and you're the first person I've told." LooAnne looked back to where Cullen Luther lay. "To think that because he was chosen out of so many other little boys to be taken and raised as a Luther he lays there now, a true criminal. Those people were terrible." She shook her head, her heart saddened. "I wish I had never been a part of this."

Ricky stopped his slow pace and wrapped LooAnne in hug, holding her tightly. "So do I, my dear. But if you hadn't been born a Luther and hadn't been part of this, I would be dead and the Luthers would be alive to take even more young children."

LooAnne nodded, "And I wouldn't have been given the chance at a life I've always wanted."

At that moment Chris walked up and asked Ricky, "So does this mean we win, sir?"

Ricky looked at Chris and smiled. "It certainly does, Mr. Block. We've beaten the Luthers!"

Hearing this the whole town yelled and cheered, throwing their hats up into the early morning sky.

As Ricky, Chris, and LooAnne stood in the street the Stacey brothers approached them.

"Ricky," Alec said, "we'd like to apologize for thinking that you killed our brother. We're very much obliged to you and LooAnne for catchin' Devin."

Ricky smiled, "You're very welcome, Alec." Ricky turned to Red and said, "Thank you for what you did for Robert. The doctor said that it wasn't a bad wound, but that he owes you his life."

"It was gonna be completely different had I let LooAnne have her way, I was gonna be the one to shoot the gun

210

and she was gonna pull Robert in off the street."

Ricky smiled down at his nice and said, "And believe it or not she would have been able to do it. She pulled me out of the estate window when it burned."

Red looked impressed, "That was you?"

LooAnne nodded.

"You didn't mention anything about it during the trial."

"It wasn't important," was all LooAnne said, afraid the true answer would reveal too much of her past.

Ricky suddenly smiled, "Speaking of the estate, I haven't seen it yet, and I'm itching..." Ricky scratched his beard, "...to shave in my bathroom, or to shave anywhere for that matter. If I was to invite you Stacey's over would you come home with us once we get LooAnne's head on the mend?"

The Stacey brothers nodded enthusiastically and the group turned towards the east in time to see the sun rising over the horizon. LooAnne paused and smiled, "Without the Luther shadow hanging over us," she said, "that sunrise is a lot brighter."

Ricky nodded. "It's a new sunrise."

"Indeed it is," Red agreed. He then turned to LooAnne and smiled, "And on the dawn of such an occasion I believe the young lady who brought it all about deserves a reward. Therefor, LooAnne, I told you that you had to make yourself worthy of such knowledge and you have, my real name is Absalom."

LooAnne's eyes brightened and she grinned broadly at her cousin, "Absalom!" she exclaimed. "I never would have guessed. Why in the world don't you like it?"

Red wrinkled his nose and said, "In the good book

Absalom wasn't such a great fella. He tried to kill his own father!"

LooAnne nodded, "But his father loved him," she pointed out. "No matter his mistakes his father would still give his life for him."

Red smiled thoughtfully and nodded, "Indeed he did. Thanks, LooAnne."

LooAnne smiled and nodded, knowing that was all Absalom Stacey had ever wanted to hear.

SIXTEEN

An Unexpected Return

Husbands love your wives just as
Christ loved the church and gave
Himself for her.
Ephesians 5:25

Who can find a virtuous wife? For her
worth is far above rubies. The heart of
her husband safely trusts her; so he will
have no lack of gain. She does good and
not evil all the days of her life.
Proverbs 31:10-12

"**A**ren't you done with that dusting yet, Daisy? He's due any minute!"

"I'm hurrying, Mr. Block," said Daisy Brown who was hurriedly dusting the study.

Ricky had been in New York City for a little over three weeks on business and was due to arrive home at any moment. Chris donned his suit coat and stuffed his arms down into the sleeves as he practically ran to the door to meet his employer. He arrived just as the Huckster pulled into the driveway. Chris stepped out into the cold winter wind that swirled around the house and grounds. One of the ranch hands opened the Huckster door for Ricky who stepped out and strode towards the house, inhaling the crisp, fresh country air.

"Welcome home, sir," Chris said as he met Ricky on the porch and held the door open for him.

"Good morning, Chris," Ricky said cheerfully as he entered the house. "I assume that everything's in order?"

"Of course, sir," Chris assured as he followed Ricky into the living room.

Ricky removed his coat, hat, and gloves and handed them to one of the maids then called into the kitchen, "Coffee in the study, Mrs. Moore."

"Coming, sir," Mary Moore called back.

Ricky strode down the hall to the study with Chris close behind him.

"Amarie still in Oklahoma with her aunt?" Ricky asked Chris as he sat down in his desk chair and leaned back restfully.

"Yes sir, she is," Chris said. Amarie had recently been sent a letter from her grandmother's sister requesting that she come and visit her during Christmas so Amarie had been gone since the weekend.

"How was your trip, sir?" Chris asked.

"Tiring, Mr. Block," Ricky said, closing his eyes. "It certainly is good to be home. Where's LooAnne?"

"Um – she's out, sir," Chris answered flatly.

Ricky opened one eye and looked at his steward questioningly then he opened the other and sat up.

"What's the matter?" he asked.

"Nothing, sir, why should anything be the matter?"

Chris denied.

"When you get that look on your face it means that you're about to tell me something that I'm not going to like, now out with it."

"There's nothing wrong, sir," Chris insisted with a slight shake of his head.

Ricky frowned, "There is something wrong and it has something to do with LooAnne not being here. Where is she?"

"I believe she's doing some last minute Christmas shopping, sir."

Ricky stood up and looked Chris in the eye, "Why is it that when there's something amiss I always have to wheedle it out of the person who is supposed to tell me on the spot before I even have to ask?"

Chris cast his employer an uncertain smile, "You know I've noticed that too, sir," he said innocently.

Ricky nodded, "I'll just bet you have, now how about telling me what's wrong? Because if you don't I'll just have to keep threatening you in various ways that have worked in the past, like you getting fired or me docking your pay or making you a ranch hand or maybe even a maid?"

"Okay, I'll tell you," Chris gave in.

Ricky smiled, "I thought you might."

"Well you see, sir, Miss Nash's birthday is in a month and she's turning eighteen."

"I'm well aware of that, Chris, now what does that have to do with anything?"

"Do you remember what happens when she turns eighteen?"

Ricky raised his eyebrows, "She's a year older?"

"Well yes but that's not quite what I'm talking about, sir."

"Chris I don't want to play guessing games with you. Now you tell me what the problem is and you do it right this minute!"

Chris inhaled deeply and said, "Kyle Denson came back yesterday, sir."

A deep frown immediately swept across Ricky's face. "Kyle Denson?"

Chris nodded soberly.

"But he hasn't finished his term yet."

"He says he quit college since LooAnne was almost eighteen and he wanted them to get married on her birthday."

This statement seemed to strike Ricky hard, taking him completely off guard, "Married? LooAnne?"

"Yes, sir," Chris admitted grudgingly. "She's engaged to him."

Ricky pushed out of his chair and paced to the middle of the room where he stood and starred at Chris. Finally he sighed deeply and shook himself out of his trance. "I guess I always knew that Kyle would come back for LooAnne. I did more or less tell him he could." Ricky returned to his desk and dropped down in his chair wearily. "I wish she was still a child, Chris. I wish I didn't have to think about her getting married."

"Well, sir, you can tell her not to."

Ricky shook his head in disagreement. "I couldn't take away her happiness like that. Besides, it wouldn't work. I told Amanda no and you see what good it did me."

"Yes, sir, I do. It did you a lot of good."

Ricky smiled wanly, "More good than I deserve, that's for sure. I suppose I should just grin and bear it, Mr. Block, that's life you know, having your children get married."

Chris nodded understandingly.

"I assume that LooAnne took Kyle with her?"

Again Chris nodded.

"How long has she been gone?"

"About two hours, sir. They should be back any time now."

Daisy came into the study with Ricky's coffee and said, "Miss Nash just arrived home, sir."

Ricky looked at Chris and said, "You were right on the money, I guess I'd better go have a talk with her." He got up and left Chris in the study. LooAnne was in the living room taking off her coat, looking flushed from the cold weather outside. When she saw her uncle she smiled.

"Uncle Ricky, you're home!" LooAnne embraced her uncle happily but frowned when she saw his despondent expression. "What's the matter?" she asked, her arms still around his neck.

"Nothing, dear," Ricky said.

"You don't look in the least bit happy. Was your trip alright?"

"Yes it was fine," Ricky assured her. "Did you get all your Christmas shopping done?"

LooAnne nodded but she was still frowning as she stepped back and said, "Mr. Block told you, didn't he?"

"About you and Kyle Denson? Yes." Ricky answered.

LooAnne sighed. "I'm sorry I didn't mention it in my

letter. I wanted to wait and tell you in person. We're getting married on my birthday. Kyle wants a big wedding."

"Married on your birthday?" Ricky thought aloud. "That's not too far away you know?"

"I think that's why he wants to have it then. You'll never believe this but Kyle came into contact with one of his brothers while he was away! He's going to the same college that Kyle was and they met for the first time since Kyle was little." LooAnne looked down at her feet and asked, "Are you angery?"

Ricky put his hand on his niece's shoulder and smiled wanly, "Of course not. I just wish you hadn't grown up so fast is all. To think that you're almost eighteen and are going to be married is more than a bit overwhelming. I'm glad to hear though that Kyle found one of his brothers."

"But you're not upset?"

"No, I just can't seem to forget the past. You should still be that little girl that found me out in the field that day." LooAnne smiled, "Seems like it was only yesterday and yet so many things have happened since then. Everything that happened before that day seems like it was a lifetime ago."

Ricky nodded, thinking of Amanda running away, and the death his father and Susan, William, and Cindy.

"Yes, my dear," he said, "anything and everything that happened before that seems like it took place a very long time ago, but still it's so fresh in my memory."

LooAnne nodded soberly. "I'm rather surprised that we've made it this far."

"I happen to know that if it wasn't for a certain young Luther I *wouldn't* have made it this far."

"And if it wasn't for a certain Texas millionaire I wouldn't have either."

"I guess we're even then?" Ricky smiled.

"Not quite," LooAnne grinned.

"What do you mean, not quite?"

"Well, tomorrow's the annual Nash Christmas party isn't it?"

Ricky nodded.

"Well since I'm coming to your Christmas party then you have to help me put up one of the Christmas trees."

Ricky frowned, "It's the twenty-second of December, haven't the maids already done that?"

"No there's still the one in the sun room to be done. I've never decorated a Christmas tree before so I told the maids to let me do it this year. Mr. Moore has it out on the side porch ready and waiting to be set up. Will you help me?"

"You know what? I've never put up a Christmas tree either," Ricky admitted.

LooAnne gasped, "You haven't!"

"No, when I was little I'd help the maids decorate it on occasion but that's it."

"Let's do it now!" LooAnne exclaimed enthusiastically.

Ricky frowned, "I don't put up Christmas trees, my dear."

"There's a first time for everything, Uncle Ricky, and if you don't help me put up the tree then I'm not going to your Christmas party."

Ricky raised his eyebrows. "Are you threatening me,

young lady?"

"No," LooAnne grinned, "just offering you a fare deal."

Ricky laughed, "You'll make a good businesswoman one day, girl."

"I get it from you."

Ricky smiled at her complement, "I hope not. Shall we put up that tree now?"

LooAnne smiled, "Yes, lets." She drug her uncle into the sun room and then out onto the porch where a beautiful Cedar lay. "You bring it inside and I'll get the stand ready." LooAnne turned and ran back through the door. Ricky stared down at the tree and frowned in uncertainty.

"Would you like me to take that in for you sir?" asked the guard.

"No thank you Bobby, I think I've got it."

Ricky looked at the tree for a moment then said, "Give me your gloves."

Bob Millson removed his work gloves and handed them to Ricky who slid his hands into them and hefted the green Cedar up over his shoulder, he then turned to the door and squeezed through into the sun room where LooAnne was standing with one of the maids, both of them watching Ricky as he set the tree down into it's stand. Ricky straitened up and smiled triumphantly at his niece and the maid. "That wasn't hard," he said as he took of Millson's gloves and tossed them to the maid. "Give those to Bob, Alexandra."

"And then pop us some popcorn," LooAnne added excitedly.

"Popcorn?" Ricky asked, "What for?"

"For the tree."

"You mean we have to make that stringed popcorn ourselves?"

LooAnne laughed, "Yes, Uncle Ricky. When you said you had never put up a tree before you weren't kidding."

Ricky shrugged. "I haven't decorated a Christmas tree since I was three years old. That's been..." Ricky paused and counted the years in his head, "... forty two years." he shook his head in exasperation. "I'm getting kind of old when you think about it."

"You are not," LooAnne scolded.

"I am too, now are we going to decorate that tree or not?"

LooAnne smiled and picked up a box of ornaments. Ricky laid down on the sofa and put his feet up, laying his hands behind his head he closed his eyes restfully.

"Uncle Ricky," LooAnne huffed, "you're supposed to be helping me, and you're going to tear a hole in the couch with your boots on."

"I'll buy another one," Ricky mumbled sleepily.

LooAnne smiled and shook her head. "Alright then, I'll decorate the tree, you string the popcorn."

Ricky's eyes shot open and he sat up saying, "Oh no you don't. I'll decorate the tree you sow the popcorn. I'm libel to stick myself with a needle."

So LooAnne strung the popcorn and Ricky decorated the Christmas tree for the first time in many years. Both of them enjoyed each others company, a luxury Ricky knew was soon to be lessened.

After lunch the next afternoon LooAnne went outside to

wait for Amarie's return from her visit with her great aunt. She seated herself on the front porch swing and wrapped her wool coat around her shivering shoulders, listening to the distant cawing of cranes as they migrated south.

"Aren't you cold?" came Kyle's now very low, gruff voice taking LooAnne by surprise as she was not yet used to it's masculine ring.

"Not really," she answered, giving her fiance a loving smile.

Kyle's appearance had changed somewhat within the two years that he had been away. He looked more like a man now. He was very tall, broad, and his muscles toned. There was a bit of stubble on his chiseled jaw which he had yet to shave off, giving him a gruff appearance. Though his boyish features were no longer there, LooAnne could still detect the mischievous look in his light blue eyes, and she found herself deeply intrigued by it.

"You waiting for Amarie?" Kyle asked as he took a seat beside LooAnne on the porch swing.

"Yes, I am. She should be here pretty soon."

Kyle put his arm around LooAnne's shoulders, causing an instant warmth from his body to encase her frame. "I haven't seen Amarie in forever," he commented "How old is she now?"

"She turned sixteen in July."

"Wow, I remember when we used to have her taggin' along where ever we went."

LooAnne laughed. "Indeed we did. But I'm glad Amarie will be here with Uncle Ricky after we're married. He would get so lonely if he had no one here to keep him company, and I'd worry about him endlessly." LooAnne looked up at Kyle and asked, "You know I've been meaning to ask, what ever happened to your other brother? Did Jake ever say where he went?"

Kyle nodded, "They split up and Bob headed north. Jake had a job in Dallas and wasn't about to leave it just because his brother wanted to move out o' Texas."

"Did Bob say why he left?"

"Yeah, he wanted a change o' things. He wanted to see the world and finally he had the money to do it. Jake's married and has a family so he wasn't gonna pull up stakes and follow Bob. They haven't seen each other in almost three years."

"I'm sorry you didn't get to meet him, but maybe you will one day."

Kyle nodded, the anticipation of such a thought exciting him, "Jake's gonna send Bob a letter and tell him that we met in Dallas. I hope I get to meet him. Jake talks a ton about him."

At that moment the Nash sedan pulled into the driveway, cutting the couple's conversation short as it came to a halt by the walkway. One of the ranch hands alighted and opened the back door for Amarie. LooAnne ran off the porch with Kyle at her heals.

"LooAnne!" Amarie called waving and smiling happily. The two girls embraced and then LooAnne asked anxiously, "How was your trip?"

"It was lovely," Amarie said, her cheeks flushed with cold. "My great aunt is absolutely wonderful! We had a grand time."

It was then that Amarie looked over LooAnne's shoulder and noticed Kyle for the first time, "Why Kyle Denson!" she exclaimed. "When did you get home?"

"A couple o' days ago," Kyle answered.

LooAnne nodded, "We're engaged!" she said, holding up her left hand so that Amarie could see her ring, a thin golden band with an ever so small diamond attached to it, something Kyle had been saving up for since he left the estate.

"We're going to be married on my birthday!" LooAnne exclaimed in animation.

Amarie's eyes lit up, "That's only a month away!" she said excitedly. "Oh, LooAnne I'm so happy for you!"

LooAnne smiled. "Come on I can't wait to tell you all about it." She took Amarie's hand and the trio ran inside. Because of the Nash Christmas party that was being held that night the maids were hurrying about making preparations. Wonderful smells coming from the kitchen swirled throughout the house, wetting everyone's appetites. Maids were dusting, sweeping, mopping, and preparing Ricky, LooAnne, and Amarie's best clothes. Mrs. Moore, Mrs. Saunders, and Gladys Jacobs were in the kitchen cooking the meal, and a few of the ranch hands were helping to rearrange the dining room so that it would more conveniently fit the guests that were coming. Chris was overseeing all of the goings-on and giving orders that he had been given by Ricky.

When the trio walked into the house Amarie asked, "What's going on?"

"The Christmas party," LooAnne answered. "The guests are supposed to arrive at six this evening."

224

"Oh yes, I'd forgotten that tomorrow is Christmas Eve."
Amarie sighed, "I haven't done a bit of Christmas
shopping!"

"You'd better get on with it," Kyle said.

"I know, tomorrow is the only day I'll have left. Can you
take me, LooAnne?"

"No I can't," LooAnne admitted grudgingly.
"Tomorrow's Uncle Ricky's Christmas Eve broadcast on
the Harry Milton Show, I've got to go with him."

"What will I do then?" Amarie asked in distress.
"Shopping along is dreadfully unpleasent."

"Ask one of the maids to go with you," LooAnne
suggested.

"I suppose that's the only option," Amarie sighed.

"I could go?" Kyle offered. "I'm off work tomorrow and
don't have nothin' better to do."

Amarie's eyes lit up. "Kyle that would be wonderful of
you!"

LooAnne frowned, "What in the world would you want
to go shopping for, Kyle?"

Her fiance shrugged, "I still got some presents to get and
I was planin' on going tomorrow anyhow."

"Hm," LooAnne thought aloud, "You take a maid with
you anyway Amarie. It wouldn't be very proper to go
alone with a young man."

Amarie sighed and rolled her eyes, "You're just like
Uncle Ricky, LooAnne. This is the twentieth century, no
one cares for escorts anymore. Where's your sense of the
new age? Plus, Kyle is your fiance, surely you wouldn't
think -"

"I trust the both of you to act decently, Amarie, but

225

what's proper is proper."

"Oh Loo, come on," Kyle scolded. "No one cares about that stuff anymore."

"Maybe not, but when it comes to things such as this a lady should take the extra step to protect her decorum." Amarie shook her head, "Fine, we'll take Daisy with us and Kyle can drive."

LooAnne nodded her approval and the threesome continued into the sun room.

SEVENTEEN

The Christmas Party

Do not lay up for yourselves treasures
on earth where moth and rust destroy
and where thieves break in and steal; but
lay up for yourselves treasures in heaven,
where neither moth nor rust destroy and
where thieves do not break in and steal,
for where your treasure is there your heart
shall be also.
Matthew 6:19-21

At precisely six o'clock that evening the guests
began arriving for the Christmas Party. Ricky, LooAnne,
and Amarie stood at the front door greeting each of them
as they filed in. There was Walter Thompson, the
president of Nash and Nash National Bank, Raymond
Lloyd, the manager of Dancing Meadow Inn; Johnny
Julian and Jessa Bradley the foreman and housekeeper
of Quinn Creek Manor; Charlie Herman, foreman of
Lone Star Ranch; Benjamin Frederics, foreman of
Flying N Ranch; Harry Milton, host of the Harry Milton
show; Melvin Ray, manager of Nash/Hearten Clothes
Factory; Lucille Cue, manager of Peaceful Inn; Stephan

Russell, manager of the Nash Hotel; Chester Donner, manager of the John Hearten Hotel; Trevor Mason, a state representative; Eliot Duncan, Ricky's new lawyer; Dr. Millard Noel, one of the town doctors all of whom brought their spouses and some of their elder children. The last person to arrive was Robert, his wife, and their two girls, who were staying for the holidays.

The house looked like a Christmas wonderland with it's glistening Christmas trees and roaring fires. Holly branches decked the banisters and door frames, wreaths hung from the lintels of the main entryways, and the house was ablaze with lights. Guests mingled throughout the rooms, conversing cheerily to one another and laughing gaily. Ricky was standing by the fire talking with Eliot Duncan, Robert, and a few others about the trial and his narrow escape.

"I certainly am glad you hired me, Mr. Nash," Eliot was saying. "No offense but Mr. Mason's reputation misinterpreted him."

"You can say that again," Robert mumbled under his breath.

"You'll do fine, Eliot," Ricky assured him, "though I can't throw too many rocks at Zeke. With that much evidence displayed there wasn't a man on earth who could have cleared me besides Devin Luther. I just hated that Zeke himself didn't believe me innocent."

"I for one am curious as to how your gun fell into Luther's hands, Mr. Nash," said one of the men.

"Ah yes, we found out not long after Devin's death that one of my guards had been convinced to retrieve the combination for Devin. He threatened to kill the poor

228

man's wife. The guard sneaked into the house just as my niece was opening the safe. He watched her turn the dial and wrote down the combination which he later gave to Devin who got the gun while he was dousing the house in kerosene."

The men present shook there's heads in amazement as one woman exclaimed, "He certainly had some nerve!" Ricky nodded in agreement as Chris approached him, standing tall and looking very elegant in his suit.

"Dinner is served, sir," he said, bowing his head slightly. "Thank you Chris," Ricky said and soon everyone was seated at the two long dining tables which had been moved in to replace the one that usually sat in the dining room.

As the group sat and chatted with one another LooAnne, who was sitting on Ricky's right, heard something just barely over the noise of the party. She listened intently for a moment and then realized that it was coming from the front porch! The noise sounded like the animated voices of several men. She looked towards the front door and out the window and could see the guard arguing with a man on the porch. The man seemed to be demanding entry which the guard was obviously refusing. LooAnne looked up at her uncle who was deeply engrossed in a conversation with the bank president. Not wanting to interrupt him and knowing it would cause a disturbance should he leave, she craned her neck in search of Chris who she soon found standing off to the side talking to one of the maids. LooAnne got his attention easily and nodded towards the front door where the commotion was taking place. Chris immediately turned in that direction and subtly made his way across the dining room and out onto the front porch. LooAnne watched as the guard and stranger were pulled out of sight of the window so they could not be seen by the guests. Less than a minute later Chris returned looking a bit disconcerted. He approached Ricky's chair and caught his employer's immediate attention.

"Forgive me, sir," he whispered so that only Ricky and LooAnne could hear him, "but there's a gentlemen outside who needs to see you."

Ricky frowned, "Can you tell him to come back tomorrow?"

"He says that today is the only day he'll be in town, sir." Ricky huffed under his breath, seeming quite annoyed at the disturbance. "Well who is he?" he asked.

Chris was hesitant in answering and when he did it was an almost unintelligible whisper. "*Philip Newton*, sir." Ricky's reaction was nothing like LooAnne expected. His entire face took on a look of shock. He paled slightly and drew in a breath before answering his steward in a voice of forced calmness. "Bring him in the back entrance and into the study."

Chris nodded and made his way back to the front door. Ricky remained seated for only a moment before rising from his chair, drawing the attention of his guests. He addressed none of them but instead kept his face void of emotion as he walked through the dining room and into the living room without a word!

The room was now in silence and all eyes were on the door that Ricky had disappeared through. Only a moment afterward Chris appeared at the door and said,

"Please continue with your meal ladies and gentlemen. We've had a slight business related incident that must be tented to immediately if you'll be so kind as to excuse us." Chris closed the door to the dining room as he exited, leaving Robert to act as host for the party.

In the study Ricky stood next to the fireplace, leaning heavily on the mantel as his mind whirled with memories that he had tried to push away. He was about to come face to face with Philip Newton, his brother-in-law! Though he had supported his wife's parents until their death many years before he had long since lost contact with their children. Had he ever expected to see them again, he wondered? But how could he not? They were, after all, the family he had married into so long ago. And now, with the visit of his wife's brother, he was about to taste a bit of the past.
Ricky was stirred from his deep thoughts by a soft knocking on the open door. He turned, and there, in the doorway, stood a man he had not seen in almost twenty years. His appearance had changed drastically with age and though he was only in his late fifties he was stooped slightly and wrinkles lined his face. His tired eyes stared at Ricky, seeming to absorb every bit of him.
"It's been a long time, Mr. Nash," he addressed Ricky gruffly as the two faced each other.
Ricky nodded, "It has indeed. Please come in and take a seat."
Philip entered the room and seated himself on the settee directly across from Ricky's desk. He was quiet at first, looking around the room and taking in the warmth of the

231

estate's interior. He sighed audibly before looking back at Ricky. "It's still got her touch, even after twenty years," he whispered.

Ricky felt a knot grow in his throat at the mention of his wife, at the thought of their home still reminding Philip of her.

Ricky let out a shaky sigh, "I'm glad you think so."

Philip nodded, "She loved this place, always did. But I didn't come here to bring back bad memories." Ricky sat down at the desk and listened intently as Philip continued, "I reckon you remember Judith?"

Ricky nodded, "Yes of course. The last time I saw her was at your mother's funeral. She was going with that young man....Josh Nobel I believe."

Philip nodded, "She married that fella not long after our ma's funeral, that's one o' the reasons I'm here. You see they just had their forth youngun and things ain't real easy right now. He lost his job 'bout three years ago and they've long since run dry o' cash. I reckon you know what I'm gettin' at?"

Ricky nodded, "She needs money."

Philip nodded and continued, "Now I know this is right rude comin' to you after twenty years and askin' such a thing, but I can't support 'em no more. The boys sold the carpenter shop when pa died and we been runin' a ranch but there's a real bad drought up north in Oklahoma and we ain't harvested a good crop in two years. I know I'm over stepping my bounds but-"

"Certainly not," Ricky interrupted. "You're my brother-in-law, Philip. You Newtons are my family and I would never turn you away, especially when I can so easily lend my help. I would like to know though, why didn't Judith come to me herself?"

Philip sighed deeply and said, "She and Josh are right ashamed of askin' help from even me, they sure weren't about to come beggin' to you."

Ricky turned to his desk and pulled out a checkbook from the top drawer. He jotted down a substantial amount and handed it to Philip. "You tell Judith I said it's my absolute pleasure and I consider you all as much my family as you ever were."

Philip rose from his seat, looking at the check in his hands and then up at Ricky. "I don't know how to thank ya, Mr. Nash."

"There's no need. If you need anything else until you get back on your feet, you let me know, yeah?"

Philip extended his hand to Ricky who shook it instantly. "I will, Mr. Nash." He looked around the room one more time and said, "I asked my sister once, when money was hard, to take advantage of your love for her. Now here I am taking it from you. You don't know how ashamed I am."

"There's no need to be ashamed. You did it with good intentions, and I can't scold you for encouraging the love of my life to marry me, no matter the reason."

Philip chuckled slightly at this before his face became serious again. He looked his brother-in-law in the eye and said, "She loved you, you know?"

Ricky nodded, withholding the tears that threatened to fall. "I know. I loved her as well, I still do, with all of my heart."

"I know you do, and believe me, Mr. Nash, she loves

you too."

Ricky nodded gratefully and Philip left without another word.

Ricky watched after him for a moment, thinking of his wife who he would be reunited with one glorious day.

"Ricky are you okay?" Robert's voice broke into his brother's thoughts and Ricky turned to find him standing in the doorway.

He nodded, "I'm fine, Robert."

"Was that Philip Newton that just left?"

"It was. He needed money."

Robert raised his eyebrows, "And you gave it to him?"

"Why wouldn't I?" Ricky questioned.

"Wasn't Philip the one that asked Susan to marry you for your money?"

"He meant well, Robert, plus I wasn't giving him the money, I was giving it to Judith. He was here on her behalf."

"Don't you think that Philip was imposing just a little?"

"No," Ricky shook his head. "If I were in the same predicament I would have done the same thing. 'Don't lay up for yourselves treasures on earth where moth and rust destroy and where thieves break in and steal; but lay up for yourselves treasures in heaven where neither moth nor rust destroys and where thieves do not break in and steal. For where your treasure is there your heart shall be also.' They're my family just like you are, Robert, from a whole other lifetime ago. If you needed the money you wouldn't hesitate to ask so he shouldn't either. Out of the seven of us that got sick that day in Oklahoma only three of us survived, Judith and I being two of them. Whether it's right or not I feel closer to her than to any of the other Newton children just because of it. Seeing Philip reminds me of the old Rick Nash, no matter how long it's been. I know that I'm not him anymore, nor will I ever be again. Now let's forget about this and get back to the party."

"What will you tell, LooAnne?" Robert asked.

Ricky sighed and paused a moment as he thought, "I don't want her to know. She's had such a hard life and to tell her of my hardships and heartbreaks would certainly sadden her and fill her with questions and uncertainty. I don't want to hurt her, Robert." With that Ricky rejoined his guests.

After apologizing to them for the disturbance he took his seat and resumed his conversation with the bank president. LooAnne looked up at him questioningly but he offered no explanation as to his actions. He was extremely cheerful but LooAnne could see down deep in his eyes where there was a sad look that shadowed his face. It was a tired, grieving sort of look that gave LooAnne an uneasy feeling.

The rest of the party went well, LooAnne spent most of her time talking with Robert's younger daughter Cecily, who was going to turn eighteen that spring. Ricky acted as though nothing had happened and by eleven o'clock everyone had left. The maids went to work cleaning up the house, Ricky sat in the living room talking to Robert and Katherine who's oldest girl was soon to be married. Cecily and Amarie were deep in a conversation about school so LooAnne decided to find Chris and ask him what had happened that evening. She found him in the dining room with his clipboard in his hands flipping through the pages that he had on it as the maids cleared the tables.

"Mr. Block," LooAnne said as she approached him. Chris looked up and asked, "Yes, Miss Nash?"

"Who was that man that came during supper?"

Chris raised his eyebrows nervously, "Um – well that man wanted money, Miss Nash."

"I sort of figured that, but why did Uncle Ricky act the way he did?"

"What way, Miss Nash?"

"The way he acted when he saw that man. He was upset and I think he still is."

"Miss Nash I don't know very much about the situation. Why don't you ask him?"

"Because he would either get mad at me for butting in or he'd tell me something that was close to the truth but not quite there."

"Why don't you try me?" came a voice from behind Chris and LooAnne.

They both looked up and saw Ricky standing in the doorway. He leaned against the door frame and crossed his arms. "I knew that man's sister a long time ago. That's how I met him. His family was desperately in need of money at the time so I helped them along. Later they moved to Oklahoma and ran one of my businesses until they bought it from me. Now they've lost that business due to some difficulty with the drought and Philip came to me to ask for some more money. I hadn't seen him in years and thought that he was better off now. I was surprised when he showed up and sorry that he and his family were still in need."

LooAnne grinned, "Like I was saying to Mr. Block, you didn't get mad but you did tell me only half the truth. I can see it in your eyes and hear it in your voice, but if you're that determined to keep it from me then I suppose you've got a good reason and I'll wait until you're ready to tell me." LooAnne looked up at the clock and said, "I'm going to bed, goodnight Uncle Ricky, goodnight Mr. Block."

With that LooAnne turned and left the dining room. Ricky and Chris looked at one another and Ricky shook his head, smiling. "Sometimes I just don't understand that girl."

"She knows what it's like to have deep secrets that are too precious to divulge, and she respects that you want privacy."

Ricky nodded, "And I can't be more appreciative to her for it. I suppose one day I'll have to tell her."

Chris nodded, "If you don't she'll find out."

"I know, but I can't bring myself to do it, not only for her sake, but mine. I can't bear to relive it again."

EIGHTEEN

Deception

*But the Lord said to Samuel, "Do not
look at his outward appearance or at
his physical stature, because I have
refused him. For the Lord does not see
as man sees; for man looks on the outward
appearance but the Lord looks on
the heart. 1 Samuel 16:7*

*Do not be deceived: God is not mocked, for
whatever one sows, that will he also reap.
For the one who sows to his won flesh will
from the flesh reap corruption, but the one
who sows to the Spirit will from the Spirit reap
eternal life. Galatians 6:7-8*

Early the next morning Kyle came to the house with
the Sedan and picked up Amaire so that she could do her
Christmas shopping. Daisy went along per LooAnne's
request. She did not want to admit I but LooAnne highly
disliked the idea of Kyle and Amarie going alone into
town though she could not quiet determine why. She
trusted Kyle wholeheartedly but could not quite forget
how Amarie had treated her when they first met.

Shortly after they left Ricky and LooAnne drove to the radio station for Ricky's Christmas Eve broadcast on the Harry Milton Show. The whole town always tuned in to listen to one of the Nash traditions, Ricky speaking about Christ's birth. Hours later when LooAnne and her uncle returned home Amarie was in her room wrapping presents. It was supper time and the sun had already gone down. A cold frost had blanketed the fields. LooAnne trudged upstairs and dropped down on her bed, exhausted from the long day in town. She closed her eyes and sighed restfully but she was soon interrupted by her bedroom door flying open and Amarie running inside, "LooAnne," she exclaimed, "we had so much fun shopping for presents! Kyle was a huge help! I got him a leather wallet, I got Uncle Robert a blue tie, Aunt Katherine a silk scarf with fringe on the ends, Uncle Ricky a new pare of those boots that he likes; Malinda I got a navy blue handbag, Cecily was hard so I just got her a box of chocolates, and of course I can't tell you what your present is but I know that you'll love it!"

LooAnne rolled over on her stomach and mumbled, "That's nice."

Amarie huffed, "What's the matter with you?"

"I'm tired, I've been in town all day long."

"But aren't you excited? Tomorrow's Christmas!"

"I know, I'm very excited, just tired."

"Oh, well I'm hungry, let's go down and see if supper's ready."

LooAnne sighed deeply and sat up, "Alright," she agreed. The two went downstairs where they found

Cecily talking with her sister, Malinda who was twenty two and engaged to be married that coming summer. "Uncle Ricky did really good on the radio today," Cecily said when the girls entered the room. "And so did you, LooAnne."

LooAnne smiled, "Thank you, Cecily, but I didn't do anything except say hello and goodbye."

"You said a thing or two in the middle," Cecily corrected.

"But that wasn't very important."

"I think it was." Cecily sighed happily, "I can't wait for today to be over, Christmas is my favorite time of the year!"

"Mine too," Amaire agreed.

"Summer is going to be my new favorite," Malinda stated thinking of her wedding that was to take place in the next few months.

At that moment Chris walked through on his way to the study, "Supper's ready, ladies." he said as he passed. The foursome thanked him and started for the dining room. Just as they were about to be seated at the table Kyle walked in. "Howdy, gals," he said smiling. "Am I late?"

"No," said LooAnne, "we haven't stated yet. Thank you again for taking Amarie to town, Kyle."

"No problem. We had a right good time." Kyle insisted, smiling at Amarie. "Girls sure do take their good ol' time when it comes to Christmas shoppin' though."

"It didn't take that long," Amarie defended herself.

At that moment Ricky, Robert, and Katherine walked in and everyone began the evening meal. As they ate

240

Amarie asked, "Can we get up at midnight like we used to, Uncle Ricky?"

Ricky frowned, "Absolutely not," he stated.

"But you used to let us do it," Amarie begged.

Robert raised his eyebrows, "Did you indeed, big brother?"

"I did once and that was it," Ricky insisted, huffing disapprovingly at Amarie for disclosing the secret.

LooAnne laughed, "We've done that quite a few times, Uncle Ricky."

"We most certainly have not," Ricky said ignoring the giggles from the girls.

At ten o'clock everyone went to bed but the girls' sleep was allusive. They lie in bed thinking about the next morning and knowing that it couldn't come soon enough. The heat from the fire below in the study swirled up through a vent in LooAnne's floor and warmed her room. She looked down from her bed at the vent and smiled. Slowly she slipped out from under her warm covers and knelt next to the small hole, peering through it's intricately designed mettle bars down into the study where she could hear the faint voices of her uncle, Chris, and Robert. She could see her uncle arranging gifts under the tree and could hear Chris adding wood to the fire.

"What do you think, Robert?" Ricky was asking his brother whom LooAnne could not see.

"Looks fine to me, but it is kinda hard for presents under a Christmas tree to look bad."

"You know how I feel about things that have to be arranged," Ricky reminded his brother.

"Yes, I know, everything must be uniform."
LooAnne smiled, knowing how precise her uncle always was with everything. She assumed this quality was essential when it came to running a business as large as his. But the next thing he said took her aback.
"This is LooAnne's last Christmas here you know. She's marrying Kyle Denson next month."
LooAnne sat back and looked up at the wall, reality striking her heart. This was her last Christmas at the Nash Estate! Ricky was right, in exactly a month she was going to be marrying Kyle Denson and then they would have their own home and their own family. LooAnne looked around her room and sadness gripped her. Then she thought of Kyle and how happy they would be. She knew this was part of getting married, leaving your home and your family, but until this night she had never actually realized it. LooAnne stood and crawled back into bed, pulling the covers over her head. The second she got them there she threw them back off, her first instinct to be able to see the door. When she realized what she had just done she groaned out of disappointment, "What kind of person am I?" she asked herself closing her eyes tightly. "When will I understand that I'm safe and I don't have to watch the door? How long am I going to be trapped in this Luther world?" LooAnne just couldn't seem to rid herself of the Luthers even though they were gone, they still lived inside her, just as much a Luther as they were.
LooAnne buried her face in her pillow and soon she had drifted off to sleep. When she woke up sunlight had flooded her room and the warm smell of pancakes

swirled up though the vent. Amarie came bursting through the door crying, "LooAnne! LooAnne! It's Christmas, come on lets go downstairs!"

LooAnne smiled, momentarily forgetting her thoughts from the previous night. Amarie yanked her out of bed and stuffed her bathrobe into her arms. "Hurry, LooAnne, let's go!"

She followed Amarie into the upper hall where Malinda and Cecily were just coming out of their bedroom. LooAnne put on her robe and the girls descended the steps, going straight into the study where they immediately halted in the doorway and stared at the Christmas tree and the presents beneath it. The sight was beautiful, as though it were spring in December.

Amarie dropped down beside the tree to find one that was addressed to her. Ricky, Robert, and Katherine soon appeared and the opening began. It was a wonderful morning full of laughter and bliss. Breakfast was pancakes and bacon with coffee and hot chocolate. Kyle arrived just before lunch and after he had opened his presents he gave the girls theirs. LooAnne, Kyle, Amarie, Cecily, and Malinda played cards while Ricky, Robert, and Katherine conversed merrily in the sun room. They played game after game and soon the sun had sunk below the tall mountain and a cold wind began to howl through the fields.

"I want the eight of hearts," Amarie sighed with exasperation when Malinda laid down a nine of spades. "Amar, you aren't supposed to tell us what you want," LooAnne pointed out. "Then we won't give it to you."

"Why?" Amarie wined.

243

"Because we don't want you to win."

"That's not very nice," Amarie huffed.

"You know what I mean," LooAnne scolded.

Amarie groaned when LooAnne laid down an ace of spades. "I don't want to draw out of the deck. I just end up laying it down anyway."

Amarie drew a card and then slapped it back down into the discard pile. "Your turn, Kyle," she said, but Kyle didn't seem to hear her. He was looking out the window at the full moon that glowed in the cold night sky. He seemed to be deeply engrossed in his thoughts.

"Kyle, it's your turn," Amarie repeated.

Kyle snapped out of his musing and drew out of the deck then laid down the eight of hearts. Amarie squealed with delight and waited patiently while the turn went around the table. LooAnne frowned as she watched Kyle continue to look out the window. It was quite obvious he was paying no attention to the game and LooAnne was inclined to think that something was wrong.

"Is something the matter, Kyle?" she asked.

Kyle turned and looked at LooAnne, his face wore a troubled expression. "Can I talk to you privately, LooAnne?" he asked in a low voice so that only those at the table heard him.

LooAnne raised her eyebrows in surprise. "Of course, Kyle." The two rose and left the room. LooAnne followed him through the living room and into the hallway where he turned and faced her. "LooAnne," he said, "I have something I need to tell you."

"Alright," LooAnne said. "What is it?"

Kyle sighed and said plainly, "I can't marry you."

LooAnne took a step back and looked at Kyle in disbelief, feeling her heart beginning to drop. "W-what do you mean you can't marry me?"

"I can't tell you why, but I just can't marry you," Kyle stated, his face void of emotion.

"But – but this makes no sense. I waited for you for almost three years and now that your back you're telling me that it was all for nothing? You've got to be joking, Kyle Denson!"

"I'm afraid I'm not joking. I'm sorry but I'm not going to marry you, LooAnne," Kyle was very firm in his insistence.

LooAnne could barely believe this was taking place. Why was Kyle refusing to marry her? "You could at least tell me why?" she demanded.

Kyle looked at the floor. "I – I have someone else in mind. I don't love you anymore," were his shocking words that stunned LooAnne so much that she could barely breathe.

"You – you what?"

"You'll find out about it sooner or later, but I'm marrying someone else."

LooAnne could feel hot tears gathering in her eyes. She yanked Kyle's engagement ring off her finger and threw it down at his feet. "There's your worthless hunk of gold, Kyle Denson. I hope your wife enjoys it!"

With that LooAnne rushed past Kyle and bounded up the stairs to her room, slamming the door behind her!

NINTEEN

Pearls Before Swine

*There is no fear in love, but perfect
love casts out fear, because fear involves
torment. But he who fears has not been
made perfect in love.*
1 John 4:18

*Do not give what is holy to the dogs,
not cast your pearls before swine,
lest they trample them under their feet and
turn and tear you in pieces.*
Matthew 7:6

"**W**here's LooAnne?" Ricky asked when Kyle
returned to the sun room alone.
"Oh, um, she said that she'd eaten too much and was
gonna lie down for a little while," Kyle lied effortlessly.
Ricky nodded, satisfied with Kyle's answer, but as the
day grew later Ricky began to wonder if there was
something wrong with his niece. By seven o'clock he
decided to check on her welfare. Ricky went to
LooAnne's room and knocked on the door. "LooAnne,
it's me. Can I come in?"

246

When there was no answer Ricky tried the door which was unlocked. He opened it quietly and looked in. LooAnne was laying on her bed, asleep. Ricky decided not to awaken her and returned downstairs. At nine thirty Amarie and Cecily went to bed, being careful not to bother LooAnne who they assumed was still sleeping. LooAnne however had just been pretending when she had heard her uncle at the door. She didn't feel like talking to anyone much less telling them that Kyle had more or less betrayed her when she had given him all of her trust. She lay on the floor next to the vent and listened to her uncles, aunt, and cousin talk in the study. Malinda soon came up to bed and Robert and Katherine followed about thirty minutes later. Ricky however stayed up and talked with Chris.

"I wonder if LooAnne and Kyle had a fight," Ricky was saying to his steward.

"What makes you think that, sir?"

"Kyle left right after he talked with LooAnne. She went to bed and didn't come back down. I suppose it's natural for couples to fight, but on Christmas day?" Ricky shook his head. "I guess I'm off to bed too, Chris. Good night and Merry Christmas."

"Good night, sir. Merry Christmas."

LooAnne saw her uncle leave the study and heard his bedroom door close. She then saw the study light go out and heard Chris walking down the hall and through the kitchen toward his bedroom. LooAnne sat back on her heals and rubbed her forehead which ached with a splitting pain. She decided that since everyone had gone to bed she would go down into the kitchen and take some aspirin. She put her robe on over her nightgown and wrapped her shawl around her shoulders. Then she quietly opened her bedroom door and tiptoed down the stairs, being careful not to step on the ones that creaked. The first floor was colder than the second. LooAnne looked into the study and saw that the fire was nothing but a small glow, as it normally was during the night. The floor beneath her bare feet felt cold but she continued to the kitchen, running her hand along the walls to feel her way through the dark yet familiar house. When she reached the kitchen she turned on one of the lamps and found the medicine, then she turned and looked out the small window. The moon was a perfect circle high in the sky surrounded by small, twinkling stars that reminded LooAnne of the birth of their Savior when the star had guided the wise men and shepherds. The black mountain was silhouetted against the night sky, and the bare trees seemed to dance in the wind that caused the house to creak and groan. LooAnne thought about Kyle Denson and how she had been completely taken in by his smooth, seemingly loving persona and then dropped for another girl after nearly three long years of waiting.

Suddenly she felt a strange sensation that someone was standing behind her! LooAnne whirled around and came face to face with her uncle who was still fully dressed standing beside the icebox.

"I thought that if we both went to bed you'd come down," he said.

LooAnne lowered her head but remained silent.

"Did you and Kyle have a disagreement?" Ricky asked.

LooAnne nodded.

"Everyone has fights some time, you can work it out." LooAnne tried hard to hold in her tears but there were so many they began to overflow, running down her face. Her emotions burst and she looked up at her uncle in anguish, "He told me he couldn't marry me!" she cried. "He said there was another woman and that he was in love with her."

Ricky was shocked, "He said what?"

"He told me he won't marry me, Uncle Ricky. After all this time he's leaving me for another woman!" LooAnne buried her face in her uncle's shoulder and sobbed, holding onto him tightly. She could feel his body stiffen as he held her. "That worthless, no account, swine!" Ricky growled. "Did he give you an explanation as to his uncalled for actions?"

LooAnne took a deep breath and dried her eyes on her sleeve. "He's not in love with me anymore," she said as she looked down at her cold feet. "He said so himself."

"I knew I didn't like that man," Ricky said through grit teeth.

"I wish I had the same discernment that you did. I should have. I've been trained to be careful of people, but apparently I couldn't retain anything good I was taught. I bet that's the whole reason he broke up with me. He saw that other woman and realized that she wasn't a no good Luther."

"That had nothing to do with it, LooAnne," Ricky said sternly. "Whatever his reasons were for breaking up with you, it had nothing to do with you being a Luther."

"You don't know that."

"LooAnne, you don't want someone like him anyway. He's a no account lowlife and doesn't deserve the shoes on his feet much less you."

LooAnne sighed and dried her eyes, "I guess I should be glad that I found out what he was really like before I married him, but I thought he loved me and I thought I loved him. I guess I was just being foolish. Now I don't know where to go or what to do. My life was all planned out hours ago and now it's just a huge mess!"

Ricky smiled at his niece. "How about you go to bed and get some rest? Everything will look better in the morning."

LooAnne sniffled and nodded, "Alright, but I don't ever want to see him again."

Ricky nodded, "After I'm done with him you won't have to worry about that."

LooAnne gave her uncle a half smile, "Don't do anything that will get you thrown in jail again, alright?"

Ricky smiled and planted a kiss on his niece's forehead, "I won't, I promise. Now you get on to bed. I'll see you in the morning."

LooAnne nodded and left the kitchen. Ricky watched her go, his heart aching along with her's. "I'll fix that boy," he said under his breath. "He'll regret ever entering my house."

Ricky woke early the next morning before anyone else and ate breakfast alone. Just as he was finishing, LooAnne appeared, looking very tired and still upset. She sat down in her chair next to Ricky and sighed, staring at the food as though it were not there.

"How'd you sleep?" Ricky asked.

"I didn't," LooAnne said closing her eyes and sinking lower in her chair.

At that moment the butler came in and said, "Mr. Denson's here to see you, sir."

Ricky and LooAnne looked at each other and then LooAnne said, "I'll be outside," and left.

Ricky told the butler to show Kyle in, preparing himself for a heated confrontation.

When he appeared he said, "I've got to talk to you, sir, it's very important."

Ricky looked up at Kyle and said, "And I'd like to talk to you about something very important."

Kyle knit his brow, "What is it, sir?"

Ricky stood and walked across the room towards Kyle. "You've been weighed in the balances and found wanting, young man."

"Excuse me, sir?" Kyle asked, looking a bit bewildered.

"I'm not partial to men that pledge their loyalty to a girl, make her wait years, and then throw her aside at the last minute."

Kyle's eyes widened. "Please, sir, I promise you that's not the way it happened. Please let me explain?"

"You had better have a good explanation!"

"I do, really."

"Then how about telling me what it is?" Ricky almost yelled.

Before Kyle could answer Amarie came in from the living room, "What's all the angry voices for? Did you tell him, Kyle?"

"Amarie you get out of -" Ricky stopped in the middle of his sentence and narrowed his eyes at his ward,

251

"What did you say, Amarie?"

"Kyle said he'd tell -"

"Sh!" Kyle cut her off but it did him no good.

Ricky looked Kyle in the eye and demanded, "Tell me what, Kyle?"

Kyle looked at Amarie then at Ricky but said nothing.

Ricky looked at Amarie and asked, "What is it that he's going to tell me, Amarie?"

Amarie glanced at Kyle and then back at Ricky and said, "I promised that I wouldn't say anything to you."

Ricky turned to Kyle and grabbed his shirt forcefully, pulling Kyle toward him until his face was inches away from his own. "You tell me this instant or I'll have you thrown out!"

Kyle gulped nervously, "We – that is, Amarie and I – we're – *engaged*, Mr. Nash."

Ricky's face inflamed with anger upon hearing this outrage and he shoved Kyle away from him! "Are you trying to tell me that you broke my niece's heart and then turned right around and proposed to Amarie?"

Kyle shook his head vigorously. "No, sir!" he insisted. "LooAnne admitted that she didn't have feelings for me anymore and we agreed to break off the engagement!"

"Unfortunately for you, Kyle Denson, I've talked with my niece and she told me quite a different story," Ricky informed the young man. "And I harbor a great distaste for liars."

Kyle started to say something but stumbled over his words, unable to further defend himself.

"You get out of my house and off my property, boy!" Ricky yelled.

252

"But what about Amarie?" Kyle asked, becoming defensive.

"I try not to make it a habit to cast my pearls before swine!"

"You mean I can't go?" Amarie asked.

"That's exactly what I mean!"

"Mr. Nash," said Kyle, "you can't deny me the right to get married to the woman I love."

"Ha!" Ricky scoffed upon hearing this. "Well you can't marry her without my permission. Now get out!"

"But Uncle Ricky!" Amarie protested. "I -"

"Don't backtalk, young lady!" Ricky snapped.

"You can't keep me from marrying her, Mr. Nash," Kyle insisted angrily. "I might leave but I'll come back for her!"

In an instant images of his little sister began to flood Ricky's mind. This entire scenario reminded him of the night she left to marry Jason Luther. He had failed in stopping her so many years before and now he knew he had to stop Amarie, no matter what the cost. "Kyle," Ricky said, anger sounding in his voice, "I'm giving you a fare warning, get out right now and never come back or I'll throw you out myself!"

Kyle stood firm, seeming undaunted. "I won't leave without her, sir."

"Fine then, but don't say I didn't warn you." Ricky grabbed Kyle by the shirt and shoved him across the room where he punched the young man across the face! Kyle went flying backward, smashing through the dining room windows as they shattered against his weight! He landed in a bed of glass on the side porch right at the guard's feet. Chris came running into the dining room with Mrs. Moore, Robert, and three of the maids behind him, "Are you alright, sir?" he asked. "Never better, Mr. Block," Ricky said as he yanked open the front door and hurriedly strode around the corner of the house were Kyle was just getting to his feet. When he saw Ricky coming towards him he ran for the road. Ricky, Chris, Amarie, and the guard stood on the side porch watching him run. When he reached the road he turned and called, "I'll be back! Bet on it!" Then he continued down the road towards town just as LooAnne came running from the back of the house. Upon seeing the shattered window, the stunned guard, and her enraged uncle her eyes grew wide and she asked, "What in the world happened?"

Before anyone could answer Amarie burst into tears and Ricky erupted into an angry tirade, "Amarie Hearten, you go to your room! Kane, if you see that man on the property again shoot him! Chris, have those windows fixed by tomorrow afternoon!" With that Ricky turned and stormed away. Amarie ran, sobbing, to her room. Robert came to the broken window and looked out questioningly, and Chris and the guard stood on the porch in a stunned silence.

LooAnne looked at Chris and asked, "What happened?" Chris shrugged. "I have no idea, Miss Nash."

LooAnne went into the house and ran up to Amarie's room, determined to find out what had happened between her uncle and Kyle. Amarie was lying on her bed with her pillow over her head, shaking with sobs. LooAnne went to her side and asked worriedly, "What happened, Amarie?"

Amarie lifted her head and sniffed then she said, "We told Uncle Ricky that we were going to be married and he got really mad and punched Kyle out the window!"

The color drained from LooAnne's face. "You mean you and Kyle?"

Amarie nodded and then began crying harder.

LooAnne felt a knot in her chest and her head began to pound. Amarie, her own friend, was the one that Kyle had been speaking of when he said he had another woman that he loved.

"Amarie, what happened on Saturday when you were shopping?" LooAnne asked, certain that any understanding they might have made would have taken place when they were together away from the watchful eye of her uncle and herself.

"He – he said he had something he wanted t-to talk to me about in p-privet and so I asked Daisy to go across the street to get us both a bottle of R-Root Beer." Amarie swallowed hard and continued, "Once she was gone Kyle told me a-about how you and he had b-broken up and that he-he was s-so lonely. He said that he-he had loved me from the m-moment he last saw me at the estate b-before he left. He said that y-you knew he was gonna propose to me and – and you were h-happy for him."

"Amarie why didn't you come and tell me about this?" LooAnne asked, feeling her heart breaking further as she listened to Kyle's lies.

"H-he said you were st-still upset a-about the breakup and he d-didn't want me to bring is up and h-hurt you."

Amarie pulled her head from the pillow and looked up LooAnne. "He loves me, LooAnne, he said he needed me and I feel the same way. I can't believe Uncle Ricky could be so cruel to him."

LooAnne sat back on the bed and looked straight ahead at the wall, staring into nothing. She could not believe Kyle had told so many lies, knowing that Amaire's gullible, naive nature would believe him. LooAnne despised him for what he had done to her family. There was no security with an inconstant man like Kyle. She didn't know what to do, but she knew that she had to find her uncle and calm him so that he could help her ease the pain in her own heart. LooAnne made her way downstairs and grabbed her coat then she ran from the house in the direction her uncle had gone. She walked down towards the creek and caught sight of him standing next to the gully looking down into it at the rushing water. LooAnne came up behind him and slipped her arm into his, looking up at his face. He looked down at her and smiled wanly, seeming calmed by the easy rushing of the creek. They were both silent for a long while before Ricky said, "I assume that someone told you what happened?"

LooAnne nodded and rested her head against her uncle's arm. "You're cold," she said.

Ricky shook his head, "I hadn't noticed." He sighed and said, "You know, Kyle Denson is like this gully. When you're standing over here you can only see the good side that isn't eroded. In order to see the side that is eroded you have to cross the creek. But when you're looking at the good side you have to be either standing on the bad side or down in the gully, neither of which are safe positions to be in. Eventually this side will collapse and take the other side with it, exposing the real true person and letting the world know that it's dangerous to come too close to the edge."

LooAnne nodded, "And I crossed the creek to get a good look at the erosion but I crossed in deep water and nearly sank. Now I'm on dry land and I've looked at the side that was eroded. I've stepped back away from the creek. If only Amarie could see the bad side of Kyle Denson before the gully collapses on her and she's buried down so deep that she can't get out."

Ricky shook his head, "I might be able to stop her for now, but when she's older I have no power over her. Kyle said he'd be back and a time is coming when I won't be able to prevent him from marrying her."

"I can't believe that Amarie is silly enough to actually want to go through with marrying him after all he's done."

"Maybe she'll learn with time, maybe she'll see his true colors as you did."

LooAnne sighed, "I didn't see them though, they were shown to me."

"As they have been to her. She should know that it was wrong of him to lead you on as he did."

"I know that I didn't like Amarie at the beginning, but she's the closest to a sister as I'm ever going to get and I don't want to see anything bad happen to her."

Ricky put his arm around his niece's shoulders and squeezed her gently, "Me either, LooAnne, me either."

TWENTY

The Root of All Evil

*For the love of money is the root of
all evil, for which some have strayed
from the faith in they're greediness,
and pierced themselves through with
many sorrows.
1 Timothy 6:10*

*For what profit is it to a man if he
gains the whole world and is himself
destroyed or lost? Luke 9:25*

 The two made their way back to the house where
they found some of the ranch hands sweeping up the
broken glass on the side porch. Amarie came down for
lunch but was in a poor mood all throughout the day.
She went out a little after lunch and returned just before
supper. She seemed to be feeling a bit better but she was
still quiet through the rest of the day and went to bed
earlier then normal. LooAnne went to bed at ten and
slept peacefully through the night though she did dream
of Kyle marrying Amarie and running off together just
as her parents had. This dream awoke her at six,

smelling hot chocolate wafting up from downstairs. Amarie's door was still closed so LooAnne assumed she was still in bed. She walked downstairs and peered into the study where her uncle was standing by the fireplace, staring into the roaring fire with his hand on the mantle. LooAnne watched the fire glowing in her uncle's eyes and the thoughtful look on his face. She smiled at the sight of Ricky standing there, watching the fire with his soft brown eyes. He looked so contented standing there in his study.

"Uncle Ricky?" LooAnne said as she leaned on the doorpost. Ricky turned around and smiled a weary smile. "Good morning." LooAnne walked to the fireside and looked down into the leaping flames. "Fire certainly is pretty when it's not burning your house."

Ricky nodded, "It certainly is." He looked at his niece and asked, "Did you sleep better?"

"I did, but I dreamed that Kyle and Amarie were married." LooAnne shook her head, "I don't know what to think about this whole thing. My mind's in a quandary."

Ricky nodded, "Mine too I must admit. I know this sounds bad but I just don't know what Kyle saw in Amarie. I mean, she had nothing that might -" Ricky stopped and frowned.

"What?" LooAnne asked.

"Amarie's turning eighteen in two years," Ricky said, rubbing his smooth chin. He turned and sat down at his desk. Opening one of the bottom drawers he shuffled through a stack of papers until he found a small folder which read:

"The Last Will and Testament of John Frederick Hearten."

Ricky opened the folder and turned to the second page which he scanned for a certain paragraph. Finding it he read through it several times and then sank back in his chair and sighed, letting the folder drop onto his lap.

"What's the matter?" LooAnne asked anxiously.

"I have a feeling this is why Kyle wanted to marry Amarie."

"Why?"

"The will states that when she is eighteen she receives her father's inheritance, providing she is unmarried; however, if she should marry before her eighteenth birthday she *and* her husband obtain control of her interests." Ricky looked up at his niece who was looking at him in disbelief.

"Do you mean to say that Kyle wants to marry her to get his hands on her money?" LooAnne asked, almost refusing to believe it.

"It's just a stab in the dark, LooAnne, but that could very well be."

"Then why would he break up with me, the niece of the millionaire, to marry Amarie for her smaller fortune?"

Ricky raised his eyebrows. "He can have her money as soon as he marries her, but if he were to marry you, well, certain undesirable events must occur before he gets control of your money."

LooAnne's eyes widened, "You mean...?"

Ricky nodded, "My death. If he married Amarie he could be very rich very quickly. If he married you he'd have to wait until I die."

LooAnne felt her heart drop. "Do you think that those

were his intentions the entire time? To marry me for my money?"

"I'm not sure of any of this, mind you. It just makes sense. I may be completely wrong."

"I must admit that for once in my life I hope you are."

Ricky sighed, "Me too. I'd like to take that Kyle Denson and wring his neck!"

"Uncle Ricky," LooAnne scolded.

Ricky sighed, "I know, I know, but he hurt you and now he's hurting Amarie. He's a ruthless, no account, swine and he deserves to be hit a few times over the head."

"I think I'm going to go talk to Amarie and see how she's feeling. Maybe I'll find out just exactly what happened and what made Kyle suddenly change his mind about me and want to marry her. I'd like to find out, too, how he knew about the money if this is the case."

"Alright, come tell me if you learn anything."

"I will." LooAnne went back upstairs and knocked on Amarie's door, when she didn't answer LooAnne called, "Amar, let me in." Still there was no answer. Cecily and Malinda came out of their bedroom and asked what was wrong. LooAnne said that Amarie was upset and wouldn't come to the door. She tried opening it but it was locked. "Cecily, would you go down and get Uncle Ricky?" LooAnne asked her cousin.

Cecily nodded and ran downstairs returning a moment later with Ricky in the lead. "Amarie, open this door," he commanded. There was no answer to his demand so he tried the door which was indeed locked. He then turned and walked down the hall, turned right and entered the bathroom through the hall door with

LooAnne, Cecily, and Malinda right behind him. He
went to the door at the other end of the large bathroom
that led to Amarie's room. It too was locked but the key
was still laying on the molding over top of the door.
Ricky unlocked the door and the foursome went in. The
closets and dresser drawers were open and their contents
gone! The bed was a mess with some dresses strewn on
the floor, and a note on the desk. LooAnne saw it
immediately and began to read:

Dear LooAnne,

*Kyle came for me last night and I went with him.
We're to be married as soon as possible. I'm sorry
things worked out the way they did between you and
Kyle and I hope that some day we can all be friends.
He is such a nice man. I love him so much. I suppose
that this is just the way things were meant to be.
Thank you for everything!*
Amarie.

LooAnne handed the note to her uncle who read it and
then looked at his niece, despair showing in his eyes.
His fist tightened around the paper, crumpling it in his
hand, then Ricky turned and stormed down the stairs, his
teeth clenched. LooAnne followed him hurriedly. He
went straight into the study and bellowed for Chris who
came running, "Is something wrong, sir?" he asked.
"Yes something's wrong! You get me James Orn, Steve
Peterson, Bill Maker, and Carter Thomas right now!"
"Yes sir," Chris left the study to get the second shift

262

guards who were sleeping in the bunkhouse.

LooAnne watched Ricky pace the floor with his hands on the back of his head. She didn't know what to say to him and she knew that nothing she could say would make him feel better. Chris soon arrived with the four guards. They all looked tired but they listened while Ricky spoke. "My ward left this house last night," he said, "Which one of you let her out without telling me she was leaving?"

The guards all looked at each other clueless as to what their employer was asking. Apparently none of them had let Amarie out, or if they had the guilty one was not willing to confess. Ricky looked at all of them and said, "She couldn't have left this house without one of you knowing about it. Now if I'm not told who did it I'll fire the lot of you!"

The men still looked blank, all except Carter Thomas, the front guard. He looked down at his feet and said, "It was me, sir. She left about midnight, maybe a little earlier. She told me not to tell anyone and payed me good money to keep my mouth shut."

Ricky locked eyes with the guard and said, "Get out. Get out and don't come back!"

Thomas turned and immediately left the house. The other three guards were excused leaving Ricky, Chris, and LooAnne standing in the study alone.

Chris looked up at his employer, his eyes wide with disbelief, "Is Miss Hearten gone, sir?" he asked, astonished.

"Yes, she's gone!" Ricky yelled, "History repeating itself, Chris! It's not enough that I mess up once, I've got to do it three or four times! Maybe now LooAnne can run away and with any luck after that I'll have learned that when young girls threaten to leave with useless scoundrels I need to lock them in their room and post a trustworthy guard in front of the door! My life has been nothing but a huge mistake! I've done nothing but ruin it, and everyone in it! Everything that ever happened in my life has happened because of me! I wish I had never-"

"Will you stop yelling for a minute and listen to yourself?" LooAnne interrupted.

Ricky immediately ceased his tirade and looked at his niece in a stunned silence.

"I'm tired of listening to you insist that everything is your fault! It's like you want it to be! Standing there and saying that your whole life has been a mistake is like telling me that I was a mistake! Your life was nothing of the sort. If it wasn't for you a lot of things would be different and just plain wrong. I'd either be with the Luthers or out on the street dying of cold and starvation! You're not the only one that was hurt by Amarie leaving. What about her? She *has* ruined her life and all you can do is stand there and feel sorry for yourself. If you must say those things then for pity's sake don't say them in front of me. I'm not Mr. Block, I'm not paid to stand here and listen to your selfishness!" LooAnne turned and started to leave but she stopped short of the door and said, "And I'd like to apologize in advance for yelling at you, because later when I've thought about all the disrespectful things I'm saying I'll be too humiliated to. So I'm sorry – sir." LooAnne ran out of the study and disappeared around the corner.

Ricky and Chris stood in silence, staring at the door wide-eyed. After a moment Ricky sank down onto the couch and buried his face in his hands.

"She didn't mean it, sir," Chris assured gently. "She's just upset. She's been through a lot in the last few days and she just needed to blow off some steam."

Ricky nodded, "I know," he said in a near whisper. "She was right though, I am being selfish. Chris do you know how I wish I could go back to the beginning and change it all?"

Chris nodded. "I do, sir. I'm sorry."

Ricky looked up at his steward and asked earnestly, "Has my life really been such a waste? So pointless that the devil seems to control it?"

Chris shook his head, "No, sir. Your life is what saved the people from the Luthers. What saved many a needy family with your generosity. You've added to this world more then any of us may ever know just by the things you do everyday. And most importantly, you saved that little Luther and grew her into a beautiful and intelligent young lady, a girl who may go on to do great things all because you saved her life."

Ricky smiled slightly at Chris, "You don't know how much I appreciate those words, Mr. Block. You've done more for me then anyone alive in the world."

At that moment Kane came in and said, "That man is here, sir, the one that you told me to shoot, and Miss Hearten is with him."

Ricky and Chris looked at each other and simultaneously ran to the door! Upon reaching it they were taken aback by the sight of Kyle and Amarie standing in the yard, hand-in-hand. When Ricky stepped out onto the porch Kyle said, "Mr. Nash, you've got something I want."

"And what might that be?" Ricky demanded not wanting to believe that it was what he thought it was.

"My wife's money!" Kyle stated.

Ricky stiffened. He had been right about Kyle's intentions, he had married Amarie for her money!

He took a deep breath and said, "I want to see the marriage certificate first, Denson."

Kyle reached into his pocket and pulled out a piece of paper. He handed it to the guard who handed it to Ricky who read it thoroughly. He looked at the paper in sorrow, a knot in his throat as his eyes scanned it. As he looked it over for a second time he felt LooAnne's arm slip into his. She looked over his shoulder at the certificate and closed her eyes in order to hold back her tears. Ricky crumpled up the paper and threw it at Kyle's feet while Amarie looked down at the grass and remained silent.

Looking at Amarie, Ricky said, "Don't do this, Amarie. You're ruining your life."

"No, I'm not," Amarie insisted. "Kyle's a wonderful man, and I know that we'll be very happy!"

"I'm giving you one last chance to change your mind, Amarie, because if you don't I'll never have you or your husband on my property again."

"I love Kyle, and where he goes I go.....Mr. Nash."

Ricky sighed. "I'll have to inform my lawyer and he will handle the legal papers before you can claim anything, though I assure you your share of the company and any money Mr. Hearten had will be handed over to you in due time."

Kyle nodded, his face plain but his eyes full of victory, "Thank you, sir."

"Don't thank me, just get out, and don't show up again."

Kyle nodded and turned back towards town, Amarie following with her head hung low.

As Ricky looked after them he said, "All Kyle wanted was the money. I would have payed him that same amount to leave Amaire alone had I known what his true intentions were."

"Maybe things will work out different than we think they will?" LooAnne said, trying to help the situation.

Ricky shook his head, "I don't have enough faith in them to think that. But I do understand now that maybe this wasn't all my fault." Ricky looked down at LooAnne who looked up at him and said, "Please forgive me, Uncle Ricky, I didn't mean to snap at you. I just have so many strange feelings and they all bubbled out at once."

Ricky put his arm around LooAnne's shoulder as he so often did and said, "I know you do, dear. Do you feel better?"

LooAnne shook her head, "I feel worse, I just can't imagine Kyle being so crooked and Amarie so naive as to blindly follow him. I wish my whole life had been different."

"Now wait just a minute, girl," Ricky said looking her in the eye. "Just a little while ago you told me not to say that my life was a mistake, now you're saying practically

the same thing. I don't think that's very fair do you?"
LooAnne sighed and looked down at the ground. "No it's not," she admitted. "But when I look back at the past I can hardly believe it all happened and yet I know it did. I've got physical and mental scars that tell me so."
Ricky thought for a minute and said, "You know what I think you need?"
"What?" LooAnne asked, looking up at her uncle questioningly.
"A change of scenery. A break from all of these bad memories, and nothing takes your mind off of things like college does."
"College?" LooAnne asked, taken completely by surprise at her uncle's proposal. "I've not even graduated yet."
"But you will come summer, and there's a great college in Dallas."
"Dallas!" LooAnne cried. "I couldn't leave here, not in a million years!"
"You were going to when you married Kyle," Ricky pointed out.
"Things were different then. Kyle was leaving with me and Amarie was here and – and things were just different. Kyle and Amarie are gone now and for the first time in six years it's just you and me. We need each other and me leaving just doesn't make sense anymore."
"If you're worried about me don't, I'm going to miss you more then anything, but I know that this is the right thing to do. I have Chris here with me and I've got a business to run, I've got plenty to keep me busy until you come home."

"It's not just you," LooAnne admitted, "I can't leave this safe world, I have too much Luther in me. I only fit in here because I'm your niece and everyone around us does what we say without question. After twelve years of living with those cruel Luthers, I've finally found a place where I'm safe and it would be completely insane to leave it. My name isn't even LooAnne Nash, it's Beth Luther and always will be. No one can change the fact that I'm the daughter of Jason and Amanda Luther and all I've been doing for the past six years is deceiving people, lying to them about who I really am. I can't go to Dallas and trick those people there just as I have the ones here, I live a lie and I've got to do all I can to keep it from growing and becoming uncontrollable."

"You do not live a lie, LooAnne. You are my full-fledged niece just as much as if you *were* Robert's daughter."

"But I'm not Uncle Robert's daughter, I'm the daughter of Jason Luther!"

"LooAnne you are my niece," Ricky persisted. "And you are a wonderful person, you being a Luther does not change who you are on the inside and it never will. Now I have never made you do anything before in my life, but if you refuse to do this for me I will. I know that this is the right thing to do and you must trust me, I know what I'm doing."

"Why do you feel so strongly about this?" LooAnne demanded.

"I must admit that I'm not sure, but something is telling me that you need to go to college, you have to know how to run this business and there's more to it then I can teach you."

LooAnne looked out the window and across the cold pastures, then she looked up at her uncle and said, "If you say so, Uncle Ricky. I suppose it's about time I had a look at everyone else's world. Though I'll miss you more then anything."

Ricky smiled, "I'll miss you as well, my dear. But you never know, maybe you'll find that young man who will make Kyle look like the scum he is."

LooAnne shook her head sadly, "I fear that's a long way off yet. Maybe even nonexistent."

"Don't think like that," Ricky scolded gently. "he's out there, LooAnne, and he's one hundred times better then any other man in the world, especially Kyle. The Almighty will bring the two of you together at the right time."

"But what if that time never comes?" LooAnne asked.

Ricky squeezed her shoulders reassuringly. "It will, and the love of your life, will come along with it."

TWENTY ONE

The Unforgotten Past

*Let us hear the conclusion of the
whole matter, fear God and keep
His commandments for this is man's
all. For God will bring every work
into judgment, including every secret
thing, whether good or evil.
Ecclesiastes 12:13 and 14*

"LooAnne we're going to be late!" Ricky called up
the stairs. "The train leaves in half an hour."
It was a hot summer morning six months later. LooAnne
was leaving Decatur for the first time in her life on the
one fifteen, bound for Dallas, Texas. Her college classes
began very soon and she wanted to be settled in before
they started.
"LooAnne!" Ricky called again, but his niece didn't
seem to hear him. She was standing in her room looking
out her back window at the lush green fields of the Nash
Estate. The wind caused the trees to sway and the tall,
seed tufted grass seemed to dance through the pastures.
The mountains in the distance were a beautiful sight

silhouetted against the blue sky, white puffy clouds settling over them.

As LooAnne stood looking at her home she felt her uncle's hand on her shoulder. Turning she looked up into his face and sighed, "What in the world am I doing?" she asked. "Leaving all of this, it's madness."

Ricky looked out the window at his fields and said, "It will all be here when you come home, LooAnne, every bit of it. And I know that you'll love Dallas. The engaging life of a big city can be an amazing thing. Now we've come this far, we must not rethink it at this point." LooAnne nodded. "I'm not rethinking it. I know that this is the right thing to do, but I wish it weren't." She took one more look out her window and said, "We'd better get going, Uncle Ricky."

Together the two walked down the stairs, passed the study, the living room, Ricky's bedroom, the welcoming hall, and out the side door onto the porch, where all the maids, ranch hands, cooks, and guards stood. Mrs. Moore was dabbing her eyes with the hem of her apron and Sam Moore held their three-year-old son Sammy. Chris pulled up in the Huckster and honked. LooAnne said goodbye to all the staff before she and Ricky got into the Huckster and the three started for town.

As they rounded the corner LooAnne looked back and smiled, remembering the day she had first laid eyes on her beautiful home. She sighed as she thought of the warm summer nights that she and Amarie had run to the house when they heard a coyote and then laugh happily when they were safe within it's walls. She remembered the day that Chris' voice had awakened her and Amarie had come bursting into her room screaming that the beautiful house was ablaze. She remembered running in amongst the flames and finding her uncle unconscious in his room as a result of saving the ring that LooAnne now wore always on her finger, never to remove it. The scar on her arm a further reminder of that day. Soon the Estate disappeared from view and LooAnne turned to face the front only to see her uncle looking back at it as well, a sad look on his face as he recalled days passed. The morning his father had called him from the barn to tell him that he was to take Patty Barson to the picnic, and him refusing to go because he wanted to have his own picnic. A picnic with Susan. It had been the next day that he had first heard of Jason Luther and now he thought of the vital role the rogue had played in his life. Ricky turned from looking at the estate and leaned back in his seat, a strange feeling coming over him and he realized in that moment he no longer hated Jason for running off with his sister, nor did he blame Amanda for leaving and causing such grief to their family. Ricky could honestly say that he had forgiven them both without the slightest doubt in his mind.

He had finally awakened from the nightmare that he had been caught in that night his sister left. He was surprised to find this was a great weight off his shoulders. He knew just having their daughter with him had compensated for anything Jason and Amanda had ever done to him. Ricky looked down at LooAnne who sat on the seat next to him and smiled.

LooAnne could feel his eyes on her and looked up into them. "What are you smiling at?" she asked.

Ricky shook his head, "The daughter of Jason Luther," he sighed. "I can still see his dark brown eyes staring at me from within the shadows of the house that night he came for Amanda. The same soft brown eyes that are staring at me now."

LooAnne smiled, "Mama used to tell me that I had my father's eyes. She loved him more then anything in the world."

"I've been wanting to ask this question for a long time, LooAnne," Ricky said. "And now I have to know. Did he love her?"

LooAnne looked out the window at the houses of Decatur that were growing closer and closer. She seemed to be thinking hard about something that was hidden within her that she had to draw out. Finally she looked back at her uncle and said, "Yes he did, he rarely showed it, especially in front of the others, but he loved her more then anything in the world."

Ricky smiled, "And what about you?"

"Me? Well, no one ever loved me but Mama. Papa was a Luther and there was nothing anyone could do to change that. But of all of them, he was the best."

Ricky shook his head in disagreement, "I'm afraid not. *You're* the best, LooAnne Nash, and there's nothing anyone can do to change that either."

LooAnne smiled, "Thank you, Uncle Ricky."

Ricky shook his head, "Thank you, LooAnne, for being able to tell me something I've wanted to know for years."

LooAnne sighed, "I used to think that I didn't know what love was, but I do now. *Real* love bares all things, believes all things, hopes all things, and endures all things. It can get buried down in the bottom of your heart where you can't see it for a while, but it never goes away. It's always there. The love I had for Kyle wasn't real because it went away, but the love my father had for my mother was real, just pushed down by his family's cruelness, because he didn't know how to keep it up. He did the best he could do, but it was real. Love like that never goes away, it's always going to be there."

At that moment Chris pulled up to the train station. There was a crowd of people getting on and off and a gush of steam shot up into the air. Ricky, Chris, and LooAnne walked over to one of the passenger cars just as everyone began to board. LooAnne looked at the train and said, "I can't believe I'm doing this."

Ricky wrapped his arms around his niece and hugged her until the conductor called, "All aboard!" and the train slowly began to pull out of the station.

LooAnne looked up at her uncle and said, "Are you sure you don't want to think it over a little longer, Uncle Ricky?"

"I'm positive, everything will work out wonderfully. You said that you were okay with it, remember?"

LooAnne nodded, remembering quite well, "I am okay with it," she assured him, "I just can't wait to get home again."

"And I can't wait to have you home again."

LooAnne hugged her uncle once more, her eyes beginning to drip with tears. "I love you, Uncle Ricky."

"I love you too, my dear."

LooAnne pulled away from her uncle and ran towards

the slowly moving train. She took hold of the grab rails on the back platform of the caboose and swung herself aboard the train, standing just outside the door as the whistle blasted and the wind blew her bright red hair across her freckled face. She stood there waving until the train disappeared into the sunset taking her to Dallas, to a knew life and the young man who was destined to spend it with her.

As Ricky and Chris watched and waved Ricky thought about his first little boy Joseph, Susan, William, Cindy, and the seventeen years that had passed since their deaths. He finally understood that all things *were* working together for good and he was finally able to forgive all that had happened to him. He knew that he would never stop grieving, he would never stop missing them, but his unending love for them would override any pain he felt, knowing he would one day see them again. Ricky dried his eyes on the cuff of his shirt as he felt yet another weight lift from his shoulders. "Mr. Block," he said.

"Yes sir?" Chris asked as he looked up at his employer. "Even though my story is nothing but *The Unforgotten Past*, I have a feeling that her story is just beginning." Chris smiled, "Indeed it is, sir. And had it not been for you and your need for her so many years ago, she wouldn't be here now, fulfilling the plans the Almighty has for her."

Ricky put his hand on Chris' shoulder as he watched the train caring his niece disappear and said, "What would I do without you, Mr. Block?"

Chris grinned his playful grin and said, "You wouldn't

do without me, sir."
The two laughed happily and started back for the estate, with only one thought left in Ricky's mind; LooAnne had long since deserved to know his entire past, the things that he had kept concealed from her for years and the things that caused him the most heartache and the most joy. He made up his mind right then and there to tell her when she returned.

The End

ONE
The Torching Flames

TWO
Triple Creek Hall

THREE
Never Forgiven

FOUR
Honor and Pride

FIVE
A Shocking Accusation

SIX
The Sheriff's Arrest

SEVEN
Guilty or Not Guilty

EIGHT
Secret Payoff

NINE
Apologies

Made in the USA
Charleston, SC
06 March 2016